Riquet. — Dessin de Gaulquod, d'après une gravure du temps (Cabinet des estampes).

Pierre-Paul Riquet

This is a work of fiction. Many of the characters are real people who lived and died in seventeenth century France, but this is not a biographical work. The author's intent is to portray a plausible historical scenario of the forces and personalities that produced this monumental human endeavor and to honor those who played key roles. Some dialog is adapted from letters of record. Many characters are totally fictitious and appear only as a means to describe the extant culture. Some characters are compounded from several disparate people of the time.

ISBN: 979-8648693418

CANAL

OF THE

SUN KING

THE BIRTH OF THE CANAL DU MIDI

A Novel

by Les Smith

Dedicated to my editor and publisher and the love of my life,

Deb Smith

CONTENTS

Introduction

A broad valley sprawls across southern France from Bordeaux on the Atlantic to Narbonne on the Mediterranean, brushing the foothills of the Pyrénées to the south and the toes of the *Massif Central* to the north.

There is a natural threshold that runs northerly through the valley from the Pyrénées to the *Massif Central*. The valley floor falls westerly from the divide to the Atlantic coast and the cities of La Rochelle, Rochefort and Bordeaux. Easterly from the divide it falls toward the Mediterranean coastal cities of Sète, Agde and Narbonne. Rain falling along that nebulous break line must flow either westward, ultimately to the Atlantic, or eastward, ultimately to the Mediterranean.

Rain falling in the watershed of the Garonne River, high in the middle of the Pyrénées, forms rivers that flow northerly into that valley through Toulouse via the Garonne, then westerly and northwesterly to the Atlantic. Rain falling in the watershed of the Aude River, just a few miles east of the headwaters of the Garonne, feeds rivers that flow northerly via the Aude to Carcassonne thence easterly to the Mediterranean.

Toulouse was the capital of the ancient province of Languedoc, where people traditionally spoke the "*Langue d' Oc*" or Occitan, as many do today. At the beginning of the Christian Era, the Garonne was navigable from Toulouse to Bordeaux. The Aude was yet untamed.

***

Roman contemporaries of Christ built a bridge over the Cavalon river in what is now Provence, a region of France lying east of Languedoc. The *Pont Julien* was constructed from cut stone set in place without benefit of mortar. Three arches support the roadbed, the central arch being nearly thirty feet high. The support columns between the arches feature openings just below the roadbed to facilitate passage of twenty-five-foot-deep flood waters. This bridge carried traffic continuously for two thousand years, modern tractor-trailer rigs included, and could serve even now if needed.

Engineers of the Roman Empire bridged the Gardon river in Provence with an aqueduct resting on three tiers of arches rising a total of one hundred sixty feet above the river. The aqueduct was part of a system that carried water thirty-one miles from Uzès to Nîmes. As it crossed the Gardon its water channel dropped roughly one inch in that quarter mile. The structure was part of a system of tunnels and aqueducts that brought nine million gallons of water per day to the city of Nîmes for over five hundred years and stands intact, ready, with minor refurbishment, to serve today.

Engineers of the Roman Empire, who created so many great works in Rome and throughout her provinces, clearly were highly skilled in hydraulics. They dug canals and built such aqueducts that brought water from miles away by gravity alone to serve urban centers.

Engineers of the Roman Empire investigated the feasibility of building a canal across southern France to link the Garonne at Toulouse to the Aude near Carcassonne, thereby linking the Mediterranean and the Atlantic. Such a canal would have greatly facilitated trade between Rome and her French and Britannic provinces as well as enforcement of her will. But finding no water supply to feed locks at the summit of such a canal, those highly skilled Roman engineers deemed the concept to be impossible.

Nearly seventeen hundred years later, during the reign of The Sun King, Louis XIV, the men and women remembered here made the impossible happen.

FRANCE

ATLANTIC
OCEAN

La Rochelle
Rochefort

Limoges

Bordeaux

Seine

Versailles · Paris

Loire

Briare

MASSIF
CENTRAL

Garonne

Cahors

Toulouse

Montagne
Noir

Carcassonne

Sète

Agde
Narbonne

Marseille

Perpignan

PYRÉNÉES

Aude

MEDITERRANEAN
SEA

SPAIN

Scale of Miles

0   150   300

N

FIRST ENTERPRISE

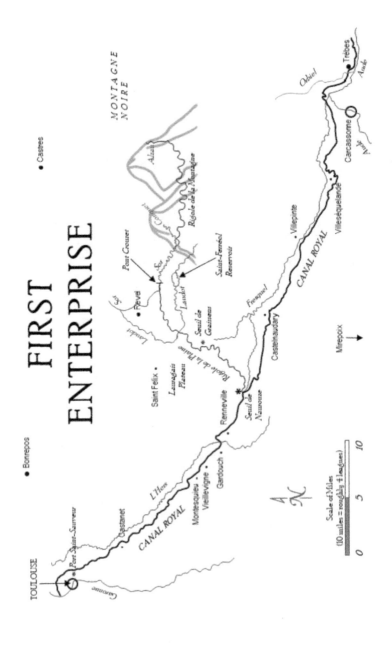

Bonrepos

Castres

MONTAGNE NOIRE

TOULOUSE

Port Saint-Sauveur

Garonne

Castanet

L'Hers

CANAL ROYAL

Montesquieu

Vieilvigne

Gardouch

Renneville

Seuil de Naurouze

Saint Félix

Lauragais Plateau

Rigole de la Plaine

Seuil de Gaissou

Laudot

Laudot

Rivel

Sor

Rigole de la Montagne

Pont Crouzet

Sor

Alzau

Conquet

Saint-Ferréol Reservoir

Castelnaudary

Freaquel

Villepinte

Mirepoix

CANAL ROYAL

Villesèquelande

Carcassonne

Orbiel

Trèbes

Aude

Aude

Scale of Miles
(10 miles = roughly 4 leagues)

0   5   10

N

SECOND
ENTERPRISE

Étang de Thau
Sète
(Cette)

Hérault
Agde
Bessan
Round Lock

Béziers
Orb
Malpas
Tunnel
Fonseranes
Lock
Montady
Aude
Capestang
Robine Canal
Argeliers
CANAL ROYAL
Narbonne
Cesse
Saint-Nazaire
Répudre
Pechlaurier
Rock
Argens

Aude
Puicheric
Marseillette
Orbiel
Trèbes

MEDITERRANEAN SEA

N

Scale of Miles
(10 miles = roughly 4 leagues)

0   5   10

Book I

Dreams

One

The Sea Route.

Jean-Luc Ruscino dreamed of the sea.

As he filled his basket with full ripe grapes plucked from his father's vineyard in the hot September sun of Languedoc, his mind would often wander to the nearby Mediterranean and he would imagine that he heard the cries of the seabirds and felt the cool salty breeze on his skin.

The Ruscinos' vineyard lay in eastern Languedoc on a rocky hillside above the village of Bessan on the Hérault River. The Hérault rose in the *Massif Central* and met the Mediterranean near Agde just six miles to the south of their home. The rocky soil of their hill above Bessan was ideal for the Carignan grapes that swelled every summer with the lifeblood of their winery.

But young Jean-Luc Ruscino dreamed of the sea. All through the hot Languedoc summer he worked the vineyards with his father, pruning and shaping the vines for maximum yield. He did not mind the work or even the hot summer sun. His father was strict about proper care of the vines and the grapes they bore but generous with praise when Jean-Luc did well.

But Jean-Luc dreamed of the sea. At the age of ten he had begun riding alongside his father to the port at Agde to bring their wine to the quay of the Hérault. The route was not difficult for their dray: the road dropped down to Bessan, then along the right bank of the Hérault until it crossed the Agde bridge, then south, along the left bank to the quay just two miles from the river's mouth.

Jean-Luc's father, Gaspard, could have sold his wine in Bessan but preferred to endure the extra few leagues cartage for a better price in Agde. They were always paid a premium for their wine. Gaspard, like his father before him, had been selling his export wine here all his life. He boasted of the best wine in Languedoc.

But every year as they approached the sea the first sharp cries of the gulls would echo through Jean-Luc's soul and feed his wanderlust. Gaspard always shipped his wine in March as soon as the road was passable. It was important for the wine to reach its destination before it was vulnerable to the hot summer sun. With the wagon off-loaded, weather permitting, they would sit on the quay and enjoy the bread, cheese and Carignan red his mother, Evelyne, had packed for their lunch. Jean-Luc loved the soft, tangy cheese his mother made from ewes' milk, the bread she baked daily, and the mellow red wine that came from their vineyard. In fact, he loved his life: his indulgent mother, his gruff, soft-hearted father, his sweet little sister, Collette, and their home in the hills outside Bessan.

But he dreamed of the sea.

One sunny afternoon, as they lunched on the quay, with the fresh sea breeze wafting through the limp sails of the schooners and the brazen birds begging them for morsels, his father praised his progress as a young vintner-to-be.

"Someday this will be your wine standing on the quay," he would say "The vineyards will be yours and the winery as well.

"You will carry on for me as did I for my father."

But once Jean-Luc had smelled the fresh salt breeze off the Mediterranean, once he had seen the majestic graceful three masted ships, he dreamed only of sailing to exotic far-away lands in search of adventure and unimaginable treasures, far from the sweaty toil of his father's vineyard. He would smile and nod as his father described his grape-filled future, knowing that to tell his father that his true love was the sea would only evoke anger and disappointment.

As they sat on the quay finishing the last of their simple meal, he casually asked his father, "Have you ever wondered what it would be like to sign on to one of these ships and sail to other lands?"

"No," his father replied curtly. "If you're curious about the life of a seaman, you have only to sit at yonder inn of an evening and listen to their tales of working the rigging in a storm, the scourge of Barbary pirates, losing teeth to scurvy, and someday, a cold burial at sea. I have no taste for that life!"

Jean-Luc said nothing. "An adventure can't be totally safe," he thought, "and still *be* an adventure." But he saw the folly in continuing the discussion, and let it be. He was amiable by nature, not inclined to argue and so, quickly liked by those he met.

In the autumn of his sixteenth year, the sun was unusually hot for September. The sweat ran from all his pores into rivulets drenching his face, his hair, and his back as he filled his basket with ripe grapes. He longed for the fresh cool breeze off the Mediterranean and dreamt of standing on the deck of a three-master with the sun on his face, the wind in his hair, and the cries of the gulls in his ears. His father's voice brought him back to reality.

"Luc! Come say hello to your uncle, Matthieu, home from the wars at last!"

Jean-Luc cautiously approached their visitor, still carrying his basket of ripe grapes, stunned to be suddenly facing, in the flesh, the uncle he had heard so much about. Matthieu's rare letter home was always shared after supper as Jean-Luc, his mother and his little sister clustered around the fire while his father read Matthieu's tales of adventure: both conquest and defeat. Gaspard's younger brother had not been destined to inherit the family vineyards, so he had joined the army seeking a vocation.

"He's come to help with the harvest!" his father beamed.

His uncle Matthieu was handsome in a roguish way. He dressed in the military fashion: white blouse, black doublet and dark blue cloak, boots that rose above the knee, all well-worn. At his side, the aptly named mortuary sword with a silver basket hilt, and in his belt, a flintlock pistol. The plume that had once lent a touch of white panache to his hat now showed the abuse of hard years of service to King and country. But Jean-Luc would have recognized Matthieu anywhere as his father's brother. He had the same classic nose, the same long dark hair falling in curls past his shoulders and his thin moustache curved up in a permanent smile. He was somewhat more gaunt. He had an angry scar on his left cheek, the result of a near death experience in the Spanish Netherlands. But he was clearly kin to Gaspard.

* * *

The Thirty Years War, embroiling all of Europe in religious war since 1618, had been grinding out corpses for twenty-five years when Matthieu joined the fray, and he soon found more adventure than he had sought. He served under Louis de Bourbon. Not the King of that name, but Louis II, Prince of Condé and a distant relative of the five-year-old Louis XIV. Le Grand Condé, a military prodigy at twenty-one, was a bold and brilliant strategist, who had earned Matthieu's respect.

When the Thirty-Years War was over it was followed by two consecutive uprisings against the young King – actually against the King's mother, the Queen Regent, and the hated Cardinal Mazarin. Condé led the second "Fronde" and Matthieu's decision to follow the Prince left him jobless and far from home after the defeat of Condé's coalition at Dunkirk, and the signing of the Treaty of the Pyrénées, which finally ended the Fronde and the war with Spain in favor of Louis XIV.

Matthieu left the army in Ypres and made his way to Antwerp, bouncing from one job to the next, missing more and more the home of his childhood. Eventually his military experience landed him a berth on a French merchant ship headed for Marseille with a belly filled with German steel. The ship's captain knew he could always use one more musketeer if boarded by pirates. That trip took nearly two months, and Matthieu seized the opportunity to learn as much as he could of the skills of a merchant seaman.

The passage was stormy, the work was hard and dangerous, and the food was *merde*. (He had acquired fluency in French while in the army, although he still preferred his native Occitan).

He was signed on for his military experience, but when storms struck every able body was needed. He found himself hauling on lines, scrambling up rope-ladder rigging and reefing sails under the worst weather conditions. He learned quickly and by the time his ship reached Marseille he was a reasonably competent seaman. But his goal in signing on was primarily passage back to his ancestral home in Languedoc, so when they docked in Marseille he gathered all he owned, stowed it in the heavy woolen bag he had picked up in Duffel, Flanders, hoisted the bag over his shoulder, said goodbye to captain and crew, and struck out for Bessan, in pursuit of a quieter life.

* * *

Matthieu and Jean-Luc took to each other immediately. They enjoyed working the harvest together and, during every spare moment, Jean-Luc would press his uncle for stories of battle and of life on the sea. Matthieu embellished nothing. If anything, he stressed the hardships of both lives. He had no desire to put the bellows to the boy's obvious fire for adventure.

Throughout the next year, whenever Jean-Luc found a moment alone with his uncle, he would always ask about the skills expected of a merchant seaman. Finally, Matthieu agreed to show him some basic knots, just to appease him. He deftly demonstrated the square, bowline, half hitch, taut line, clove hitch, figure eight, and sheet bend. At times when he was alone, Jean-Luc practiced until his fingers were raw, and, eventually mastered all seven.

Matthieu's stories of the sea provided opportunities to learn about terms used aboard ship such as the differences between lines, ropes and hawsers. Matthieu's knowledge was limited to the barque he had sailed on from Antwerp, but most of the terms were universal sailing jargon. He described jibs, lugsails, square sails and lateens. He described tack, hatch, deck, bulkhead, block, and belay. Jean-Luc absorbed it all like a thirsty grapevine in a warm summer rain.

As Matthieu had passed through the Gibraltar Strait, from the Atlantic Ocean to the Mediterranean Sea, en route to Marseille, he heard stories of the ruthless Barbary pirates who terrorized any ships that dared to travel those waters. The Berbers also pillaged Spanish coastal towns at will. They took slaves to power their galleys or to sell in the Moorish slave markets of North Africa. Matthieu's ship passed safely through the danger zone, but all his shipmates were clearly on edge until they reached Marseille. Matthieu hoped these stories would have cautionary value, but they could not pierce the rosy veil of Jean-Luc's idealized dream of life on the sea.

* * *

Jean-Luc was determined to follow his dream. He decided January would be the best time to depart. He had completed his second harvest with his uncle and the vines had been trimmed for winter. Vineyard maintenance was at an ebb, and one less mouth to feed would be of some help to his family through the winter. Wishing to avoid rancor and tears, he planned no goodbyes. Instead he wrote four letters.

In his letter to his father, he confessed that the sea had always drawn him, that if he did not go, he would forever regret not seeing whatever wonders were to be found in the world outside Bessan. He speculated that he would, in all probability, return in a few years to settle into the vintner's life.

To his mother, he expressed his devotion, and appreciation for all she had taught him. He thanked her for his literacy, and near fluency in French, Spanish, and Italian. He promised to write her and assured her that he expected to return in a few years.

To his sister, he apologized for leaving without a goodbye, but explained that to do otherwise would only have caused more pain all around. He reminisced some about his memories of growing up with her, told her how much he would miss her, and that he expected to be home in a few years. He promised to write often.

In his letter to his uncle, he thanked him for the insights that would ease his journey, assuring him that he was not complicit.

> *"My departure was inevitable. You have merely given me tools that make success more likely. By just being here you have eased my mind regarding the burden I leave my father."*

He promised to write often and reiterated his intent to be home in a few years.

He packed his possessions in the cloth bag his mother had made for his journey years ago to the *École de Langues* in Béziers. It was fashioned from a durable cotton fabric from Nîmes that she had acquired specifically for that purpose. The cloth was dyed blue with woad from Carcassonne and known throughout Languedoc as "*le sergé bleu de Nîmes.*" He slipped out just pre-dawn, left the letters on his pillow, and, with the naïve confidence of youth strode off toward Bessan.

It was a cold crisp winter morning and the sky was clear and blue-black as he passed row upon row of naked grape stalks trimmed back for the winter. Nocturnal creatures who had not yet read the dawn scurried from the road as he approached, forager and predator alike. The air was fresh and filled his lungs with the hope of finally living his dream.

The road was dry and firm and the first hour of daylight found him in Bessan. The sweet smell of the Hérault mixed with smoke from village chimneys filled his nostrils with anticipation. He made for the riverfront hoping to catch a ride to Agde. A bottle of wine persuaded the captain of a south-bound barge to carry him the rest of the way. Although he could have easily walked the distance, the roads of Occitania were not always safe for a traveler alone.

Upon arrival in Agde, he asked an innkeeper on the quay about securing a berth on a merchant ship.

"The *Dama de España* just tied up, lad," said the Innkeeper. "Captain Diaz usually finds his way here for rum 'n coffee while they lade his cargo. He's the only one comes to mind might be needing a hand. You got papers?"

"I have writing papers."

The innkeeper chuckled. "I was meanin' your Able-Bodied Seaman's papers, lad. I thought not. No matter; if he's in need, he won't be too fussy; if he is not, papers wouldn't help none."

"Sit yourself over in that corner there, and I'll give a nod when he shows."

True to form, the Captain arrived within minutes, and called to the innkeeper for bread, rum, and coffee. The innkeeper gave Jean-Luc a nod, but Jean-Luc decided to wait until the rum was gone before approaching. He had always found his father more amenable after a *pinte* or so of wine and assumed the rum might have similar effect.

The Captain was stout, olive-toned and heavily bearded. His hair was black except for the beginnings of gray in his beard. The exposed features of his face were heavily weathered, and at the corners of his eyes were deep creases suggesting either laughter or perennial squinting. Jean-Luc guessed squinting was more likely. The rum was gone almost before it hit the table and Diaz ordered another. When that, too, disappeared, the time seemed right, so Jean-Luc approached cautiously.

"*Qué quieres?*" growled Captain Diaz, without looking up. In the same language, Spanish, Jean-Luc responded that he was looking for a berth.

"*Siento, niño,*" said Diaz with a somewhat softened tone. "Got all the crew I need. Just waiting for the last of the stone to be stowed, then I'm off for Marseille."

Jean-Luc apologized for the intrusion, then retired despondently to his table to consider his next move.

Before long, a tall, blond, leather-faced man entered the inn and approached the Captain.

"Rodriguez is gone, *Capitan*," he said, obviously agitated.

"Gone?! Gone where?!" demanded the Captain.

"Not sure, *Capitan*," replied the blond. "His people are from Perpignan, and I'm thinking that might be his plan."

"*Madre de Christo*! Is the stone on board?"

"*Si, Capitan.*"

"We need to weigh anchor, or we'll miss the morning tide."

With only a momentary pause for thought, Diaz turned to scan the room.

He called out to Jean-Luc, "*Niño*! You got papers?"

The boy jumped from his chair as if it had caught fire. "*No, Capitan*, (mimicking the blond's form of address), but my uncle is a seaman and taught me the ropes." A minor stretch of the truth.

"Can you tie a bowline?"

"*Si, Capitan*!"

"Show me." (Throwing him a short length of rope.)

He did.

"What rope would you haul to raise the mainsail?"

"The halyard is not a rope, *Capitan*, it is a line."

The Captain chuckled with satisfaction, "I guess you'll do, and if you don't, we can always use you for shark bait. Let's go sailing, *niño*!"

And with that, they vacated the inn and were under way within the hour. As they sailed out the mouth of the Hérault, headed for Marseille, an old dray pulled up outside the inn. The driver and his passenger stepped inside to inquire of the innkeeper if he had seen a boy of seventeen around the quay today.

"A handsome, good mannered lad with dark hair and a fine Roman nose like your own?"

"That would be him."

"I'm afraid you just missed him. He's on the *Dama de España*, yonder, headed out to sea."

Gaspard and Matthieu turned to see the ship just vanishing behind the point, then stared at each other in stunned disbelief.

When Jean-Luc was uncharacteristically absent at breakfast they had checked his room but did not notice the letters. Matthieu suggested that he might be in the barn grooming the horses, but he was not. Returning to the house, they found Evelyne in tears with her letter in hand.

"His bag is gone," she said. "And there are letters for each of you and for Collette."

Once they realized what had happened, they wasted no time hitching the wagon and driving into Bessan. Finding no trace there, they decided to press on to Agde. They arrived not more than thirty minutes too late.

"All we can do now," said Matthieu, "is trust that we've taught him well."

Gaspard wept silently in despair.

* * *

A full crew for the *Dama* was thirty-six men including the Captain and First Mate. Most of the men were Spaniards, with only a few Italians, one German (the First Mate), and one other Occitanian.

Claude Durant was a young man from Montpellier who looked upon Jean-Luc as his countryman and was relieved to have a shipmate who shared his native tongue. Diaz recognized the bond at once and encouraged Claude to school the lad in seamanship.

Sailing to Marseille, the *Dama de España* never lost sight of land, and the trip should have been a gentle apprenticeship for Jean-Luc. But Neptune had other plans.

Halfway to Marseille a violent thunderstorm caught them. At its peak, Diaz feared loss of the mainmast and ordered the mainsail furled. Furling sail in a storm was the acid test for any seaman, so Jean-Luc found himself high in the rigging gathering and tying off the mainsail and trying desperately not to be borne away by the wind. It was the most terrifying experience of his life, but his shipmates shared his terror and, admiring his courage, helped him through the ordeal. Claude was by his side almost constantly, and at one point his firm grip saved Jean-Luc's life when he lost his footing high in the rigging.

Fortunately, the stone in the hold gave the *Dama* extra stability, and she was able, in due course, to ride out the storm. By then Jean-Luc had breathed his fill of fresh salt air.

It was obvious to all concerned that Jean-Luc had much to learn about seamanship. Thanks to his uncle's tutoring he gave a first impression of knowledge he did not possess. Also, Spanish was not his native tongue, which complicated the learning process when Claude was not involved. The word "*pendejo*," however, was always clear: he knew when he had done something stupid. His work as an apprentice seaman was demanding and sometimes frightening, but pure joy. He was living his dream at last! He relished every task and every learning experience. Even ineptitude could not dull the joy of being at sea.

The *Dama* tied up at the quay in Marseille to take on additional cargo, bales of le sergé bleu de Nîmes bound for Rome. Helping with the lading, Jean-Luc noticed a salty-looking youth approach the Mate on the quay carrying a sea bag much like his uncle's. He could not hear the conversation but guessed its nature. He was relieved to see the Mate shake his head and the stranger turn and walk away. It seemed clear that the Mate had not chosen to replace him with an experienced seaman. Apparently, he had not been deemed "shark bait" yet.

The Mate was a tall, blond German, "Dutch," who had sailed with Diaz since before he had been given command of the *Dama* by the Barcelona Shipping Company, and when that day had come, Diaz had picked Dutch to be his First Mate. The two shared a bond that can only be forged in the face of imminent death. Luckily for Jean-Luc, they had both instantly taken a liking to him. That initial impression had since been reinforced by his quickness, his courage, and his cheerful nature.

The denim was laded in time to catch the evening tide, but Diaz didn't like the look of the eastern skies and decided to lay over until morning. Another storm came that night and howled around them for two days before subsiding. Diaz spent the time at an inn on the quay while Dutch supervised the ship's watch.

Jean-Luc and Claude used the free time to share stories of growing up in Occitan. Claude was the son of a Montpellier fisherman and could not understand why Jean-Luc would have left the vineyards of Bessan and a life that Claude imagined as idyllic.

As they lay in their hammocks off watch, Claude would run through various ship's procedures. He would not just describe proper procedure, but also the most dangerous mistakes and how to avoid them.

Finally, fair weather gave them leave to embark for Rome.

In three days, with fair winds, they reached Portus at the mouth of the Tiber River. As the ship was being offloaded,

Jean-Luc asked Claude, "I thought our cargo was bound for Rome?"

"It is," Claude replied. "But this is as far as we go. We're too tall to make it past the bridges 'cross the Tiber 'tween here and Rome, so we offload here, and it's barged or carted up to Rome." Jean-Luc realized with dismay that he would not have an opportunity to visit the exotic Rome. The fabled, Eternal City.

At midday Diaz announced a change in their itinerary. He had planned to return to Marseille laden with Italian cheese and wine, but while in port he learned of a large shipment of Murano mirrors needing transport from Venice to Paris. Such a shipment would pay dearly. The journey would take six to eight weeks and would require passage through the Gibraltar Strait. Spanish warships were not a concern for the *Dama*, but the Barbary pirates were always a threat. The Barbary pirates were known to prey on merchant ships passing through the waters off the north coast of Africa bound for Gibraltar.

Expecting to be well compensated for the risk, Diaz took on some miscellaneous cargo bound for the Venetian city-state and set sail south, east, and north, around the boot, to the port of Venice.

Before leaving port, Jean-Luc found a ship bound for Marseille and gave the Captain four letters to carry.

* * *

The mirrors had been ferried over from Murano to Venice for export. The artisans of Murano produced mirrors by a closely guarded secret process that rendered the glass flawless. The mirrors were prized throughout Europe. The fee for carrying them to Paris would reward Diaz and the Barcelona Shipping Company well for the long and hazardous voyage. Varying in size, they were packed three to five to a crate and were lashed securely in the hold to prevent any shifting or breakage during the journey. They would be worth tens of thousands of *livres* in Paris.

It was late afternoon before their cargo was secured, so Diaz gave the crew leave to explore Venice but for a minimal ship's watch, planning to embark with the morning tide.

Jean-Luc wanted to explore the city some before sunset and Claude agreed to join him. Just off the quay, they found the Piazza San Marco. While most of the crew sought bars and brothels, Claude and Jean-Luc strolled the Piazza marveling at the beautiful stonework. The clock tower seemed by far the most beautiful structure Jean-Luc had ever beheld. It rose five stories above the Piazza, the first two forming an arch to pass through to the Rialto, the commercial and financial center of the city. Above the arch, workmen were restoring the vibrant golden signs of the Zodiac circling the rich blue of the clock face. Above that, the Virgin sat in an alcove holding the baby Jesus. The face of the next story featured an alcove containing the statue of a man Jean-Luc took to be a king kneeling before a great winged lion. Above all this grandeur rose a great bell of tarnished bronze bracketed by two great bronze statues holding long-handled hammers.

As the two young men stood agape, the clock's sunburst pointer reached the top of the hour and the two bronze giants began to sound the hour with their great hammers. At the same time, to their astonishment, a door opened on each side of the Virgin and the three Magi sortied out of the door on the left, disappearing through the door on the right led by an angel.

With that spectacle at an end, they turned toward the Basilica and were greeted by the last rays of the sun lighting what appeared to be four great golden horses standing over the entrance.

"This city is rich beyond measure," exclaimed Claude.

"In many ways!" agreed Jean-Luc.

They explored the walkways of Venice for hours, down narrow streets crossing and re-crossing the network of small canals that were the arteries of this great city. After his disappointment from not being allowed to see Rome, now he eagerly drank in the art and architecture – the culture of Venice. This was the sort of experience Jean-Luc had hoped for when he escaped Bessan. He dragged Claude up one alley and down another until his friend begged for relief.

Finally, returning to the quay, Claude went to find their shipmates at a nearby inn, but Jean-Luc chose to return to the ship to find his hammock and ponder the wonders he had seen that day.

With the morning tide, they set sail for Paris, via Gibraltar, perforce. Diaz held their course tight to the boot of the Apennine Peninsula, avoiding the north African lairs of the Barbary pirates. The weather held, and within a week they were off Mallorca and setting a course for Gibraltar. As they were passing the isle of Ibiza, the lookout shouted "Sail, ho! Off the starboard bow!" Diaz recognized the ship immediately as a Barbary corsair.

The pirates favored galleys because their single sail was augmented by oars and they could usually outrun unassisted sail power even in a fair wind. The Berbers' main trade was in slaves, and captured crews were valuable in that market.

"*Sangre de Christo!*" Diaz cursed. "She must have been just laying up in a cove there on Ibiza waiting for prey like us! With all that glass in our belly, those oars'll catch us even under full sail! They're wanting slaves more than mirrors, I'll wager. We don't want to be taken alive. To the armory, Dutch! Arm the men!"

Jean-Luc suddenly realized there was an aspect of his uncle's life he had neglected to learn. His father never owned a gun. The only wild game that ever found their table was the occasional snared rabbit. He had held his uncle's sword but had never wielded it.

Claude guessed they would be outnumbered two or three to one. He gave Jean-Luc a quick course in loading and firing his weapon. As to the cutlass, he said, "Show them no mercy! They'll sure as hell show you none. It's kill or be killed, or worse, made a galley slave!"

The sails were full, but the wind was not strong, and the corsair soon pulled alongside, and grappling hooks came flying over the rail. Jean-Luc was trying to cut one of the lines when a large, turbaned, black-skinned pirate with a cutlass in his teeth jumped the gap. Terrified, Jean-Luc plunged his cutlass into the pirate's chest as hard and as deep as he could. The sword lodged in the man's spine, and Jean-Luc lost hold of it as the man fell from the rail. He grabbed his musket and shot the next boarder point-blank but had no time to reload before the next attacker appeared. Desperate, he grabbed a belaying pin and, gripping it with both hands, struck the next one in the center of his forehead with all his strength. He turned in time to see another boarder with his sword raised over Claude as Claude was frantically trying to reload his weapon. Jean-Luc felled the giant with his cudgel, but as he spun back to face his next victim, a cutlass crossed his throat and he knew that he was dead. As he lay on the deck with his blood and his life ebbing onto the teak, he dreamed he was in the hot sun on the hill above Bessan, picking grapes.

Two

The Land Route.

The hot climate was harsh for the people of Languedoc, but it was ideal for the woad and the wine produced there during the reign of the Sun King. The yellow woad blossoms belied the rich blue dye harbored in the leaves. Blue dye was rare before the introduction of the indigo plant from Asia, and those woad leaves made Languedoc very wealthy.

But the Ruscinos were vintners. Wine was the lifeblood of France in the seventeenth century, as it is today. Then, as now, each region took great pride in their local *vin de pays*. Each of the many wine regions of Languedoc judged their local wine to be superior to all the rest. Although Gaspard Ruscino's Carignan grapes had come from Spain generations ago, by his day their flavor was rooted in the soil and climate, the *terroir*, of Bessan. His wine was appreciated in the Italian republics, in Spain, in Toulouse, and even in Bordeaux.

Transporting his wine to anyplace outside his immediate locale was dangerous by any route. By sea lay the threat of storms, Barbary pirates and, in time of war, Spanish warships. The overland option was plagued by a different sort of pirate and by storms that turned the roads of Occitania to clinging quagmires that could grasp wagon wheels in a death grip.

Still, each year Gaspard shipped one-third of his vintage to Rome or, in times of peace, Barcelona. One-third he kept for personal use and local sale, and the rest he sold to a Toulousain wine merchant. Each year Henri Duvall and his son, Jean-Henri would arrive in the spring when the weather relented enough to render the road from Toulouse passable. It was a trip Henri had made with his father for many years, but once Jean-Henri was old enough he had relieved his grandfather of the arduous trek. They would load up the portion of that year's vintage reserved for the markets of

Toulouse and Bordeaux. Once in Toulouse, the wine could be shipped more easily to Bordeaux via the Garonne River which was navigable below Toulouse.

When Jean-Henri had been deemed old enough to handle a pistol, he began to accompany his father to Bessan in his grandfather's stead. At fourteen Jean-Henri went with his father to an abandoned quarry near Toulouse to learn how to clean, load and fire pistols and arquebusses. By fifteen he had become proficient and his father enlisted him as guard on the perilous roads of Occitania. He carried two pistols as did his father and they kept a loaded arquebus in a sling at the side of their dray.

Jean-Luc and Collette Ruscino admired the younger Duvall. Although only a year senior to Jean-Luc, he seemed vastly more worldly. They knew of his role on the journey from Toulouse and were in awe.

Once the wine was on the dray, Jean-Henri and Jean-Luc would make straight for the pond nestled in a small dale near the vineyard where they would spend the afternoon fishing while Collette, who refused to be left behind, sat nearby on the grass and braided coronets of wild lavender. Collette did not care for fishing. She felt sympathy for the worms as well as the fish. Jean-Henri was a skillful angler and often provided fare for the table he and his father shared with the Ruscinos.

As the years passed and Collette grew older, Jean-Henri was more and more drawn to the younger Ruscino. He received the news of Jean-Luc's departure on the *Dama* with mixed emotions. He missed his young friend, but was not disappointed to realize that now it would be just he and Collette at the fishing hole, and at fourteen she had blossomed into a stunning young woman, although as she sat braiding her coronets while Jean-Henri fished, he could still see the young girl.

They would often stroll the vineyards at sunset after supper. The tendrils that would bear this year's grapes reached out from the central stalks like arms outstretched with a yawn as they awoke from winter. New leaves were forming as the winter's barren stalks came to life. The contrast of the dying day and the rebirth of the vines was to the young couple an irresistibly romantic setting. They talked of the virtues and curses of country life and of the curses and virtues of city life. Henri shared his dreams of great fortune; Collette shared her dreams of family.

One evening, as the sun settled on the horizon, he turned to face her.

"Do you think you could be happy living in Toulouse?" he asked.

Her heart nearly stopped as she realized his intent.

"I think I would be happy anywhere if you were there," she replied.

He did not even try to suppress the broad grin that exploded from his soul.

No one was surprised when Jean-Henri asked for Collette's hand. In fact, both families found the prospect divinely inspired. The senior Duvall and Gaspard had become good friends over the years as their fathers had been before them and Evelyne always looked forward to the rare visit from Theresa Duvall when she was able to persuade Henri to bring her along. Henri was reluctant, of course, because the roads of Languedoc were not safe.

It was agreed that the two would wed in Toulouse the following spring. The Ruscinos would bring the season's wine shipment to Toulouse and save the Duvalls their annual trek.

* * *

A month before they planned to depart for Toulouse, the Ruscinos received a visit from a young man from Montpellier, one Claude Durant. He told them of the friendship he had formed with their son. He told them, with deep regret, that Jean-Luc would not be coming home.

"My mother insisted that I must bring you these ill tidings," he explained. "She was certain that you would want to know your son's fate."

The Ruscinos had not received letters for over a year and had suspected the worst. The uncertainty had, indeed, been harder to bear than was the terrible truth.

"When the accursed Berbers boarded us, he fought well and bravely," Claude continued. "He saved my own life just before he, himself, was slain. I received a blow from behind and fell unconscious after that. Taken prisoner, I managed to convince the Berbers that my parents would pay more in ransom than I would fetch in their slave markets. The ransom was arranged through an intermediary in Málaga, and I was delivered home in January.

"I was loathe to bring you this worst possible news, but mother insisted and I hoped you would find comfort knowing that Jean-Luc was liked by all on the *Dama* and that he showed true strength and courage in the battle that took his life."

Evelyne and Collette, overwhelmed by grief, broke into uncontrollable sobbing while Gaspard simply sat in stony silence. Claude just sat quietly not knowing what to say or do next.

"We thank you for your kindness in performing this odious task," said Matthieu, the only Ruscino able to find words. "Now you must stay the night and share our table. I am certain you have stories to tell of my nephew that will be less tragic in nature, and we shall want to hear them all."

"Y-yes, certainly," stammered Gaspard, his senses starting to return. "Stay the night. Share our table. Tell us your stories."

He spoke as in a dream, or more as if he had been pole-axed, which, in a way, he had.

This news cast a pall over the Ruscino home. Their worst fears had been realized. And soon they must embark upon their own dangerous journey. A journey that would result either in great healing joy in Toulouse, or in total devastation on the roads of Languedoc. All depended on the fortunes of their travels. When the day of departure arrived, Matthieu carried a second pistol in his belt, thinking that he might lend fortune a hand.

It would be a difficult six-day journey, assuming the roads were sound, the dray held up and the horses stayed healthy. But knowing that the roads were seldom sound this early in the year, they had allowed ten days. They were praying that they would be spared a spring storm that would turn the clay of Languedoc into grasping muck that would hold a dray like theirs beyond retrieval even by their team of two strong horses.

"I should have four horses for this journey," thought Gaspard. "If I ever make this trip again, I must have two more."

But the weather was kind and the roads stayed dry. Passing through Béziers, they spent the first night at an *auberge* south of the city near the Orb River where there were stables for their horses and secure storage for their wagon. The second day brought them safely to Villedaigne where they found similar accommodations. In the evening of the third day, they arrived in Trèbes and again found a secure *auberge* for the night. The fourth day found them in Villepinte and the fifth in Villefranche. Here they enjoyed their host's company at supper and shared with him the purpose of their journey.

His face darkened.

"Would there was another route from here to Toulouse," he warned. "I would not travel that road of late for love nor for money. Highwaymen camped in secret forest lairs sortie out to waylay innocent travelers at random. Your wine and your women will be sorely tempting. Do not tarry on the road for any reason."

"We thank you for your counsel, monsieur," replied Gaspard, "and we shall use all care. But fortune leaves us no choice: we must be on to Toulouse."

On the sixth and final day of travel they learned the wisdom of the innkeeper's warning.

* * *

Richard Garat was former army, mustered out for crimes committed against French citizens while in uniform. He had fled Paris to escape the hangman's noose. He and his band of brigands lived in the forest east of Toulouse. From there they preyed upon travelers on the road that ran between Villefranche and Toulouse.

There was a ready black market for salt from the salt pans along the Mediterranean coast, wine from the Rhone, Languedoc or Roussillon, or woad balls from the golden triangle formed by Toulouse, Carcassonne and Albi. Of course, they preferred coin from travelers' purses. And any women they waylaid would provide them days of entertainment before they ultimately slit their throats to make way for new stock.

Today they had their sights on a large dray full of barrels, drawn by a team of two horses. Riding beside the driver were another man and two women.

"Don't kill the women," cautioned Garat. "They're no fun if they're dead. And use your steel on the men, it's cheaper and quieter."

When the seven bandits rode out from the woods to block the road, Gaspard reined in the horses. Matthieu's first thoughts were of the pistols in his belt and the musket mounted within reach on the side of the wagon, but he quickly realized that those meager arms would provide little protection against seven.

"Don't anyone be a hero," warned Garat. "We just want your wagon and your goods. You can walk to town from here."

Matthieu doubted it. He had seen renegade soldiers before and knew the look. These men were not planning to leave any witnesses.

Matthieu dropped to the ground. The man who appeared to be the leader rode toward him, unsheathing his sword as he came. A second advanced toward Gaspard. They had not seen the pistols under Matthieu's coat. The dray separated Matthieu from his brother and the women. As Garat approached, Matthieu saw his doom clearly. He calmly drew both pistols from his belt and shot the brigand through the chest left-handed. Garat was dead before he hit the ground. The second pistol he turned on the cur who had targeted Gaspard and dropped him in similar fashion.

Forgetting the other three victims for the moment, a third bandit charged, sword raised. Instinctively, Matthieu dropped the empty pistols and drew his own sword in defense.

Suddenly, three more shots roared in unison, and three more of the brigands fell, including the one attacking Matthieu. The force of the musket ball drove him forward, off his horse, and full onto Matthieu. As he fell, his sword glanced harmlessly off Matthieu's, but the falling rider splayed Matthieu on his back with his attacker atop him.

The two remaining thieves, on seeing a dozen men wearing the Sun King's livery galloping toward them, broke for the forest, but one was dropped by a sixth shot before reaching the cover of the trees. Two of the rescuers rode after the last man, and before long a seventh shot was heard, and then no more.

Gaspard, seeing that his wife and daughter were safe, fairly vaulted the dray to reach his brother's side. Rolling the villain off, he was horrified to see his blood-soaked brother.

"Where are you hurt?" he asked, fearing what the answer might be.

"*Mon cul!*" Matthieu grumbled as he rose, "I fell on a rather hard stone. All this blood's from his vile heart, it's none of mine own."

The rest of the rescuers came forward to greet the travelers. A distinguished looking gentleman who appeared to be in charge approached Matthieu. He was well dressed, almost foppish, and had dark curly hair that fell below his shoulders, typical of the fashion of the day. He had the full round face of a man who doesn't miss many meals, and the creases in the corners of his eyes seemed more likely from laughter than from squinting. He wore a large, broad-brimmed black hat and a cape that draped from his shoulders to the haunches of his steed.

"Well met, my friends," he said. "Are you all unscathed? Allow me to introduce myself…"

"I know well who you are, my lord," injected Gaspard. "You're the Baron Pierre-Paul Riquet, the *Fermier General* of Languedoc, to whom my little winery pays a premium for the salt that sustains us. You may recall searching our home for contraband on occasion. In honesty, I haven't enjoyed our meetings much before today."

Riquet laughed deeply and amiably. He was a man people found difficult to dislike, despite his hateful occupation. The *gabelle*, or salt tax, was the most hated tax in France -- more so in Languedoc, where allegiance to the Sun King was gossamer thin. Neither people nor livestock could live without salt, and the *gabelle* was a duty on that vital commodity. It was a royal monopoly that required the King's subjects to buy from the King's salt banks at a price that included his substantial duty. Salt "farmers" collected the *gabelle* in the name of the King, adding a somewhat discretionary amount to the price as an administrative commission. Riquet was fundamentally an honest man, not greedy like many of his counterparts in other provinces, but still earned a comfortable living.

"Ah, yes," said Riquet. "*Monsieur* Ruscino of Bessan. I remember now. But *monsieur*, I am but a humble businessman like yourself. It is for the King and for France that I collect the tax you find so odious."

"That aside," said Gaspard, "we are most pleased to meet you and your men so fortuitously. I fear our lives were forfeit without your intervention. We are in your debt."

Again, Riquet laughed. "And you may be assured that I shall be by to collect that debt in due course, monsieur! It is, after all, what I do. But for now, please allow me to send four of my men with you to Toulouse. Now that we've dispatched this bunch, I doubt you'll have any more troubles between here and the city gates, but I would be loath to have our auspicious meeting be for naught. I'm sure the eight who stay with me will be adequate to protect the King's revenues. It is the Sun King's coin they are here to protect, not his humble *fermier*."

The two guards who had left in pursuit of the last bandit returned. One was leading the last of the brigands on foot, hands tied behind his back and a noose around his neck. The captor was Hugo Hérault, the captain of Riquet's guard. Riquet had hired him years ago, upon his appointment as *Fermier General* for Languedoc. Hugo had been recommended by Riquet's uncle, François de Portugniares, who had known Hérault's family and considered Hugo to be an ethical, competent soldier whose loyalty could be relied upon. Hugo had a tall muscular frame and the scars of one who has survived many battles. He had the easy confidence of a man who was in his element in combat. Over their years together, Hugo had proven his courage and his loyalty to Riquet many times. While Hugo was away at war, his entire family had been slain by marauders just such as these.

"Claude here, missed the thief but shot his horse," chuckled Hugo. "Clean head shot. Dropped like a stone. This rat turd seems to have a new appreciation for the sweetness of life, having dodged the ball. I thought maybe we could persuade him to lead us to their lair?"

"Excellent idea," agreed Riquet. "We'll attend to that once these travelers are safely on their way." Turning to the Ruscinos, "This has indeed been a fortuitous meeting. We must arrange a visit at Bonrepos, my estate near Verfeil, just five leagues east of Toulouse. We shall properly celebrate our good fortune. But for now, as you say, I am a salt farmer and it is harvest season, so I must be off to gather the King's crop. My parting advice to you, Monsieur Ruscino, would be to consider shipping your wine around Spain to Bordeaux and thence up the Garonne to Toulouse. It might cost more in coin, but less in lives."

"With respect, Monsieur le Baron, you know naught of what you speak," replied Gaspard. "My only son was lost to that route just last year. The Berbers slew him. We just learned of his death on the fifth of March. One of his shipmates brought us the news. As he tells the story, my son died bravely defending against the boarding. But died nonetheless. There is no safe route from Agde to Toulouse."

"I am truly sorry for your loss, monsieur, replied Riquet. "I should have kept my counsel to myself. That said, let me assure you that as we speak our King is considering a bold plan to provide a safe route from the riviera to Toulouse, and even to Bordeaux. But for now, *bon voyage*! Better fortune to you all!"

He put his valet, Gerome, in charge of the guard he had leant to the Ruscinos, then he and the guard he retained headed into the woods in search of the lair of the highway pirates. The Ruscinos climbed back aboard the dray and, this time with an armed escort, proceeded to Toulouse for Collette's wedding. Later that year, upon returning to Bonrepos, after an adventure to be recounted later, Riquet found a cask of Carignan in his cellar that had not been there when he left.

* * *

Riquet's sortie into the woods that day proved all too fruitful. They did indeed find the lair, six more highwaymen, a dirty, sickly lot, and four female prisoners who had clearly been sorely misused. Hugo's men quickly disarmed the lot and lined them up before the Baron.

"Now what shall we do with you then?" Riquet asked no one in particular.

"Put the brigands to the sword," volunteered Hugo. "Save us the trouble taking 'em in and save the court the trouble of hanging 'em."

"Probably good advice," agreed Riquet, "but I am well beyond the bounds of my Barony here and I am not certain into which fief this forest falls but there can be no doubt that the courts of Toulouse have judicial powers here. We must conduct the ladies to safety anyway, so I think we shall let those courts deal with this lot. Gather their horses and put the ladies on the best four. Bind the brigands together in a chain and we'll let them walk to Toulouse. If there's anything here worth the salvage, lade it onto the free horses and we'll confiscate it in the King's name."

The women, half insane, were at first loath to be touched even by their saviors. Eventually they realized that these men meant them no harm and were persuaded to mount the horses that would carry them to Toulouse and safety.

They half-dragged their chain of thieves to Toulouse. There wasn't much fight left in the ragged brigands when they staggered into the prison. Riquet signed a warrant charging them with highway robbery, rape, and murder, and left them in the care of the magistrate.

The women he entrusted to the church, knowing that the sisters would care for them until their families could be located and contacted.

Once his business in Toulouse was concluded, Riquet spoke briefly with his Captain.

"I have received word of a very distinguished visitor who is on his way to Bonrepos as we speak. I must ride there in haste," he told Hugo, "but I would like you to continue the harvest in my name. There is no one I would trust more with the King's coin than you, but I ask that you keep in mind that it is a burdensome and unpopular tax and endeavor to be strict but compassionate with our countrymen."

The Ruscinos had been delivered safely to Toulouse, and Riquet's troop had thereafter been reunited. He and Gerome set out for Bonrepos, leaving Hugo to continue the harvest with the rest of his force. Riquet was confident that Gerome would provide all the security he needed for his person.

The distinguished visitor he rode to meet at Bonrepos was Hector de Boutheroüe de Bourgneuf, a man who would play a key role in the success or failure of the bold plan Riquet had mentioned to Gaspard.

Three

The Canal.

Pierre-Paul Riquet dreamed of a canal.

The summer sun of Sorèze was hot as he sat by a stream with his best friend, Paul Mas, fishing, unsuccessfully, while his sister, Madeleine, was content to sit and watch. She seemed happy to be wherever Paul was.

They were on release from the Jesuit school in Béziers, and staying in Sorèze with his aunt and uncle, Isabeau and François de Portugniares. Isabeau was his mother's sister who, being childless, welcomed the Riquet children as her own. François, a gentleman of substance, had been asked to serve as Pierre-Paul's godfather. François was very fond of them as well and would one day welcome his role as surrogate father.

Pierre-Paul, who was nearing the end of his school days, had persuaded Paul to join him this summer. Although the Riquet children got along well, Pierre-Paul's relationship with his brother and sisters was not the same as the bond he felt with his best friend. He and Paul seemed to think as one in all things except their studies. Paul relished his law lessons, Pierre-Paul loved math and science.

As they sat, simmering in their own sweat, Paul asked Pierre-Paul for a promise.

"If I should melt and flow into that stream, promise me that you will inform my parents of my fate."

"But if you do," countered Pierre-Paul, "I shall soon follow and not be left to tell of our demise.

"Instead, I suggest we go for a swim."

"In this little stream?" laughed Paul. "We could cool our ankles, perhaps."

Pierre-Paul rose decisively to act on an idea he had been incubating. He gathered an armload of limbs shed from nearby trees and carried them to the culvert where the rural road crossed their stream.

He built a grille across the mouth of the culvert and pulled sod from the stream bank to seal the cracks. The road crossing became a dam and a pond began to build behind it.

"*Now* shall we swim?" he asked triumphantly.

All three of them waded in and before long were enjoying a surprisingly large swimming hole.

"Who would have thought," asked Paul in amazement, "that this small stream could form such a lake so quickly."

"Obviously," said Pierre-Paul, "*I* did."

But in an hour or so he realized that his pond would soon overtop the road, and not wishing to damage the road he decided to open the culvert a little. He dove under to pull free some of the blockage he had built but it refused to budge. The tremendous weight of all that water held his grill immobile. He tried to remove just the sod, but the grass tore free leaving the root-mass caulking in place.

As the pond started to spill into the road Pierre-Paul realized that he was in real trouble and urgently flagged down a passing farmer for help. Learning what the boy had done, the farmer unhitched his horse and pulled a length of stout rope from the bed of his wagon. Pierre-Paul tied a loop in one end of the rope, dove under and managed to hook it onto his grille. The farmer tied the other end of the rope to his horse's harness, and, with some effort, the horse was able to free the blockage, the pond drained, and the road was spared any serious damage.

Pierre-Paul had learned a valuable lesson regarding the awesome power of water collected in even moderately large quantities.

* * *

Fifty-four years before he was destined to rescue the Ruscinos, Pierre-Paul Riquet began life well positioned for success. He was born in Béziers, the son of a prominent local attorney and legislator who was one of the Consuls of Béziers. His father, Guillaume, was descended from Italian nobility but his grandfather had left that status behind when he emigrated to Occitania to escape political persecution.

To support his family, Pierre-Paul's grandfather, Nicolas, had been forced to find gainful employment. Gainful employment was not allowed for members of the nobility and his grandfather's eventual success as a clothier bore the price of derogation of the family's noble status.

Despite the loss of noble status, the Riquets were well regarded in Béziers society and Nicolas' clothier business provided enough income to support Jesuit education for his sons. Guillaume chose law. He had no interest in a career as a clothier. By the time Pierre-Paul was born Guillaume had a thriving practice and was quite wealthy.

His wife, Guillaumette, gave him four children: two boys and two girls. Feeling that he had benefited greatly from his Jesuit education, Guillaume wanted his sons, Pierre and Pierre-Paul, to have the same advantage. Pierre-Paul's academic strengths lay in the sciences. Pierre, the eldest, chose a clerical life, possibly motivated by the miseries which befell his family as a result of his father's questionable ethics.

Guillaume was not above using his office for personal gain. This sometimes resulted in public confrontations, which he often opted to settle with his blade. His skill with a sword was well known and tended to deter confrontation.

His time in jail, however, was not served for murder but for an unpaid debt. He was an entrepreneur with an eye for lucrative opportunities, which did not always bring the results he expected. When he died, he left a significant fortune, but also significant debt for his family to settle.

In Pierre-Paul, the Jesuits saw Guillaume's business acumen tempered by a much stronger sense of ethics. This was, again, no doubt due to his father's negative example and the grief he had seen it bring upon his mother. The Jesuits assured Guillaume that his second son had a promising future as a businessman. They were willing to forgive his total lack of interest in languages in consideration of his love for math and science.

Pierre-Paul found particular interest in hydraulics, the study of the behavior of liquids. His first exposure to practical hydraulics came as his father recounted one of his cases at supper one evening. Guillaume had represented a local miller in a dispute over rights to a stream that powered his mill. A neighboring farmer had diverted the stream to irrigate his land, causing the mill to cease milling. Guillaume had determined that the lay of the land would permit the stream to be diverted at a point downstream from the mill, thereby affording both parties the use of the same water.

"With the proper guidance," he told his son, "water can serve many masters."

Telling the story, Guillaume focused on the fact that the miller and the farmer were both pleased by his solution. But Pierre-Paul's imagination was captured by the power that lay in redirecting a seemingly insignificant stream to serve the needs of men.

Later, his father's derision of a proposal to construct a canal from Carcassonne to Toulouse only served to further inspire Pierre-Paul's imagination.

As a Consul of Béziers, Guillaume heard a proposal put forward to connect the Aude River at Carcassonne with the Garonne at Toulouse. The Garonne was navigable from Toulouse to the Atlantic Ocean, via Bordeaux and the Gironde. As part of the plan, the Aude would be made navigable from Carcassonne to Narbonne on the Mediterranean. The proposed canal would thereby link the Mediterranean Sea with the Atlantic Ocean. The proponents of the canal set forth their case:

"The sea route from the riviera to Bordeaux by way of Gibraltar is fraught with peril. If our ships don't fall prey to the Barbary pirates, they are taken by Spanish men-of-war. The overland routes are no better. Travelers and carters are plagued by thieves and murderers. And the roads are unreliable as well as unsafe. Inclement weather renders them impassable.

"The Consuls have a responsibility to the people of Languedoc to provide for safe travel and a safe route for trade between the Mediterranean and the *Océane* . This proposal would fulfill that obligation."

This plan had resurfaced periodically since the days of the Roman Empire but was always discarded, foundering on the absence of a water source for the summit locks. To move traffic along a canal to either higher or lower elevations, the traffic was sequestered in a confined space sealed front and back by "lock" doors. Then the lock chambers were filled to raise boats or emptied to lower them. After a single use the water was, perforce, passed downstream. This process required an abundant source of water for the summit that would need to be constant through all seasons. At the proposed summit, more than six hundred feet above sea level, there was no such source.

"It's the same old plan with a new sponsor," declared one of Guillaume's colleagues. "Nearly a century ago the great da Vinci examined this route and deemed it impossible due to the absence of a water source to feed the summit locks. How many times must we flog this long dead horse?"

"And if we were to find a way to do the impossible, who benefits?" accused another. "Trade on this canal would be trade drawn away from Marseille, Béziers, Agde, and even Perpignan. "We would be undertaking great financial risk only to benefit Narbonne at the expense of the other great port cities of Languedoc."

"Clearly," observed Guillaume Riquet, "some of you find this plan impractical. Some say it is absurdly optimistic. Others see it as self-serving and detrimental to the interests of all Languedoc save Carcassonne and Narbonne. To my mind, it is all these things. My vote is with the opposition."

At supper that evening, Guillaume shared the experience with his family.

"Foolishness," scoffed his father. "François the First explored the concept one hundred and fifty years ago. He even brought the great engineer Leonardo da Vinci to evaluate the route. Da Vinci himself determined that there was no reliable water source to feed the locks at the summit. The *États du Languedoc* declined the same proposal just last year.

"Even the Romans, who left us so many great works of engineering, deemed the idea impossible."

But the younger Riquet was intrigued. The seed was sown; the dream developed. Throughout his youth he remained captivated by the idea. While his schoolmates were playing tennis, Pierre-Paul was in the school library studying lock designs and poring over every map of Occitania he could find, seeking a solution to this enigma. He dreamed of finding a way to connect the two seas.

* * *

Pierre-Paul was seventeen when his father died. This drew him closer to his aunt and uncle in Sorèze, where he began to spend more time. The village lay at the foot of the *Montagne Noire*, a great mass of granite at the southwest corner of the *Massif Central;* actually, a short range of close-set peaks considered singular by the locals. These mountains straddled the central divide of the great valley. Streams flowed from these mountains west to the Atlantic or east toward the Mediterranean. As Riquet traveled the paths of the village and the mountains, he would often wonder if the solution to the challenge of the water supply for a canal to connect the two seas might somehow be found in the abundant waters of the *Montagne Noire.*

Despite Guillaume's financial troubles he left a substantial fortune. The jail time resulting from his failure to pay a debt was due to stubbornness and spite, not inability to pay. Two years after his father's death Pierre-Paul settled the contentious debt and had enough left over to fund some investments. In 1630 his godfather, well respected in Paris, arranged for him to buy the contract to sell salt for the King in two nearby villages: Lavaur and Castres. This was his entry into the life-long occupation of administering the *gabelle* for the King.

Much of the objection to the *gabelle* was rooted in the great disparity inherent in the duty from one region to the next. The King's levy could vary by as much as a factor of thirty, which produced an irresistible incentive to smuggle salt across regional borders or north, across the Pyrénées from Spain where it could be had for a small fraction of the King's price.

Those, like Riquet, who contracted to sell salt for the King were obligated to make fixed periodic payments to the royal treasury and it was their responsibility to sell enough salt to cover that obligation and whatever profit they could manage.

To that end, these salt farmers were given broad authority to curb smuggling. They could, at will, search persons, homes and transport for salt that was not packaged, documented and stamped with the *fleur de lis* of the King. Penalties for smuggling were severe, including conscription for galley service or even death.

Abuse of this inspection authority was common, especially with regard to searching women, known to commonly secrete contraband salt on their persons when travelling from a region of lower duty to one where the duty might be thirty times higher. Riquet would brook no such abuse by his employees.

A minimum consumption of salt was ascribed to anyone over the age of eight, and records of legitimate purchase could be demanded at any time by the King's salt farmers.

Riquet extracted only a modest commission from those buying salt from the Royal Granaries he managed, satisfied with the comfortable income it provided and not wanting to be drawn into the vice of excessive greed that he had witnessed in his father.

He was ambitious and a hard worker and his *gabelle* responsibilities increased quickly, much to the annoyance of his colleague, Jean de Milhau. Milhau, like Riquet, had grown up in Béziers. He was the older brother of Riquet's childhood friend, Catherine de Milhau, and older than Riquet as well. He was senior in the administrative structure of the *gabelles* and resented Riquet's rapid rise.

* * *

Riquet was just twenty-five when he won the contract to oversee the salt bank in Mirepoix, thirty miles south of Sorèze. The position was untenable from his uncle's home, so he took up residence in a small house adjoining the salt bank of Mirepoix where he could easily keep an eye on the salt trade. Salt was almost the same as currency in seventeenth century Languedoc, thievery was common, and the workers in the salt bank needed watching.

Before he left for Mirepoix, his uncle persuaded him to hire a valet.

"Not everyone loves salt farmers," he explained. "You should have a second to aid in your defense should the need arise.

"Please allow me to introduce Gerome Barnard. He served as Aide de Camp to the Comte de Montauban until the wound that took his left leg below the knee retired him. He is an expert with both steel and powder and will serve you well."

Gerome was armed with a mortuary sword, a poniard and two pistols, and the polished ash post that completed his left leg gave him more the look of a pirate than a gentlemen's gentleman. But Riquet found his look appropriate for the valet of a salt farmer and, relying on his godfather's recommendation, hired him instantly.

* * *

Riquet's ascension to the Mirepoix salt bank did nothing to mitigate the enmity of Jean de Milhau. At supper Jean resentfully sought sympathy from his wife, Toinette.

"I applied for that post two years ago," he groused. "It should have been mine. We have family there."

"It was not meant to be, Jean," Toinette consoled, "Perhaps God has other plans for you."

"So, God wants me to trek twenty leagues every time I want to see my parents and my sister?" he scowled.

"That burden falls upon me as well," she cajoled, "and I am content to abide by God's will."

Unappeased, he finished his meal in silence.

In fact, his mother, father and sister, Catherine, now lived just down the street from Riquet's new home. They had relocated from Béziers shortly after Riquet moved to Sorèze. Catherine was a beautiful young woman and now that they were neighbors, Mirepoix was too small a village for chance to keep Pierre-Paul and Catherine apart for long. Romance soon kindled.

This did nothing to mitigate the enmity of Jean de Milhau. His father passed, leaving him at the head of the de Milhau household and Riquet would need his approval to marry Catherine.

Riquet was truly shocked at the animosity displayed by the man he hoped would soon be his *beau-frère.*

"You will never marry her while I live!" spat Jean, his face contorted in an angry scowl.

"Why, in the name of Heaven, do you despise me so?" pled Riquet, having no idea of the resentment Jean bore him.

"I still remember the time your scandalous father spent in prison in Béziers," replied Jean, not wanting to admit his baser motives. "The acorn never falls far from the tree. My sister deserves better."

"I am not my father," argued Riquet. "When he passed it was I who settled the debt for which he was incarcerated."

"My position is firm. You shall not marry."

"You care nothing for the love we feel for each other?"

"I do not need to justify myself to you. I have nothing more to say on the subject."

With that, he called to his valet to show Riquet to the door.

Riquet left in despair. He was bound by the culture and customs of his day. He and Catherine could not marry without the permission of Jean de Milhau.

Catherine, on the other hand, found the whole affair ridiculous. She loved Pierre-Paul deeply and refused to allow her domineering brother to keep them apart. She pled her case to Toinette at every opportunity, hoping that her sister-in-law might intercede on her behalf. Meanwhile, she and Pierre-Paul behaved as young lovers do. They were committed to each other for life and saw marriage as a formality that would eventually be observed. The inevitable result was the absence of Catherine's monthly visitor in May of 1637. Realizing she was carrying Riquet's child, she implored Toinette to persuade Jean to relent.

Toinette, who was fond of Riquet and had been plying her husband with subtle diplomacy for some time, decided that the time for subtle diplomacy had passed.

"You claim you want better for her," she accused Jean, "but the status of unwed mother will benefit her none. She will be relegated to the convent and that is no life for a bright young woman like Catherine. This is not the consequence of some irresponsible roll in the hay. This is the natural product of two young people who deeply love each other living in close proximity. You must dismount that proud steed of arrogance and do what is truly best for your sister. Until and unless you do, I can promise you no peace in this family!"

With that she spun on her heel and left him in his study, his brow furrowed, lips moving, groping for a word of defense. The only sound was the crackle of the fire.

Pierre-Paul and Catherine were married in Mirepoix the following week.

* * *

In January Catherine presented Pierre-Paul with his first son, Jean-Mathias, a robust infant who thrived in the care of his doting parents. In stark contrast, their second son, Pierre, born three years later was a frail child. Not long after his first birthday he contracted a fever that could not be eased by leeches. He left them before he saw his fifteenth moon.

October of 1645 brought their first daughter, Elizabeth, goddaughter to the now reconciled Jean de Milhau, and in November of the following year Pierre-Pol was born, who would be just two years old when the family moved to Revel.

In 1648, when Riquet's responsibilities were expanded to include all of *Haut-Languedoc*, thanks to his administrative skills and to the connections in Paris enjoyed by his godfather, he decided to resettle in Revel. This was again a choice that would keep him close to his work, Revel being centrally located between the salt banks he now supervised. Fatefully, the move would also bring him back into the shadow of the *Montagne Noire*.

This great sentinel drew rain clouds like flowers draw bees and they dropped their life-giving cargo in abundance, feeding the many streams that flowed east or flowed west from its shoulders. Riquet still nurtured the conviction that this

Dark Mountain, sitting astride the divide, could be the source of alimentation for a canal that would finally link the two seas.

Revel lay very near that divide, near the confluence of the Sor and the Laudot rivers which many speculated could be improved to accommodate commercial navigation. The town also offered many business opportunities for an ambitious young man.

With his income from the *gabelle* and with his inheritance, Riquet launched several business ventures in Revel. He bought a mill, as much to feed his fascination with hydraulics as to provide income. He also acquired some apartments and other commercial properties, but the mill was his pet enterprise. He was, indeed, a very successful businessman, but the prospect of linking the two seas was never far from his thoughts.

Beyond the obvious benefit of steady income from the *gabelle*, his success administering his salt stores demonstrated his reliability to the King's court. This eventually provided him an entry into the lucrative business of supplying matériel to the King's armies fighting in Roussillon and Spain. He provided uniforms dyed with woad from Carcassonne, beef, mutton, grain, and wine from the farms and vineyards of Languedoc, and leather goods and munitions from Toulouse. The trade made him a wealthy man. Some speculated that he might be the wealthiest man in all Languedoc.

As his income grew, so did his family. Within a week of their resettlement in Revel, Catherine gave Pierre-Paul another daughter, Marie.

Not long after the expansion of his role with the *gabelle* Riquet realized that he needed help managing the salt banks. He decided to approach his brother-in-law, Paul Mas, his best friend since his days at Jesuit school in Béziers. Paul was now an attorney in Béziers and well respected. More than friends now, they were family, Mas having married Riquet's sister,

Madeleine. Paul and Madeleine were childless and loved Riquet's children as if they were their own.

One evening after supper, in the mellow mood of pipes and cognac, Riquet asked his brother-in-law to act as his deputy for eastern Languedoc, knowing that he was totally trustworthy, and that the King's coin would never stick to his fingers. Paul was not immediately sanguine for the prospect of administering the *gabelle*.

"I am not certain I have the temperament to be a tax farmer," hedged Paul. "Tax farmer" was a term applied by many to the role Riquet viewed as "salt farmer," an essentially semantical distinction.

"Your role would be administrative, not confrontational," explained Riquet. "Others will collect; you will receive the collections for deposit with the *États* and maintain accounts of the receipts."

"I cannot decide a thing like this on the moment. Let me discuss it with Madeleine, and let the idea mellow some overnight. I expect that I shall have an answer for you in the morning."

In the morning, having realized that it would be a service to Riquet which he was uniquely qualified to perform, Paul agreed.

Riquet's greatly expanded *gabelle* territory greatly increased the demand on his time, so Catherine assumed more duties with estate business. She managed the staff and the accounts, collected rents and saw to procurement of supplies. She was a natural administrator and eventually her skills came into play managing the staff of the *gabelle* as well.

Returning, exhausted from a trip to Narbonne where the salt bank was headless, its manager having been found shot dead by the side of the road, Riquet asked her, "Are there any promising applicants to manage the salt bank in Narbonne?"

"One," she said. "This young man, François Andréossy, looks promising. He's young, but so were you when you managed Mirepoix."

Riquet eagerly scanned the application. "Barely twenty-one," he mused. "But he has a letter of recommendation from the Bishop of Castres, Monseigneur Charles-François d'Anglure de Bourlemont. This was the cleric my godfather approached to have my name put forward for Mirepoix. A young man with such connections might prove useful. It would be a blessing to be relieved of the need to personally manage Narbonne."

"Like you, he has roots in Italy," she offered.

This seemed a minor decision like those we all make occasionally with no concept of the magnitude of their ultimate significance. The appointment of François Andréossy to manage the salt bank in Narbonne introduced an essential element to the complex alloy that would ultimately be forged into the destiny of Pierre-Paul Riquet.

Four

The Forge.

Several key elements needed to coalesce in the forge of history before Riquet's dream could transmuted to reality. Realization of so great a dream would require collaboration of great minds possessing special knowledge, special skills, inspiration and the political influence required to bring these talents to light.

While living in Revel, Riquet encountered another of these: the local *fontainier*, Pierre Campmas. As *fontainier* of Revel, Campmas was responsible for maintaining the region's water supply. He was also charged with efforts to mitigate the impact of floods. Riquet had occasion to employ him when changes in the channel of the Sor River cut off the water supply to his mill.

Riquet liked Campmas immediately. He was tall, broad shouldered and the sort of muscular that comes with hard work. His hair was cropped in an almost monastic cut, but he had a full black beard. His eyes sparkled with good humor and showed creases at the corners that Riquet deemed likely to have been born of laughter more than squinting, although his face was darkly weather-tanned, like leather. Above all, Riquet was drawn to him through their shared passion for hydraulics.

"The river has abandoned me," complained Riquet. "The flood brought too much water to allow the mill to run, then when the flood waters departed so did the Sor. My mill no longer mills. Can the old channel be restored?"

"It seems a simple matter," replied Campmas. "We shall remove the silt from the intake for your mill and install a weir in the new channel just upstream from it. The weir will redirect the flow toward the intake."

Pierre's simple diversionary weir solved the problem and made an immediate impression on his client. Riquet's penchant for hydrology drew them together, but their compatible personalities cemented a friendship that lasted through decades. They supped together on many occasions and Riquet shared his dream of a canal that would link the Mediterranean and the Atlantic, speculating that the Fresquel River, destined for the Mediterranean, and the Atlantic-bound Laudot River might be joined to that end. The two spent many evenings engaged in passionate discussions about the practical aspects of building such a canal and supplying it with alimentation. They both believed that the abundant waters of the *Montagne Noire* could somehow be harnessed for the task.

Later, after moving his family to Toulouse, Riquet would still maintain his friendship with the *fontainier*, visiting at Pierre's home as often as Pierre visited his, despite the miles that separated them.

Campmas' home in Revel lay in the shadow of the *Montagne Noire*. The waters of the northern slopes of the mountain fed the Laudot River and those of the south face fed the Fresquel. Those two rivers were separated by a narrow divide near Revel – essentially a sill which was on the break line of the divide of the great valley. This sill was known as the *seuil de Graissens*. Riquet envisioned a canal that would link the two rivers by crossing that sill. Combined with improvements to those two river channels and the rivers they fed, navigation between the two seas might at last become a reality. Earlier plans had been designed to cross the threshold farther south at the *seuil de Naurouze*, which separated the Aude watershed from the Garonne watershed. The *seuil de Graissens* was at a higher elevation than the *seuil de Naurouze*, and would therefore require more locks, but the availability of alimentation for the summit locks was the key factor for feasibility, and Riquet believed that the *Montagne Noire* could provide an adequate water supply to the *seuil de Graissens*, although he was not yet sure how it could be done.

Unfortunately, although Campmas agreed with Riquet, neither had a specific plan to put forward nor the political status to put the concept before the Sun King for further study. Lacking any avenue to proceed, they could only ponder, discuss, and trust that someone or something would show them the way forward.

* * *

Another key element gathered in Revel was the master builder Isaac Roux.

As Riquet's income grew, he began to plan for the security of his children's future. The loss of nobility his family had suffered upon fleeing political persecution in Italy had been a painful memory for his father and grandfather and he dreamed of restoring his family's noble status.

To that end, in 1651, he bought the fief of Bonrepos, twenty-four miles northwest of Revel, near the village of Verfeil, only ten miles east of Toulouse. As the new Baron of Bonrepos he was immediately endowed with "nobility of the robe" (as opposed to "nobility of the sword," which was acquired only genetically). It did not bring him acceptance by those of the latter class, more in the nature of contempt. But he saw it as a step toward reclamation of his family's honor. In his mind the Riquets were indeed "nobility of the sword."

The fief included an old chateau which was not livable, but the structure was sound and he could easily afford the needed renovations. The moat had been backfilled long ago and he liked it that way. He contracted with Roux to rebuild the chateau as more of a manor than a fortress. Over the years of renovation, he spent many nights there and engaged in lengthy discussions of design with Roux.

"I want a comfortable home for my family, not a castle," he told Isaac. "I want to be able to entertain guests in style. I am acquiring farms, forests and streams to enhance the estate and provide food for a grand table."

"I understand your meaning, *Monsieur le Baron*," said Isaac, "and I am certain that I can create the structure you desire. The foundation of the chateau is sound. I shall build cookstoves and ovens in the basement along with pantries to supply them."

"And an icehouse on the north side for keeping perishables in the summertime," interjected Riquet.

"The parlor, ballroom, cabinet, library and dining will be next, at ground level, with a fire in every room," continued Roux. "The family and guest quarters will be next, on the first floor, then an attic level for staff."

"Clearly I have picked the right man for the job!" exclaimed Riquet.

As the mill restoration had been with Campmas, this project would be the foundation of a long, strong friendship between Riquet and Roux.

The project was immense, and Roux and his wife would soon resettle in the village of Bonrepos until the renovations were completed in 1663. Later, despite beautiful homes in Revel and Toulouse, this would always be the place the Riquet family called "home."

* * *

As the work on Bonrepos progressed, the plague struck Languedoc. After years of poor harvests resulting in widespread famine and poverty -- the *plague*.

It struck first in Narbonne and did not threaten Revel for several years, but it was a time of poor harvests and hardship for all, even landlords like Riquet. Impoverished tenants could not pay rents. They could be evicted, but that would not replace the rents. It was only his contract administering the *gabelle* that carried Riquet through this time. The fixed price of salt was not diminished by poor harvests and salt was an essential commodity.

Nonetheless, he did not escape all suffering. It was during these hard years that Catherine bore him twins. The girl was named after her mother; the boy, named Guillaume for Riquet's father, was stillborn.

Eventually the impact on Riquet's workforce from both famine and plague left too few workers to spread, dry and harvest the salt derived from seawater in the salt pans south of Narbonne. To remedy the situation, Riquet found himself working elbow to elbow with the spreaders, driers and harvesters, regardless of the threat of contagion, to assure the supply of salt for the Sun King's salt banks.

Also working by his side was young François Andréossy, whom he had recently hired to manage the salt bank of Narbonne. A young man in his twenties, he wore the clothes of a gentleman. His boots were of fine leather and the hilt of his rapier was gilded and bejeweled. Impressed by the young man's courage and industry, Riquet asked him to join him for supper one evening.

The inn they chose was dimly lit but cozy, and their table was near the fire. They were both exhausted from a long day in the salt pans, but an uncharacteristically robust Côtes du Rhône revived them quickly.

As they sipped the wine from pewter goblets waiting for their supper, Riquet's curiosity opened the conversation.

"I was impressed by the recommendation provided you by the Bishop of Castres," admitted Riquet. "How did you come to be sponsored by a man of such notable influence in Paris?"

"Paris is where I was born and educated. My parents had many influential friends there and knew of the respect the Bishop enjoyed and believed his endorsement might turn your decision in my favor.

"I understand that you are interested in linking the seas," continued Andréossy, sans segue.

Riquet's face visibly brightened.

"I am indeed," he replied.

"It is an interest of mine as well," declared the young man. "I studied the sciences while I was in Paris, and hydrology was of particular interest to me.

"I only recently returned from a journey to Lombardy and Padua in the Italian republics to settle the estate of my grandmother. While there, I examined the mitered lock doors invented by the great Leonardo da Vinci. Their workings are truly remarkable.

"I understand that you, too have roots in Italy."

"I do," said Riquet. "Noble roots. I hope one day to have that nobility restored.

"I also hope one day to make communication between the seas a reality. Perhaps you would like to assist me in that endeavor?"

"I would indeed," replied the young man eagerly. Now *his* face brightened.

"Have you solved the problem of alimentation for the summit locks?" he asked.

"No, but I believe I am close to a solution. I believe it will be found in the waters of the *Montagne Noire*."

"In this, as in the *gabelle*, I am at your service, *Monsieur le Baron*," affirmed the young man.

* * *

Once his work was done in Narbonne, Riquet returned to Revel. He arrived late in the evening, exhausted, and more interested in brandy than food.

While Gerome lit the fire in the den, Catherine decanted his favorite brandy and filled his favorite pipe with his favorite tobacco.

He was too weary to piece together the extraordinary nature of this greeting until his wife volunteered more brandy.

She filled his glass and knelt beside his chair saying, "My love, I am sorry to say that I have some very bad news."

The beginnings of panic began to rise in his gut.

"I could not bear to write to you of this," explained Catherine. "I did not deem it news to be received in the post."

Her tears terrified him.

"What is it? He demanded. "Out with it, please."

"We lost dear Elizabeth, my love, to the plague."

"What?!

"Dear God!

"She is dead?! Gone?!"

"It pains me more than you can know to have to bear these tidings, but yes, she is gone from us."

"What of Cate and Marie? Are the boys well?"

"Yes, we seem to have escaped danger, all but poor Elizabeth. The sisters insisted that we put everything of hers to the fire, even her mattress. That may be what saved us."

"This cannot be – if I had known it was God's plan to spare my life in exchange for hers, I would have willed otherwise," he moaned.

Catherine knew her news would hit him hard, but he was even more shaken by the news than she had expected. It worried her.

"God does not deal, my love. When he calls, we must go. We must find consolation knowing that such an innocent soul is surely in heaven."

Finding little consolation in her words, the tax man pulled her to him, buried his face in her hair, and wept.

From that day he found their home in Revel difficult to abide. He constantly found reason to stay in Toulouse rather than return to Revel and his family. He found that the *Auberge des Trois-Anges* in the capital offered an atmosphere of jovial congeniality that helped prevent his thoughts from straying to the tragedy of his beloved daughter's death. Jean-Mathias was enrolled in the Jesuit school in Toulouse and he and his schoolmates provided youthful energy to conversations at table that helped distract Riquet from the dark thoughts always waiting to fill his mind:

"What is it all for? Why do I struggle so when life, in the end, amounts to a leaf that can be blown away by the slightest breeze?"

After several months, Catherine wrote to him.

Is our marriage now at an end, mon amour? My life is so barren here without you.

I understand that this house holds painful memories of our little Elizabeth. I share those memories. I need you with me to help me to live with them. Her sisters who still live need you as well.

It breaks my heart knowing the pain you are feeling and not being able to hold you and comfort you.

Do you, perhaps, blame me for Elizabeth's death? I am certain that there was nothing to be done to save her. Like you, I would have given my life for hers. But that was not God's will.

Please, mon cher, come home to us and we can find our way through these dark days together.

It was simply signed "Catherine."

When Riquet read the letter, he was swept by a flood of emotion realizing, finally, what he had been doing all this time. He returned to Revel that night. But that solved nothing. Everywhere he turned he saw traces and memories of his dead little girl who would never see her tenth year. He could not bear it.

"This is not working," he finally admitted to Catherine. "I cannot bear it here, but I also cannot bear life without you and Marie and Cate.

"Come with me to Toulouse. All of you."

"But where would we stay?" she asked in disbelief. Then with mild sarcasm, "In your room at the inn?"

"Actually, the *aubergiste*, Couly, has plenty of rooms available. Marie and Cate could have their own. He spreads an amazing table and there are always interesting people to talk with and laugh with and, best of all, debate with. You will love it there.

"We will be closer to the boys and only half as far from Bonrepos and our restoration project."

Catherine capitulated. They would move to Toulouse and the Inn of the Three Angels would be their home until Bonrepos was ready for residence. As construction proceeded at Bonrepos, it was during their stay at the Inn of the Three Angels that Catherine presented Pierre-Paul with their fourth daughter, Anne. Anne would be his baby girl for the rest of his life, bringing him comfort after the rest of his brood had left the nest.

* * *

Sofia Soler and Olivia Porras were clearing muck from the *rigole* that brought water to their village in the Pyrénées. The *rigole* was ancient. They never thought about who built it; they simply kept it in good repair and clear of sediment as their mothers and grandmothers had. They never thought about how this task had fallen to them; it was just part of their life.

The stone channel was about three feet wide and two feet deep. There were sluice gates every hundred yards or so that could be opened to flush accumulated silt out of the *rigole*. Each gate was a slate slab set in the right wall of the channel that could be lifted to open the wall and reset across the channel to block the flow. They then used square tipped shovels to scoop the silt out of the channel.

There were settling ponds at the catchment points on the far side of the hill where the rigole began. They were designed to keep sediment from entering the channel, but some inevitably found its way into the *rigole* and needed to be purged periodically.

They had just finished the last gate before their village when they noticed a troop of armed men halted on the road just below them. They had not heard them arrive due to their focus on their work and the noise of the water and their shovels scraping on the stone.

A footpath followed the *rigole* on the uphill side all the way to their village, and they took to it quickly trying not to display their fear.

"Don't run unless they come for us," Sofia warned quietly. "They may have just been resting their horses."

"It's that damned tax farmer," replied Olivia under her breath. "I doubt he'll molest us here. He'll just ransack our homes later looking for salt not stamped by the fucking King in Paris."

Riquet's journey to and into the Pyrénées was uneventful until, approaching a small village, he noticed two women working on a hillside not far from the road. He stopped to watch, intrigued.

Realizing that his armed party had disquieted the women, Riquet decided to continue into town, relieving them of any sense of threat from his troop of armed men.

As they entered the village, Riquet could see that the *rigole* they had followed emptied into a large cistern at the edge of town. The rim of the stone tank was breached at several points where clear water issued forth into various smaller channels to be carried to different parts of town. These channels, in turn, were separated into smaller divisions that carried some water into homes for domestic use, some into gardens and some into fields of grain. As they moved deeper into town, they came across a channel that was shrouded in steam. Dismounting to investigate, Riquet found that the water was quite hot.

"Ah yes," he mused, "I remember now. The Romans were fond of capturing natural hot springs for their baths. Besides warmth, these waters contain minerals that have healing qualities."

He saw that there was a second complete distribution system serving the baths, the open-air laundry, and for domestic use.

The village, lying close to the northern border of Spain where salt could be had for a small fraction of the French King's price, was a prime market for smugglers. Consequently, visits by Riquet's *gabelle* enforcers, his *gabelous*, involved house-to-house searches for contraband. Riquet made every effort to mitigate the process, but the intrusions, inherently rude, brought inevitable resentment.

Riquet's arrival had not gone unnoticed, and by the time they had boarded their horses and arranged accommodations for the night, there was an angry crowd gathered in the village square.

"You are not welcome here!" shouted one of the women in the crowd.

"A pox on you and your fucking *gabelle*!" shouted one of the men. "Salt is essential to our lives and our livestock! The price of your salt is taxing us to death! We cannot pay it and still feed ourselves!"

"It's not my *gabelle*," Riquet protested in defense. "It is the King's. I merely collect it in his name."

"Collect this for your King!" shouted Olivia as she leapt forward, producing a dagger from the folds of her skirt. Riquet recognized her as one of the women from the *rigole*.

The dagger was just inches from Riquet's heart when Hugo's sword flashed, and the offending hand fell to the cobbles still clutching the dagger. Without hesitation, Sofia grasped the bloody stump in a vice-like grip, ducked under Olivia's bosom as she swooned, took her left wrist in her own left hand and lifted her on her back as if she weighed nothing.

Hugo raised his sword, intent on finishing what he had started, and his men all brought their muskets to bear on the crowd. But Riquet stayed Hugo's hand.

"I think she has payed dearly for her choler," he said, "and knowing your arm and your blade I fear that you might cleave them both. Her friend is innocent."

Hugo lowered his sword but ordered the crowd to disperse, and they did so sullenly.

Sofia carried her friend to the village forge, beckoning the blacksmith to follow. Knowing what she intended, he put an iron in the forge and pumped the bellows. The hand had been removed cleanly, almost surgically at the joint. When he first touched the hot iron to the wound, the maimed woman revived briefly, uttered a scream and immediately passed out again. When the wound was fully cauterized, the smith settled the women on a bench and went up to his living quarters for two wool blankets and a linen towel. On return, he re-cauterized two veins that were weeping and bound the wound with the towel. He bundled the maimed woman in the blankets.

"You'll want to keep her warm 'til the shock passes," he said. "We'll know by sunrise if she's going to live."

After supper Riquet and Gerome went to the forge to ask about the injured woman. Gerome had been Riquet's valet for nearly twenty-five years now and had come to anticipate his master's needs intuitively. He was, as always, armed with his mortuary sword, poniard and two pistols. He had learned his trade during the Thirty Years War and had learned the value of preparedness. In view of his master's occupation, it would have been folly to disarm. He had played the same role played earlier this day by Hugo many times in service to Riquet. Angry taxpayers were an occupational hazard for the salt farmer. Having been only a moment late for the action that afternoon, he was grateful to Hugo for defending his master. Gerome and Hugo shared a bond known only to those who have survived combat.

They found the two women still resting quietly on the blacksmith's bench. Riquet's attacker lay sleeping or unconscious with her head in the lap of her savior. Riquet inquired as to the maimed woman's condition.

"We won't know 'til morning," replied her friend. "If she survives this night, I'll see her home on the morrow, unless you're thinking she'll hang."

"No, in fact, I truly regret that she has paid so high a price for a momentary lapse of reason. I hope she will be well. You showed great courage today. You probably saved her life. May I know your name?"

"I am Sofia Soler, and this is my neighbor Olivia Porras. Olivia is not violent by nature but your King's *gabelle* is particularly loathsome to us all. Our husbands have adjoining farms near here. Most years we barely survive on what the farms earn, and the *gabelle* is an odious burden."

"I appreciate that no one loves the high price our King demands for salt, but the Sun King needs revenue for maintaining roads and bridges and for other enterprises that benefit his people. Works that could never be accomplished without the revenue reaped by the *gabelle*.

"Tell me," he continued, "does it always fall to you two to maintain that *rigole*, or are your husbands just not available temporarily?"

She laughed dryly. "Our husbands are not available more or less permanently. In the autumn they are off picking someone else's grapes, and when they're home, they're tending the sheep. Olivia and I have maintained the *rigole* since we were girls. Our mothers taught us how as their mothers taught them. Mostly it's just flushing the silt. Otherwise the muck will soon enough foul the town's water supply. But heavy rains can also do damage, so we have to be mindful of needed repairs."

"Where is the source for your *rigole*?"

"Round the other side of that hill. Left to its own, the water would flow on down to the plain. The ancients built that stonework to bring it to the town. We just keep it clear and in good repair."

"The Romans?"

"I suppose."

The chance sighting of this mountain *rigole* had produced in Riquet an epiphany. He envisioned using a diversionary channel like the one these women were clearing to bring the waters from the south face of the *Montagne Noire* to join the waters of the north face and to guide them together to the *seuil de Graissens* to provide alimentation for canal locks there.

"I might have work for you designing a system such as this near Toulouse, where I live. Would you consider working for me? It would benefit all the people of Languedoc. And I could pay you thirty *sols* per day. And your friend as well."

"Thirty *sols*, you say? I would have to ask my husband. Olivia may be less inclined, if she even lives. 'Tis not uncommon to die from the loss of a limb. The shock to the soul is dire. If she survives, she may be resentful for the loss of her right hand more than she is grateful for the sparing of her life. I heard you stay the big man's sword. I know you spared her life and probably mine as well. That may soften her disposition toward you somewhat in time, but it may not."

"In the event that my need for your skills comes to pass, I shall send word. Please consider my offer, and if you and your husband decide in my favor, you can reach me at the *Auberge des Trois-Anges* in Toulouse. I shall send you an escort for the journey. Your knowledge would be very valuable to me. Now please allow me to arrange a room for the two of you at the inn tonight and an escort home in the morning. Gerome will carry your friend, with your permission, and we shall get you settled as comfortably as is possible under the circumstances."

"I would be grateful. You have been most kind under the circumstances."

Another key element was added to the forge.

Five

The Plan.

Home from the harvest, Riquet stopped in Revel to inspect his various business interests and supped with Pierre Campmas *chez* Campmas. At that supper, in the shadow of the *Montagne Noire*, the two men honed their plan for feeding the highest locks of the canal.

Once the table was cleared, they retired to chairs by the fire for port wine and bowls of tobacco.

"I have brought the summit alimentation solution home with me from the Pyrénées," claimed Riquet. "We can capture the abundant waters high on the south face of the *Montagne Noire*, on the Mediterranean side, and bring them by *rigole* around to the *Océane* side to supplement the waters of the Sor. Then the Sor could provide alimentation for the summit locks at the *seuil de Graissens* without compromising the mills the river now serves."

"Of course!" exclaimed Pierre. "We simply build a channel to follow the contours of the mountain around to the *Océane* side and the Sor!" He found the sheer simplicity of the solution difficult to grasp. Why had it ever eluded them?

"There are five separate streams we can capture. The streams all lie in canyons that could be dammed to create reservoirs for the dry months."

Riquet agreed.

"This is truly inspirational," mused Pierre, "but at the same time obvious. It should have been clear to me years ago that this is the solution."

"So we are agreed," said Riquet. "Now we must collect elevation and flow rate measurements to prove our plan to those who hold the power to implement it."

"I have already collected much of that data and I shall begin at once to fill in any gaps," agreed Pierre.

* * *

In time, Riquet found paying rent for his family to live at the Inn unacceptable from a basic business perspective. As a solution, he bought a fine home on the *Rue des Puits-Clos* that became their residence in Toulouse. Through this move he was able to retain his close ties to Parliament but cease dumping wealth into a property he did not own.

Not long after the Riquets settled in their new home the Bishop of Castres, Monseigneur Charles-François d'Anglure de Bourlemont, dined one evening in the Bishop's Palace with Father Alfonse de Bergerac, an engineering instructor at the Jesuit university in the village of Castres. Castres lay at the feet of the *Massif Central*, north of the *Montagne Noire*. The town also lay on the Agoût River about seven miles east of its confluence with the Sor and sixteen miles north of Revel. The priest, a cleric of some stature as head of the school of engineering, was nonetheless honored to be invited to dine with the Bishop. At the same time, a back corner of his mind feared this might be the venue for delivery of bad news.

"The harvests have been poor of late," opened Bourlemont, and the plague has decimated our flock."

"Indeed, your grace." The fearful back corner of the priest's mind began to gain prominence.

"We must do what we can to restore the health and wealth of this community. By so doing we shall restore our sickly tithes as well."

"I agree, your grace, but how?"

"A former colleague of yours has a plan that I find intriguing. Unfortunately, the man of whom I speak is the heretic Pierre Borel. The plan is for the establishment of navigation from our city through Montauban to the Garonne by way of the Agoût and thence the Tarn."

"I am aware of his works in that regard," replied the priest, feeling some relief.

"I understand that he also is of the belief that the Agoût can be linked through the Sor and the Laudot to the Fresquel across the *seuil de Graissens*?

"Oui."

"And you, Father, are you of the same opinion?"

"I believe it might be possible," replied the priest cautiously," but alimentation for the summit locks would need to be provided. *Monsieur* Borel has encountered strong resistance from the riparian owners along the Agoût. He may not even succeed with *that* endeavor without intervention from His Majesty..."

"...who is not likely to intercede on behalf of a heretic," finished the Bishop. "If only there were a good Catholic, like yourself, who might take an interest in the project, it might be of great commercial benefit to this town. I am sure you understand that what benefits the town benefits the church."

"With apologies, Monseigneur, I am much too old to take on such a project," demurred the priest. After a few moments and a sip or two of wine he added, "There is one who might be interested. He is not an engineer, but he has a good mind for organization, delegation and finances. He could employ engineers to advise him. I speak, of course of the Baron of Bonrepos, Pierre-Paul Riquet. He is a good Catholic and has an avocational interest in hydraulics. Communication of the two seas is a particular interest of his. His son Jean-Mathias studies law at the Jesuit school in Toulouse and is very well regarded there."

"I know of this Baron. I recommended him for the *gabelle* when he was barely more than a boy. He is godson to François Portugniares. I understand that he has acquitted himself well as a tax farmer.

"Perhaps I should pay him a visit," mused Bourlemont. "I pass near his estate every time I travel to Toulouse."

"I believe the chateau is under restoration," cautioned the priest, "but he can often be found there supervising the reconstruction. Failing that, he could be almost anywhere in Languedoc administering the *gabelle*, but if he is in Toulouse, I believe he will be found at the Inn of the Three Angels.

"I believe he might be the one you seek, Excellency."

* * *

It was not until early in 1662 that the Bishop of Castres paid an unexpected visit to Bonrepos pursuant to his conversation with Father Bergerac. Riquet had attended services in Castres from time to time when his business took him there, and he was aware that the cleric had been enlisted by his uncle to back his bid for the Mirepoix *gabelle*, but he was surprised to learn that the Bishop remembered his name. Serendipity found him at Bonrepos going over plans with Isaac Roux.

With the ground floor still in disarray, he invited the Bishop up to his chamber for a glass of wine by the fire. His chamber was well furnished, and the fire was welcome as was the rich Fronton Gerome brought them, the *vin de pays* of Toulouse.

The Bishop explained that, on the advice of Father Bergerac, he had stopped at Bonrepos to discuss the Borel plan of connecting the Fresquel and the Laudot across the *seuil de Graissens*. Such a link, he believed, would be of great benefit to Castres as well as Revel, and the priest had suggested that Riquet might be interested in pursuing the plan. Riquet, of course, knew of the plan and of Borel's failure to implement it. He and Pierre Campmas had discussed it at length.

"I am deeply honored," said Riquet, "to be considered for such a project. I am not certain, however, that it is the best plan for linking the *Océane* and the Mediterranean."

"I am bound for Toulouse," said the Bishop, "but first I would like you to accompany me to Saint-Felix. We shall discuss these matters that I believe will benefit us both and I shall show you a view that I expect will interest you."

Elated by the prospect of such a distinguished sponsor, Riquet realized immediately that this could be the avenue that he and Campmas had been hoping for. He told Gerome of his plan and asked him to follow the bishop's coach and bring along the bay for Riquet's return home. Gerome took up his position behind Bourlemont's coach with the bay in tow and Riquet joined the Bishop inside. The Bishop's guard flanked Gerome as they set off for Saint-Felix.

Bourlemont's coach had clearly been crafted by artisans. The structure was strong but delicate in appearance. The red oak panels were covered in sheer varnish exposing the exquisite grain patterns. The trim was appropriately cardinal red. Bourlemont eschewed gilding, deeming it too ostentatious for a man of the cloth. Riquet could not help but appreciate the artistry as he climbed aboard. He also noticed that this coach had much deeper upholstery than his own and made a mental note to correct that.

The road from Bonrepos to Revel traversed the Lauragais Plateau where the village of Saint-Felix lay. Riquet and the Bishop were deeply engaged in discussion of the tremendous commercial value of canals and navigable rivers when Bourlemont interrupted their conversation just outside Saint-Felix as he called to his driver to stop.

"Walk with me," said Bourlemont, and they stepped down from the carriage. It was a clear, crisp morning in early February and with every breath the frosty air formed tiny clouds of ice crystals before them. The bishop led the way to a rime-covered, grassy clearing beside the road where the Lauragais ridge broke down onto the plain of Revel. Revel could be seen to the north, in the distance, and at their feet lay the *seuil de Graissens*, the divide between the Laudot and the Fresquel.

The sky was clear and cold, and they could see for miles. In the foreground the Fresquel flowed southerly, to their right, ultimately to the Mediterranean. Ahead and just beyond the Fresquel lay the threshold of Graissens. To the north, toward Revel, the Laudot ran north to join the Sor flowing thence, ultimately, to the Atlantic. Revel lay between the Laudot and the Sor. Far off and straight ahead loomed the *Montagne Noire*, a great granite sentinel, harbinger of the *Massif Central* rising to the north and east.

"There below us you can see the Fresquel making its way to the Mediterranean, and off there to the left, across that narrow isthmus, flows the Laudot as it passes north to meet the Sor bound for the *Océane* . From this viewpoint, usually God's alone, it seems clear that the Fresquel and Laudot could be joined across that threshold and, with some improvement to those river channels, the *Océane* and Mediterranean seas would indeed be joined. The commerce this would induce would be of immeasurable benefit to Castres and Revel in particular, and, indeed, all of Languedoc."

"I am familiar with Borel's plan," agreed Riquet, "but it would require drawing water from the head of the Sor to feed the locks at the summit, a concept that has faced open rebellion from those who own mills on the Sor. Borel was nearly lynched when he tried to implement it. The key lies in finding a source for the locks that does not deplete the Sor. I believe the solution lies in the *Montagne Noire.*

"I have an idea that might accomplish that goal by diverting water from the Mediterranean side of the Dark Mountain to the *Océane* side. I have contemplated building a model at Bonrepos that would demonstrate the concept on a small scale. As yet, it is still only a vision. Until today I have had no one in mind whom I might be expecting to witness such a demonstration. The plan would ultimately need backing from the King to move forward, and I do not have status with the King to propose it.

"If you are interested, Excellency, I shall begin immediately to give my idea form and substance."

"That would be interesting indeed." agreed the Bishop, "Let me know when it is ready for demonstration. If it seems feasible, I can help you to advance your plan."

"To that end, Monseigneur, I shall beg your leave to return to Bonrepos immediately to discuss construction of the model with my builder."

"Please do," replied Bourlemont.

Riquet mounted the bay and, with Gerome, proceeded to Revel to inform Pierre Campmas of the bishop's interest and his plan to move forward with the model *rigole*. Together they returned to Bonrepos where they enlisted Isaac Roux to help plan the model.

Isaac understood the objective immediately. He and Riquet and Campmas spent the next day studying the terrain near the chateau to determine the best route for the model *rigole*.

"At this point," offered Roux "we could actually install a small-scale lock to demonstrate their workings, although I am not certain how to go about building one."

"I shall write young Andréossy in Narbonne," offered Riquet. "He is an artist with pen and ink and has studied hydrology in Paris. He knows locks and has witnessed the operation of da Vinci's mitered locks in Lombardy. I shall ask him to produce a plan for you at the appropriate scale.

"I don't want the renovation work on the chateau to suffer," he cautioned, "so I would like you to hire artisans and laborers you can dedicate to this task separately."

In the following weeks, Campmas and Roux began construction of a model canal system at Bonrepos. It would demonstrate on a small scale how the *Montagne Noire rigole* system would function. The model wrapped around a hill on the grounds of the estate and incorporated a stream that had once fed the moat before it had been filled with earth years ago.

François Andréossy soon arrived with plans for a scaled-down lock to fit the dimensions of the model and demonstrate the da Vinci style mitered lock doors.

* * *

While conducting business with the Parliament of Toulouse, Riquet had made the acquaintance of Jacques de Lombrail, Lord de Rochemontès and advisor to the Parliament. He found him to be a young man of grace and intelligence and had invited him home for supper at the Inn frequently. It seemed to Riquet that there was a connection between the young lord and his daughter, Marie, such that he began to think of him as a potential son-in-law.

After resettling on *Rue des Puits-Clos*, they often entertained the young lord and other Toulousain dignitaries. Often, however, it was Lombrail alone who shared their table.

"You should take particular care with Marie's coif for supper this evening my dove," he warned Catherine. "I believe young Lombrail might be a fine addition to the family. If you agree, I'm planning to explore the concept over brandy this evening."

"I find him very charming," she replied. "I have heard no ill word spoken against him. His family is well established in Toulouse and even Paris. I think Marie is fond of him as well. In short, I concur."

At supper Riquet studied the conversation between their guest and Marie in a new light. Marie shared her mother's quick wit and Riquet could see that the young Lord was enchanted. It also seemed certain that the attraction was mutual.

After supper, the men retired to the den for cognac and bowls, while the ladies attended to their petit point. Riquet managed a brief private moment with Catherine to confirm his assessment of the connection he had seen at supper.

"I believe they are quite taken with each other," she concurred, "and it would not seem unreasonable to move forward if that is your intent."

"My dear Lord de Rochemontès," said Riquet as the brandy began to mellow the mood, "I would be interested to know your opinion of my daughter Marie. I have always found her to be pleasant in nature and appealing to the eye, but I realize that as her father I am biased. Do you find her to have a pleasant nature?"

"Indeed, monsieur, she is truly a lovely young woman in all respects."

"Welcome words to a father's ears. Especially since a father must eventually find suitable husbands for his daughters; men of true quality such as yourself. Men who must, themselves, be very selective in choosing a mate."

"Marie will be found to be desirable by the most selective of suitors."

"Even by a man such as yourself?"

"If I am reading your meaning correctly, *monsieur*, yes, I would be honored to be considered a suitable husband for your daughter."

"I could manage a small dowry. Perhaps you would find thirty thousand *livres* sufficient?"

"Monsieur, for such a prize as Marie the dowry would be like gold leaf on a *fleur-de-lis*."

"*Tres bien*," said Riquet with a tone of finality. "Now let me be the first to raise a glass to your happy union!"

The two men talked at length of canals and cognac, women and wine until Riquet was suddenly afflicted with severe chills.

"Regretfully, I must excuse myself," he said. As much as I am enjoying the conversation, I must retire. I was spared the plague while working the salt pans of Narbonne, but I seem to have contracted the fourth fever from the bad air of the marshes. What my Italian grandfather called the *malattia de mal aria*. It comes over me from time to time and it seems to have chosen this evening to lay me low.

The link between marshlands and malaria had been known for centuries, but the role played by the mosquito was not yet understood. Instead, the "bad air" of the marsh was blamed as the cause.

Rising to retire, Riquet closed, "I hope we shall enjoy many more such evenings in the future."

Rising to depart, Jacques replied, "This evening has proved most exceptional for me, Baron Riquet. I came here tonight with no intuition of the great honor I was to receive. I hope you feel better on the morrow and I bid you *la plus bon nuit.*"

* * *

It was October before the model *rigole* was completed and Campmas and Roux gave Riquet and Andréossy a demonstration. Isaac opened the gate admitting water to their miniature *rigole.* The water then tracked around a hillock on the estate to the scaled down lock built to represent the summit locks at the *seuil de Graissens.* They had captured the outflow in a pond twenty feet above the estate's kitchen garden and the pond fed a pipe that, in turn, fed a fountain at the base of the hill. From there the water was routed to irrigate the kitchen garden and formal floral gardens planned for Bonrepos. Campmas and Roux were practical men and had decided that the model might as well serve a useful purpose beyond demonstration of their plan.

"You have indeed found the answer, *Monsieur le Baron,*" affirmed François. "You must give Monseigneur Bourlemont a demonstration. I am certain that he will want to champion your plan before the Sun King."

The following day Riquet rode to Toulouse to invite Monseigneur Bourlemont, newly ordained Archbishop of Toulouse, to visit Bonrepos and view the model.

"Gladly," replied the Archbishop, "and, if I may, I shall invite some friends of the nobility to join me. It would be helpful to demonstrate your plan to more eyes than mine alone."

"An excellent idea," agreed Riquet. "Bonrepos is not yet fully restored, but with some preparation we can accommodate you and your distinguished friends in suitable fashion."

Within the week Bourlemont arrived at the estate with an entourage of local dignitaries. Riquet provided a sumptuous feast for his noble guests and Campmas and Roux reprised their demonstration for the visitors.

They had all been invited to stay the night at Bonrepos, and the wine and debate flowed late into the evening.

"Clearly you have found a way to transport the waters of this little stream from one side of this little hill to the other," acknowledged one lord who owned a mill in Revel, "but will this scheme work on the grand scale that will be required to capture enough water to feed your canal locks without starving my mill on the Sor? I rely on the waters of the Sor to turn the stone that grinds out some meager income from that mill, and do not wish to see those waters depleted."

"I, too, have a mill on the Sor," reassured Riquet, "and have no desire to see it grind to a halt. *Monsieur* Campmas has assured me that the flow rates are adequate."

"It is November now," said another. "how much water does this stream of yours carry in mid-summer? More to the point, how much flows from the *Montagne Noire* in the dry season?"

"We plan to capture winter's abundance in reservoirs," assured Riquet, "for supplementation in the drier months. *Monsieur* Campmas has amassed much information over many years regarding the variance in flows over the span of a full year of seasons. We can make that information available to anyone who cares to study it."

"These two," offered Bourlemont, "have invested much of their time and energy into this study and I am inclined to trust their findings. However, if any of you remain unconvinced, I would suggest that we visit the canyons of the *Montagne Noire* to verify their claims."

The Catholic church was a powerful force during the reign of the Sun King. The Archbishop's endorsement carried much weight with the nobles, and they all felt a subtle pressure against strident opposition to the plan.

Wine can inspire the most sedentary creature with ambition, and as the hour grew late all agreed that a visit to the actual site of the proposed *rigole* was in order.

Of course, all those noblemen did not actually *climb* the mountain. They took up lodging in Revel while their servants examined the streams of the *Montagne Noire*. Yet they were satisfied, vicariously, that Riquet's claims were plausible, and it was agreed that the plan should be presented to the Sun King.

To that end, Bourlemont wrote to the King's Finance Minister, Jean-Baptiste Colbert, describing his findings and the concurrences of the local nobility. He also advised the Minister that he had directed Riquet to submit a proposal for the construction of a canal that would link the two seas. Riquet had neither the social nor the political status to approach Colbert directly, but once directed by Bourlemont, who enjoyed the close confidence of the Minister, he could do so. The next morning, November 15th in the year 1662, Riquet wrote to Colbert.

Six

The Empire.

The Sun King dreamed of an empire.

At the age of four, upon the death of his father, young Louis de Bourbon became King Louis XIV of France. He had no concept of "empire" and certainly no desire to build one. He had no concept of war, even though France was prosecuting one in his name at the time. But it was clear to him even then that he was special. As he grew into puberty, his tutors explained God's particular interest in his reign. He learned about all the great empires in history, from the Romans to the Persians to the Ottomans. He wanted one.

King Louis gradually came to understand that there was more to building an empire than just defeating your rivals in battle. Historically, the key to empire building, he understood, had been just that: *building*. The Romans left an amazingly durable legacy of engineering throughout their empire, nowhere beyond the Apennine peninsula more prominently than in France, and Languedoc in particular. The roads, bridges, amphitheaters and canals of Languedoc still bore witness to the glory of Rome's golden age. Even the modern name of the French region of "*Provence–Alpes–Côte d'Azur*" is rooted in the age when "*Provence*" was a Roman province.

In the spring of 1661, with the death of Cardinal Mazarin, Louis XIV at last assumed the role he was born to fill, that of ruler of a great country. At twenty-two he was bestowed with awesome power but also burdened with awesome responsibility. He aspired to greatness. He identified with Apollo, the Greek Sun God and chose the sun as his emblem.

The Sun King set about clearing the corruption that consumed his court. One of the worst offenders was his Minister of Finance, Nicolas Fouquet, who had, through malfeasance, amassed a fortune blatantly greater than the King's own. In August of the same year, the King had him arrested by the legendary captain of his musketeers, Charles d'Artagnan, and thrown into the Bastille. The King chose as Fouquet's replacement a young subordinate of the deposed Minister, Jean-Baptiste Colbert, who had shown great integrity in service to his King.

He formed a Royal Council consisting of his new Minister of Finance, his Minister of War, Michel le Tellier, and his Minister of Foreign Affairs, Hugues de Lionne. Le Tellier would be succeeded within a few months by his son, François-Michel le Tellier, Marquis du Louvois, who would be called upon to prosecute the King's perennial wars. He is remembered in France simply as "Louvois."

Born to a middleclass merchant in Reims, Jean-Baptiste Colbert had grown up in a family where honesty and loyalty were highly valued. This ethic was reinforced by his Jesuit education. After graduation, he secured a post in Louis' court under Secretary of War Michel le Tellier where he distinguished himself as a loyal and honest bureaucrat. Cardinal Mazarin recommended him to Louis as a financial advisor and in that post, again, he served his King well.

As the King's new Minister of Finance, Colbert initiated tax reforms and fought corruption. It seemed that prior to his appointment less than half the taxes collected in the King's name ever found their way to the King's coffers. Colbert was appalled by the corruption he found infecting the court of the Sun King.

Colbert, also Minister of the Navy and of Commerce, launched various efforts to enhance industry and trade throughout France, programs he deemed needed as counterpart to taxes to restore the solvency of the Sun King's reign.

He had come to know the Bishop of Castres, now Archbishop of Toulouse, quite well as they shared a common interest in restoring integrity to the court of the Sun King and promoting the economic health of the realm.

In November of 1662, he sat at his desk sorting his mail as was his custom. He had three baskets: one for discussion with the King, one for further thought and one for the trash. It seemed everyone in France had a son, daughter, niece or nephew who would be a great help to the Sun King if only Colbert could find them a suitable position at court.

His eye caught the name of Baron Pierre-Paul Riquet, *Fermier General* of Languedoc, and he wondered what the Baron could be writing about. His *gabelle* payments had always been prompt, and he hoped nothing had happened that might tarnish that record.

He broke the seal and opened the envelope. When he unfolded the letter, he saw to his astonishment that the Baron was proposing to build a canal for communication of the two seas. He gave an involuntary guffaw, shook his head in amusement and dropped the letter into the "trash" basket.

Then it dawned on him that he had seen the name of Archbishop Bourlemont referenced in the letter. He slowly and thoughtfully retrieved the letter and read it more carefully. The Baron claimed that "...the Archbishop has *directed* me to write you..." and went on to claim that he had found a source for alimentation of the summit locks that would enable communication of the two seas.

He decided to relegate the letter to the second basket for a time.

Then, deeper in the pile, he found the familiar seal of the Archbishop. He quickly opened the letter to find that Bourlemont had indeed directed Riquet to submit his proposal and that he, too, believed that Riquet had found a way to enable construction of a canal linking the two seas.

The Archbishop's endorsement demanded that Riquet's proposal be given serious consideration. Colbert felt the weight of his responsibility to strengthen the French economy and realized immediately what a profound impact Riquet's proposal would have if it were to succeed. This was the sort of bold economic development King Louis was counting on Colbert to produce. He assigned both letters to the first basket.

So it was that at twenty-four, when the Sun King's trusted Minister of Finance presented him with a proposal that, at first, seemed impossible (Hadn't the Romans, themselves, deemed this project impossible?) he immediately recognized it as precisely the sort of enterprise that would imbue his empire and the Sun King, himself, with immortality. *If* it could be done. To undertake such an arguably impossible and expensive task and fail would be unacceptable.

In his letter to Colbert, Riquet had suggested several possible routes, one linking to Toulouse, two bypassing the capital. When Colbert decided to put the proposal before the King he chose to defer route selection until the King had ruled on the viability of the concept.

"The abundant waters of the *Montagne Noire* will be redirected from the Mediterranean side to the *Océane* side," explained Colbert, "to provide alimentation for the summit locks. This removes the crucial impediment that has historically been fatal to execution of this concept."

"It would be welcome indeed," agreed Louis, "to have a way to move the Royal fleet from the Mediterranean to the *Océane* without passing the Spanish forts at Gibraltar. Also, we need a port on the Mediterranean that is our own and not subject to the vagaries of local demigods whose loyalties change with the tide. The *Chevalier* tells us that there is a fishing village, *Cette*, I believe it is called, that he could develop into a secure port for our navy. Perhaps that should be the Mediterranean terminus of this canal."

Then, musing, "We can't seem to call to mind any memory of the house of Riquet."

"They are not of the nobility of the sword, Sire," replied Colbert. "He is, in fact, a tax farmer."

"A *tax farmer*?!" exclaimed the King. "Yet he dares presume that he has found a solution where the great Leonardo da Vinci found none?"

"Monseigneur Bourlemont is convinced that he has done so, Sire.

"I share your suspicion of tax farmers, *Majesté*, but I am assured by the Archbishop that Baron Riquet is an honest man of considerable ingenuity and integrity."

Months passed while the King and his Finance Minister pondered the proposal and periodically debated one aspect or another. Finally, in January of 1663, the King reached a decision.

The King decided to test the waters. He would entertain the proposal by consulting the finest scientific and engineering minds at his disposal, and task those men with determining whether the canal deemed impossible by the great da Vinci, might, after all, be accomplished by the will of God and Louis the Great.

"We must proceed carefully," he confided to Colbert. "We shall form a Royal Commission to verify or refute the claims of this tax farmer. Perhaps it should be led by Clerville. If *Monsieur* Riquet has indeed found the answer, this could help bind Languedoc to us and at the same time end our dependence on Gibraltar for passage from sea to sea. A great boon indeed. Which route do you deem best?"

"I would leave that decision to the Commission, Sire."

"*Bien sûr!*" the King agreed with a wry smile. Choosing a route would be too much like endorsing the project. He would take no position before hearing the decision of his Commission.

"As to the Commission, Sire," continued Colbert, "if I may suggest, I think perhaps *Monsieur* Hector de Boutheroüe de Bourgneuf, Director of Operations for the Canal de Briare, might also be well placed on the Commission. He has a great reservoir of practical experience operating and maintaining that canal."

"As you see fit. But Clerville for certain."

* * *

Unaware of the King's decision, Riquet was focusing as well as he could on Marie's wedding with the Lord de Rochemontès. The contract was signed, and the ceremony was held in the chapel of the *Cathédrale Saint-Étienne* in Toulouse on January 21st. It was an impressive celebration officiated by none other than Archbishop Bourlemont. As the Bonrepos renovation was not quite complete, the Riquets hosted a lavish reception at their home on *Rue des Puits-Clos*.

Riquet had not yet received word that the King, just three days earlier, had ordered the creation of the Royal Commission to study the feasibility of his plan.

When Colbert's letter arrived informing Riquet that the King had decided to act on his proposal, and that the Royal Commission would be formed, headed by the great military engineer, *Chevalier* Louis Nicolas de Clerville, Riquet's spirits soared. Riquet knew of Clerville's work building and strengthening fortifications for the Sun King. He looked forward to his guidance in designing and building locks, dams and bridges and the other great works the canal would spawn.

Filling the Commission required some months, while Riquet could only wait to hear their decision. Meanwhile, he continued to focus on his primary responsibility, collection and enforcement of the *gabelle*.

While he waited, the renovations were completed at Bonrepos and the Riquets were able at last to settle in their family home.

Book II

Formation

Seven

The Route from Toulouse.

On the heels of his fortuitous rescue of the Ruscino family that morning in April of 1663, Riquet's abrupt departure from Toulouse had been precipitated by a visit to the Archbishop. While he was in town, Riquet decided to inquire into news of the Royal Commission.

"What brings you to Toulouse?" asked the Archbishop in surprise. "You should be at Bonrepos. Hector de Boutheroüe de Bourgneuf, who is the manager of the Canal de Briare, and the member of the Royal Commission who has the most knowledge of canals, is expecting to meet with you there very soon. Possibly even this very day. You would be wise to cultivate his favor and unwise to offend him."

"I had no idea!" exclaimed Riquet. If I had been informed of his plans I would never have left."

Obviously, Riquet must change his plans, return home in haste, and trust the duties of the harvest to Hugo.

Boutheroüe was appointed to the Royal Commission as the nation's foremost authority on canals. Construction of the Canal de Briare between the Loire River and the Seine valley was begun under Henri IV. Work on the canal was suspended after Henri's death, but completed thirty years later under Louis XIII, father of the Sun King. Boutheroüe's father, François de Boutheroüe, had finished the construction and had managed the operation of the Canal de Briare until his death. Since then, Hector had been Director of Operations. In many ways the Canal de Briare would serve as the prototype for the *Canal Royal*.

The purpose of Boutheroüe's visit to Bonrepos was to discuss his plan for determining the feasibility of Riquet's proposal. Riquet arrived back at Bonrepos less than an hour before his guest arrived and was on hand to greet him warmly.

"*Bienvenue Monsieur Boutheroüe!*" he exclaimed as Boutheroüe was shown into his cabinet. "I have been expecting you. It is a great comfort to me to have a person of your profound experience involved in these deliberations.

"It is clearly by the hand of God, through Monseigneur Bourlemont, that you find me here today. But for a chance meeting with some highwaymen and subsequent fortuitous conversation with Archbishop Bourlemont, I would be halfway to Béziers now."

"Did you not receive my letter? I wrote you of my plans two weeks ago."

"Aha," laughed Riquet. "Either it fell through some crack in Toulouse or it sits waiting there, as we speak, for enough company to warrant carrying it here with other mail bound for Saint-Felix.

"Clearly God has intervened in compensation for the French post to assure that we would meet here today."

He was genuinely pleased to have a man of Boutheroüe's experience serving on the commission. None of the others had any specific knowledge of canals. Not even Clerville, whose knowledge of hydraulics was limited to the construction and maintenance of moats. As a young man, Hector had been a participating witness to the completion of the Canal de Briare and he had gained much practical experience through years of operation and maintenance of that waterway. Riquet was certain his counsel would be priceless.

"You must be my guest while we discuss how you intend to proceed with your investigation," insisted Riquet.

As he showed his guest to a room, he invited the Commissioner to tour his model *rigole.*

Seeing Riquet's ill-veiled eagerness Boutheroüe replied, "I would be most pleased."

While their masters viewed the model *rigole*, Gerome showed Hector's valet, André, to a room near his own. André was the son of a valet who was also a son of a valet, and carried more of a "gentleman's gentleman" demeanor than Gerome's *aide de camp* style. A fundamental difference in nature that would inhibit the forming of a friendship.

Having walked the full course of the model Riquet boasted, "There can be no doubt that the waters of the *Montagne Noire* can be trained to our purposes in the same manner as this stream has been."

"Very impressive, *monsieur*," said Boutheroüe, "but perhaps more so to a novice to the workings of water. I arrived here with little doubt as to the viability of your plan."

"That pleases me to hear, *sieur*, but at least the stroll is a pleasant one, *n'est ce pas?*"

"I hope the 'stroll' upon which we are about to embark will be equally pleasant. My plan is for you to show me the entire route you have planned. As yet, all discussions of your plan have been conceptual in nature, with the exception of the specific volume calculations collected by *Monsieur* Campmas on the *Montagne Noire*. If the Commission is to make a sound decision regarding the feasibility of your proposal, either for or against, we must survey and monument the centerline and record soil types along the way. This will be an undertaking of some months. Are you prepared to undertake such a quest?"

"It will be my pleasure, *monsieur*. Now let us see what Catherine has planned for supper."

Once again, a shared interest in canals and hydrology formed the basis of a bond that would last for years. They were about to embark on an expedition that would bind them for life.

As a prelude to their expedition, Riquet took Boutheroüe to the Lauragais ridge, to the same viewpoint Bourlemont had shown him from which they could view the *seuil de Graissens* and see the proximity between the Laudot, flowing toward the Atlantic and the Fresquel, flowing toward the Mediterranean. In Riquet's mind, the shadows of random clouds gliding across the valley floor conjured images of ships sailing toward Revel.

Also before them, the *Montagne Noire* stood astride the divide just east of Revel. Rainfall on the southern slopes destined for the Mediterranean, that falling on the northern face flowing to the Atlantic.

"As you probably know," explained Riquet, "the plan is to capture the waters of the streams on the southern face of that great, dark mountain, starting at the Alzau, and guide them by means of a gently sloping *rigole* around the mountain to the *Océane* side, thence, joined by waters of the Sor, to the *seuil de Graissens*. This will provide sufficient alimentation for the summit locks, while leaving adequate supply for the mills on the Sor. We also plan to dam the streams at their respective collection points to create reservoirs for the dry season."

"It would indeed seem a simple matter to connect these two rivers," agreed Boutheroüe. "But having accomplished the connection, your true impediments will become apparent."

"How so?" Riquet felt certain that the only impediment to connection of the seas had been finding an adequate source of water for the summit. He had removed that obstacle.

"Hugues Cosnier, who designed the Canal de Briare, dissuaded King Henry's Royal Council from the use of natural watercourses arguing the continual and costly annoyance of traffic interruption due to both flood and drought and the maintenance expense of keeping the channels clear. Storms would fill the channels with rocks. Floods would make passage impossible and silt up the channels. The King's Council ultimately decided to cut new still-water canals near the natural channels but above the flood zone, so we could take just the flow we needed for navigation, but let all excess continue in its natural course."

Riquet was stunned. All the routes he had considered thus far incorporated live channels as essential elements. Excluding the use of live channels would have an enormous impact on the magnitude of the scope of all his plans.

"Of course," Boutheroüe continued, "we still needed to connect to the Loire and the Loing, which connects to the Seine, or the canal would have been pointless. To this day, navigation on the Canal Briare is confounded when either the Loire or the Loing is in flood. We are compelled to close floodgates to protect the canal from the damage of flood waters. This perforce suspends ingress and egress by canal traffic."

"I confess that I never considered the liability of too much water!" Riquet admitted. "My concern was finding sufficient water to feed the summit locks. So, for this canal you would propose cutting channels parallel to the Laudot and Fresquel?"

"As of now, I am thinking if the terrain allows it, we might want to bypass Graissens and take the collected waters from the *Montagne Noire* on through to the divide at Naurouze. The *seuil de Naurouze* is somewhat lower than the *seuil de Graissens*. Routing the canal from Toulouse through the lower divide will require fewer locks, and locks impede traffic.

"One of your proposed routes ties into the River L'Hers and the moat at Toulouse, does it not?"

"Indeed."

"I suggest we focus on that route, but I would not use the River L'Hers except for alimentation. We should plan a route from Toulouse to Naurouze and trace the route of the feeder *rigole* back to the Sor to verify that the waters of the Dark Mountain will pass Graissens without pumping.

"The route should proceed from the summit at Naurouze, thence to the Fresquel and the Aude, and on to Narbonne. But I would not use the live channels of those rivers either. Although the Aude provides more flow than the Fresquel, a plus for navigation, it poses the same problems regarding flood interruption and keeping the channel clear. I think our canal should parallel the Fresquel and the Aude above the flood level. Once our canal is completed, the Garonne, itself, although deemed navigable below Toulouse, will, I expect, be bypassed one day for the same reasons."

"*Our* canal...'" thought Riquet, "'Once *our* canal is completed...'" Clearly the Royal Commission's foremost expert on canals expected Riquet's plan to move forward. It would be a much grander enterprise than he had imagined involving the excavation of many miles of canal where he had envisioned using navigable rivers. Yet Commissioner Boutheroüe clearly believed such an enterprise was feasible. He was elated.

The political implications flashed through his mind in a flood.

"Bypassing the *seuil de Graissens,*" he thought, "would mean fewer locks and a more direct route from Toulouse to Narbonne. The cities of Revel and Castres will not benefit as directly, but Bourlemont is in Toulouse now. He may well find Boutheroüe's plan preferable."

"All that you say seems wise to me," he said aloud. "Let us proceed to evaluate the sources on the *Montagne Noire* and verify a route to bring them to Naurouze."

"I propose," Boutheroüe replied "that we leave that endeavor to *Monsieur* Campmas. "His intimate knowledge of the streams of the dark mountain will ensure success.

"Let us, you and I, begin in Toulouse to survey the route of the canal to Naurouze. While we stake that route, your *fontainier* can trace a route for your *rigoles* from Naurouze to the Alzau and verify that the terrain can be traversed by natural flow alone and confirm that the flow rates are adequate."

Isaac Roux had not taken on any new projects since completion of the renovation of Bonrepos, which suited Riquet because it meant he was a ready resource for an occasional minor addition or adjustment to the manor. Having come to trust his judgement as well as his ethics, Riquet suggested to Boutheroüe that he be assigned to partner with Campmas for the survey of the routes of the *rigoles*. The two had formed a friendship and become a very effective team while designing and building the model *rigole*.

* * *

Riquet and Boutheroüe spent the next month and a half surveying the route of the proposed canal from Toulouse to Naurouze while Campmas and Roux defined the routes of the *rigoles*.

First, over the course of the next week, Boutheroüe, acting for the Royal Commission, assembled a survey party. François Andréossy would play a key role. He had been appointed to the Commission at the request of Monseigneur Bourlemont. He would serve as *arpenteur* and *géomètre*. In the first capacity he would gather horizontal measurements, and in the second he would map them. The party also included a *nivelleur* for vertical measurements and a *géologue* to record soil types. In support of the technicians, Boutheroüe hired two chainmen, two axemen, two rodmen, a cook, a laundress and ten laborers. For security, they were accompanied by twelve men at arms. He assembled a similar crew to support Campmas and Roux in staking the routes of the *rigoles*.

Riquet had ordered four hundred oak posts from his mill in the *Montagne Noire*, which were laded onto two wagons. One was delivered to Campmas in Revel and the other to Bonrepos. These would be the monuments for his survey. Boutheroüe had a third wagonload of camping and cooking provisions assembled and had ribs fashioned for a canvas roof for that wagon. April was blossoming and the weather was fair and clear, but they were sure to encounter foul weather before this "stroll" was at an end. In Revel, he had a similar wagon outfitted for the Campmas-Roux crew. If rain did come, it would most likely come to the *Montagne Noire* first.

On the day of departure, the Boutheroüe-Riquet party assembled in front of Bonrepos for the blessing of their enterprise, provided by Monseigneur Bourlemont.

"The Sun King," began the Archbishop, "Louis XIV, King by the Grace of God, has commissioned this party for an undertaking that will change history. If your mission succeeds, the *Canal Royal des Deux Mers* will forever link the *Océane* and Mediterranean seas and bring peace and prosperity to Occitan. To that end I ask God to bless this party, this endeavor, and the visionary who leads it. In His name, amen."

Riquet knelt before the Archbishop and kissed his ring. He then stood to address the party.

"Some of the best scientific and engineering minds of the realm have assured the Sun King of the feasibility of this endeavor, yet it falls to us to prove the truth of the matter over the fields and through the forests from the Garonne to the *Montagne Noire* and from the stones of Naurouze to the Mediterranean. This journey will be difficult and there are those among our countrymen who wish us to fail. But we shall *not* fail. We shall find a route that will, in time and with industry, carry the Sun King's ships safely from sea to sea. The

Canal Royal, when completed, will also provide a safer route for the produce of Occitanian farmers and vintners to be carried to market. Travelers also will at last have a safer route through the perils which pervade the roads of Languedoc and in preference to the perils of the sea route from the riviera to Bordeaux. With God's blessing, provided us by His Excellency Monseigneur Bourlemont, God's presence here and throughout Languedoc, our endeavor shall prevail!"

A great clamor of cheers rose from the crowd, and with that the host mounted up and started for Toulouse. It was a beautiful spring day with a blue sky punctuated by wooly white clouds. The air was cold and crisp and promised good fortune.

Riquet and Boutheroüe led the way followed by Andréossy and the other technicians. They were flanked by the men of the guard. Then came their camp wagon followed by the wagon laden with oak posts. Then came the rodmen, axemen and laborers on foot, along with herdsmen to manage the various beasts they brought for the table.

The passing of their troop drew curious villagers who wanted to know their purpose. When the locals learned of the royal mission, they were generally supportive but skeptical, doubting the likelihood of the mission's success. The people of Occitania had long wished for safe travel between the riviera and Toulouse, but da Vinci's denial was firmly embedded in the oral history of Languedoc. It was common knowledge that a canal connecting the two seas was impossible. The people of Languedoc were not optimistic.

The survey party made camp about a mile southeast of Toulouse, planning to begin their survey the next day. They would start at the outer wall of the moat defending Toulouse, and monument the centerline of the proposed route toward the River L'Hers, a tributary of the Garonne that bypassed Toulouse to the east and joined the Garonne ten miles downstream from the city. They would follow a route parallel to that tributary southeasterly toward Naurouze.

In the morning the surveyors left camp and proceeded to the moat. That portion of the city lying east of the Garonne was girded by a road that ran proximate to the moat. François picked a starting point between the road and the moat near the east gate of the ramparts and in line with the north wall of the *Cathédrale Saint-Étienne*. This position could be identified on existing maps and would facilitate the mapping of their route. He had a three-foot-long oak post set flush with the surface for the starting point of their survey. He chiseled a cross mark in the wall of the moat to the left of the post and a second cross mark to the right such that the marks formed a "V" with the post itself. If the top of the post were to be buried by debris over time, the chiseled cross marks would be easy to find and could be used as references to find the post.

Seeing the first monument set was almost spiritual for Riquet. He nearly wept with joy.

"It's finally happening," he thought. "Now each day will bring this great enterprise closer to reality.

"It is as if I am dreaming that same dream that has so often visited my slumbers, save now I am wide awake. I can smell the grasses and the stone and the waters of the moat. I can feel the wind and sun on my face and the horse between my knees. I can hear the grind of the shovels, the strikes of the hammer and the communication of the men and beasts who carry this enterprise forward. This, at last, is real."

François paced easterly roughly three chains from the first post to a point still in line with the north wall of the cathedral that afforded a good line of sight to the southeast. He had another post set there in similar fashion. The north wall of the cathedral, depicted on existing maps, would provide alignment for their route map. He chose a point near two large oak trees that would serve as references to the second post like the crosses chiseled in the moat wall for the first. While the chainmen were measuring from the first post to the second post, with the help of the *nivelleur*, he supervised the positioning of a third post to the southeast.

As they progressed southeasterly, toward the River L'Hers, he maintained a level course winding the route as necessary to minimize the excavation that would be required. He allowed the route to rise only when he foresaw the need for a lock. Locks would be needed to lift the canal to Naurouze, but between the locks the canal would need to be level.

Following the progress on horseback, Riquet trotted from one post to the next and back again, fascinated by the science that seemed so complex yet almost automatic for François.

The lead chainman had a quiver of ten steel shafts, each having a length of three feet with a ring on one end and a point on the other. When the chain pulled tight, he would drive a shaft into the ground to mark the extent of the chain's reach. He would then move on to set another shaft once the rear chainman had reached the first shaft and the chain pulled tight again. The rear chainman would retrieve the shafts as he went, and they would serve to maintain a tally of the number of chain lengths traversed. Upon reaching the next post, the rear chainman would call out the number of chains and the lead chainman would announce the additional fraction. François recorded the tally in the logbook of the survey using a graphite stick wound with string. The graphite was handier and less prone to accident than quill and ink. It would prove essential for recording in the rain.

The chain in use was comprised of one hundred long links connected to each other by short links. The long links were rods about two feet long with an eye at each end and each was joined to the next by a short link just large enough to make the connection. The total chain measured two hundred twenty *pieds* end to end, or one *arpent*.

While the distance from the first post to the second was being measured, François measured the angle from the post at the moat through the second post to the third post. His instrument could only measure horizontal angles, so while he was establishing horizontal control for their survey it was left to the *nivelleur* to measure the vertical differences. François recorded the angular and vertical measurements in the log along with the chain tallies.

The axemen blazed the reference trees on the sides facing the centerline post and the chainmen measured the distances from the blazes to the post. These reference measurements could be used to find the post long after it was buried under leaves and grass. François drew a sketch of the post position and its reference trees in the logbook and recorded the reference measurements on the sketch.

The process was tedious, and they only advanced by twelve chains that first day. As the sun neared the horizon, the party returned to their campsite of the previous evening near a stream tributary to the River L'Hers. The cookfire was built and supper preparation underway when they arrived. They were still within sight of the city wall, but Riquet was thrilled to be moving forward with the design of the canal. Gerome had a fire built near Riquet's tent, and a table set for him by the time the cook had supper prepared.

André had pitched Boutheroüe's tent close by, and the tent Andréossy shared with the *nivelleur* was not far, so Riquet invited Hector and François to join him, and the three sat down to a supper of bread, cheese, stew, and wine.

"Not a great start," said François, "but tomorrow will be better. This mission we have undertaken will not be completed in a week. It will be well into next month before we reach Naurouze."

"I am glad just to have started," replied Riquet. "It brings a flavor of reality to my dream. As you know, this quest has nagged at my thoughts since I was a boy. Sometimes faint in the background, sometimes stronger in the forefront. But always there. I don't mind if it takes years as long as it progresses. As certain as I am of success, I shall rest easier when my conviction is backed by your engineering."

"Will you be with us throughout?" asked Hector. "Can you and François afford the time away from Bonrepos and from your commitments to the *gabelle*?"

"Matty has completed his studies in law and will be available to provide any assistance Catherine may require with most estate and business matters. My man Hugo has the *gabelle* in his capable hands. I shall be free to focus on the requirements of this endeavor for as long as it takes. François no longer works the *gabelle*. He and his wife now reside in Toulouse. I have replaced him at the salt bank in Narbonne and he receives his stipend as Commissioner and additional pay for his work as *arpenteur* and *géomètre* for the Commission."

Andréossy was recently wed. His wife was an actress who had not been well received by Narbonne society. Understanding that the canal project might be starting to materialize, and anxious to be free of the toxic social environment, upon his appointment to the Royal Commission he had seized the opportunity to relocate with his new wife to Toulouse.

"Good, then," said Hector, "we shall explore the specifics together."

Weary from the day's labors, they retired shortly after sunset. Except for Gerome, who tended the fire and kept watch late into the night. Hector had sentries posted as a matter of course, but Gerome was a cautious fellow.

They resumed at dawn. The sky was clear, and the sun rose on a day filled with promise. The survey party moved on, the pace quickening somewhat as the men fell into a rhythm and progress improved. The *nivelleur* took the lead, using elevation, line of sight and available references as the primary criteria for placement of posts going forward. He was assisted by a rodman and a laborer. The rodman would mark the position for the next post, based on direction from the *nivelleur,* and the laborer would take a post from the wagon and bury it flush with the surface of the ground. This left François free to sketch stations, measure angles and record them along with the chainmen's tallies.

"Note any structures that fall within sixty pieds of the centerline as we pass," said Riquet. "They must be considered in calculating the cost of taking lands for the canal. Especially mills."

Hector had convinced Riquet to parallel the path of the River L'Hers on the gentle slopes of the valley, above the floodplain, as far as Renneville. There they would cross the river and continue their ascent to the *seuil de Naurouze.* Combined with the work of the Campmas-Roux crew establishing the route of the *rigole de la plaine* to the Sor River, and the route of the *rigole de le Montagne* from the Sor to the Alzau, they would be able to prove absolutely and with specific certainty the feasibility of building a canal from Toulouse to the summit at Naurouze. It would be all downhill from there.

The land was open, and there were few obstructions to interfere with their course. As they approached the River L'Hers, they held their course well above the marshy land adjoining the river and well above any impact of potential flooding. They shadowed the river southeasterly along the southwesterly slopes of the valley. The land rose gently as they went. If their line passed through trees, the axemen removed the lower branches to open the line of sight for measuring the angles. To the extent possible, the trees themselves were spared until the route was more certain.

The *nivelleur* tracked the rise of the land in *pieds* and *pouces*, with 12 *pouces* to the *pied*. The *pied du roi* in use was based on the length of the unshod foot of Charlemagne. François recorded his measurements in the survey log.

It took three days to reach Castanet, barely three leagues from Toulouse. Hector kept track of the elevation increase. He noted lock locations based on every eight-foot rise. Riquet kept his own account, figuring one lock chamber for every fourteen feet. The two were not of one mind regarding the optimum lock depth. Riquet wanted to minimize the number of locks to facilitate traffic flow. Boutheroüe sought to minimize structural stress and the risk of collapse to ensure safety and preclude disastrous traffic interruptions.

As a brief respite and a reward for their hard work, Riquet found lodging in Castanet for most of the party, housing the laborers in the stables with the horses. Supper at the *auberge* was a welcome change from campfire fare, and the landlord honored Riquet and Boutheroüe with an excellent cognac to enjoy with their pipes afterwards.

"The land rose only fifty *pieds* in the three leagues from Toulouse to Castanet," declared Riquet as they relaxed by the fire. "This stretch will only require four locks raising the traffic fourteen *pieds* or so with each lock."

Boutheroüe differed.

"We should not risk more than eight *pieds* per chamber," he argued. "The extra six *pieds* of water will add enormous strain to the walls and doors. Six locks would be a safer design."

"But locks impede navigation, *n'est ce pas?*" parried Riquet.

"But lock failures are far more troublesome," replied Boutheroüe. "We shall need an adequate number of lock chambers, bothersome as they are."

Riquet decided not to argue the point, thinking that there would be time enough to argue specifics once the plan was sanctioned by the King.

The next day Riquet tasked Gerome with procurement of supplies in the village. Returning from this task, Gerome was livid.

"These merchants are bandits, master! They charge twice the value of the goods because they know that we must have them and that we shall not be back to buy from them again."

"It is to be expected, Gerome," replied Riquet. "They likely believe it is their own tax money they are recovering. As you observed, we have no choice."

Riquet felt the bite of extraordinary expense personally. The Royal Commission had provided a modest budget for these endeavors, but Riquet had already found the need to supplement that budget from his own funds. His wealth was such that the expense was not too troublesome, and his inherent sense of compassion would not allow him to fault the merchants of Languedoc.

* * *

They continued southeasterly toward Gardouch. Curious locals learning of their purpose either lauded them or threatened them, depending primarily on whether their lands were to be taken for the canal. Many were blasé, knowing that processions of surveyors had traveled the route before, with never a spade soiled.

Spades were soiled this time. The *géologue* took frequent samples, calling for holes up to twelve feet deep. He kept detailed records of soil types noting sand and clay content and the depth of bedrock if encountered. Riquet insisted that the test holes be backfilled when the *géologue* had collected his data, not wanting to leave pitfalls for the locals.

Just north of Vieillevigne, one angry woad farmer confronted François with a pitchfork, threatening to impale him unless he retreated at once. The young *arpenteur* was skilled with the sword and could have dispatched the old farmer easily, but chose restraint, not wanting to engender more animosity toward their enterprise.

"By what right do you trespass upon my land digging holes and planting posts?" demanded the angry old man, spittle flying from his lips.

"By right of the King's edict," replied François calmly but firmly.

He produced a copy of the edict establishing the Royal Commission for the farmer's inspection. Although illiterate, the farmer was impressed by the official appearance of the document. He had seen the King's seal before on public postings and was duly impressed. However, he was not willing to drop the issue without protest.

"I do not need, nor do I want your accursed canal cut through my woad. It will take land from me that would otherwise profit me at harvest, and it will obstruct my harvest of the land you leave me. I shall somehow have to cross your accursed canal to harvest the other side. Get off my land or I swear I'll run you through."

With that François' hand went to the hilt of his sword but with the arrival of the guards wearing the King's livery, the conversation took on a calmer tone.

"Why cut a new channel when God has provided you a natural one yonder?" the old farmer continued, waving his arm in the direction of the River L'Hers.

"Live streams are not suitable due to the damage the channel would suffer from flood waters," replied François, "and the marshy lands adjoining the river are not suitable for the towpath we shall need for the beasts that draw the barges."

In the end, it was the guard that persuaded the irate farmer to go on about his business. From that point on, the guards held close to the survey crew and Gerome found himself less occupied with the affairs of camp and more occupied as Riquet's shadow as the Baron rode to and fro monitoring progress and keeping constant watch for issues that might require his authority for resolution.

Late one afternoon Riquet called an early halt in a glade by a stream that offered respite from the hot sun. Hector decided to use the free time to revisit the issue of lock sizes. As he arrived at Riquet's tent, he found the flap open and a bit of drama unfolding inside.

"Only one *pinte*?" Riquet was asking Gerome who had his boot firmly on the neck of the young axeman who was prostrate before Riquet.

"*Oui*, master," replied Gerome.

"Still," Riquet continued, "we cannot allow pilferage in any amount. Some, I know, would simply hang a thief. In Arabie they would take his right hand, thereby denying the thief access to the communal supper pot, the left hand being deemed suitable only for the toilet."

"You are Jacques Morel?" he asked the prostrate youth.

"Mfmt."

"Please, Gerome, ease your boot some so I can communicate with the young man."

With the boot off his neck, the young man replied, "I am, *sieur*."

"Of Saint-Felix?"

"Oui, sieur."

"Your father is a cooper there?"

"Oui, sieur."

"I know him to be a man of integrity. If you were to lose your hand or your life, the loss of honor would pain him as deeply as the loss of flesh."

Turning to Gerome he ordered, "This one time we shall temper our punishment. Have this young man swaddled tightly about the torso with his right arm bound underneath but leave his left arm free. A week of this will give him a taste of what life would be like with but one hand. If he makes any attempt to free his arm, then take the hand off at the wrist. Remove his bonds at night lest the arm die and chain him to the post wagon each night lest he tire of our company."

"Merci, sieur, merci beaucoup!" cried the young man as Gerome hauled him off.

"A decision worthy of Solomon," mused Boutheroüe to himself. He decided to let the lock size issue lay for a time.

The next day, as they approached Gardouch, they were met by the Mayor of the town. Angry landowners had warned him of their approach. But the Mayor was one of a minority of Languedocian landowners who could clearly see the benefit of the canal to his community and his estate.

"Bonjour, monsieurs!" was his cheerful greeting. "And you, *Monsieur* Riquet, I see that my countrymen have not yet lynched you, praise God. I can welcome you warmly to Gardouch knowing that all my salt bears the King's *fleur de lis.*"

"And good day to you as well, *Monsieur le Maire*," replied Riquet. "I am not here for the *gabelle* today. Today we are exploring the route for the Sun King's canal to join the two seas."

"I know of your mission, *monsieur*," said the Mayor. "I am here to offer assistance if I may.

"How so?"

"I have lands near Gardouch that I would give for use as a port on your canal if it pleases you."

Pleased by the all too rare encounter with a far-sighted landowner, and hoping to encourage citizen support for the enterprise, Riquet agreed to examine the site. He and Hector, François and the *nivelleur* rode with the Mayor, under armed escort, to view the site he was proposing for the port. Without ever setting up his level, the *nivelleur* was able to determine confidently that a course through the site would be workable. He had an innate sense of the horizontal.

"I believe we shall need a lock," he predicted, "to reach the level of the proposed port, but our goal is to lift the canal to Naurouze eventually and this would be a good placement for one."

"As you know, *Monsieur le Maire*," said Riquet, "the final decision rests with the King. But I shall propose to His Majesty that his canal should employ this site for a port. We shall adjust our proposed route alignment to accommodate your request."

* * *

April warmed into May and spirits rose with the temperatures, but the work was even more exhausting in the heat of the day, and the noon meal was always accompanied by wine. Hector was not stingy with the wine, limiting it to three *pintes* per worker per day only due to concerns about safety. But on the hottest days after the noon meal and wine, they would take long naps in the shade. The warmer nights were welcome as they bedded down in their tents.

They continued through Renneville, crossing the River L'Hers, and up the northeast side of the valley. By the ides of May they reached the *seuil de Naurouze*, near the head of the south fork of the Fresquel river. When the time came to survey their route to the east, they would shadow the Fresquel on their descent toward the Mediterranean as they had previously shadowed the River L'Hers while climbing toward Naurouze.

François laid out an octagonal tract not far from the Stones of Naurouze, just east of the canal centerline. Each side of the octagon was two chains (about four hundred forty feet) long. This would be the site of the Naurouze reservoir. Riquet was in total agreement with Boutheroüe's plan that they should, if the terrain would allow it, bypass Graissens for Naurouze. He recognized that the direct route from Toulouse would probably have a political advantage as well as the hydraulic advantage: as the new Archbishop of Toulouse, Monseigneur Bourlemont might be less sanguine about bypassing the capital than he had been as Bishop of Castres, his allegiance having followed his post.

The locks of their canal would be "pound" locks. They would act as elevators for canal traffic; that is their function would be to raise or lower boats from one level of the canal to the next. For example, traffic bound for the next higher level would enter a lock chamber, the doors would close behind it and the chamber would be filled, raising the boat to the next level. When the water level in the lock chamber matched the next level of the canal, the front doors would open and the traffic could move on. Operation of these pound locks would require a source of im*pound*ed water to replace what was sent downstream as the locks were filled to raise traffic or emptied to lower traffic to the next level. The replacement water would be held in an impound of one form or another until needed to refill the locks. Ideally, the canal would have enough level length between locks to serve as the pound but, particularly at the summit, as the canal was drained to fill the locks, that water needed to be replenished.

Ultimately, at Naurouze, that replenishment would come from the *Montagne Noire*. The canal would be level at the summit for approximately three miles. That length of level channel would form a substantial pound to supply the water to operate the summit locks. But continuous resupply would be required. The plan was to create a large reservoir here at Naurouze to replenish the pound as it was depleted through normal operation. The reservoir itself would be maintained by the waters of the Dark Mountain.

The *géologue* tried a test hole just inside the perimeter of the octagon and struck stone barely one shovel deep. He tried several more scattered about the reservoir site with similar results.

"The bedrock is shallow here," reported the *géologue*. "Your reservoir may, in fact, be a quarry."

"*Très chanceux!*" exclaimed Riquet. "Good news, indeed!"

"This could be the heart of a utopian city," Riquet confided to Hector. "This reservoir could be a great harbor. The streets of the city could radiate from this harbor and be joined by avenues concentric with the central octagon. The canal would fill the city with art, culture and commerce."

"You are a far-sighted man, indeed, *monsieur*," replied Hector, "but we must not lose focus lest we lose all."

Although Boutheroüe could see the potential, he thought the idea a bit fanciful and did not want to be distracted from their primary objective: communication between the two seas.

That evening after supper Riquet, François and Hector sat by the fire enjoying their pipes and sweet red wine from Porto. Riquet shared with his companions the legend of the Stones of Naurouze.

"As the story goes, those huge stones yonder were dropped here by the giant whose name they bear. He was carrying them to Toulouse to be used in construction of the city wall," explained Riquet. "He carried them up from the east, and upon reaching the summit, exhausted, dropped them, and then, presumably, went off in search of less strenuous employment. Also, it seems the devil himself was involved in some way, imbuing the stones with so much evil that rain falling upon them fled in all directions.

"This fanciful legend is no doubt rooted in the fact that the stones lie on the threshold of Naurouze. When rain falls on these stones, some heads west, to the *Océane*, and some heads east, to the Mediterranean.

"From a more scientific perspective, it is the perfect spot to bring the waters of the Dark Mountain for alimentation of the canal."

* * *

As François was setting that first post by the moat back in Toulouse, the Campmas crew had begun a similar trek beginning at the Stones of Naurouze where Riquet now stood. That crew was comprised of Campmas, Roux, and technicians working for the Royal Commission who were tasked with verification or rebuttal of the data previously collected by Campmas. From Naurouze Campmas and Roux had monumented the route of the feeder *rigole* past the *seuil de Graissens* to the Sor.

Backtracking the route took them northerly from Naurouze along the western slopes of the valley of the north fork of the Fresquel toward Saint-Felix, situated on the Lauragais Plateau above. They confirmed that the terrain would allow the *rigole* to bypass the *seuil de Graissens* in favor of the *seuil de Naurouze*. It would, however, require artificial elevation of the watercourse through several valleys by means of raised levees or aqueducts. Campmas had speculated about the viability of the bypass from the beginning and had been hoping that the *nivelleur* would confirm the feasibility of that route.

From the base of the Lauragais Plateau south of Saint-Felix, the route of the *rigole* turned east to run south of Revel and join the Sor near Pont Crouzet east of Revel. By the time they arrived at the Sor, they had confirmed that the collected waters could, indeed, be carried by gravity alone to Naurouze. The route then followed the Sor east to Conquet then, leaving the Sor, it climbed along the forested southern faces of the *Montagne Noire* to the Alzau.

The survey into the *Montagne Noire* to the catchment point of the Alzau would allow the Royal Commission's technicians to verify Campmas' measurements of elevations and flow rates and confirm the viability of that part of the plan. The southern face was rent with canyons through which many streams cascaded toward the Fresquel. The plan was to capture those cascades high on the mountain and channel them westerly along the southern slopes around to the Atlantic side and the Sor River.

As they climbed out of the hot sun, into the shelter of the conifers, the air grew thick and sweet with the smell of the hot sap of the fir and spruce forests that gave the mountain its name. Progress was much slower on the mountain. To measure horizontal distances accurately, lacking the means to measure a vertical angle, the chain had to be held horizontally. That meant "breaking" the chain sometimes every ten feet, as the ground rose or fell six feet in that distance. The man on the downhill end was only able to raise his end about six feet to reach horizontal with the higher ground. The *nivelleur* faced similar issues and the axemen were more taxed than on the fields of the valley below. The trees were close set and the lower limbs had to be removed to enable measurement of both distances and angles. The pace ground to a crawl. The first day on the mountain they had progressed less than two chains by noon. Campmas and Roux discussed their progress at lunch. They sat by a rill and enjoyed bread and cheese washed down with wine that they had set in the cold mountain stream to chill.

"Our *rigole* is going to have a steep gradient," observed Roux.

"We could reduce the gradient by placing the catchment points lower," said Campmas, "but then the ravines will be wider and more difficult to dam."

"Which would provide more storage," offered Roux.

"In the end, these choices will have to be weighed carefully," said Campmas. "For my part, I am not certain which would be the better design."

"The *Chevalier* de Clerville will, no doubt, have an opinion," said Roux. "His experience should help the Baron find the right path."

They continued to climb until they reached the Alzau, the farthest stream they intended to capture. It was well into May before they had completed this leg of the survey. With the data gathered from the survey, they confirmed the catchment plan previously conceived by Campmas and Riquet.

On return from the Alzau, the survey party stopped in Revel, *chez* Campmas, where they found the Riquet party camped and awaiting their arrival. Riquet was pleased that the King's own men had confirmed their plan and immediately wrote Bourlemont to inform him of the good news. Boutheroüe dismissed both crews, thanking them for their service. Escorted by the guard, Riquet then set out with Gerome, Hector and Isaac for Bonrepos.

* * *

Bourlemont was preparing to journey to Paris when he received Riquet's letter informing him of the unqualified success of the survey. Bourlemont had been invited to a gala at Versailles to celebrate and promulgate progress on the great renovation. In view of the successful completion of the survey, he decided it would be wise to bring the Baron of Bonrepos along to explain his plan to the Finance Minister in person and in detail.

Before setting out for Bonrepos he decided to stop by Riquet's house on *Rue des Puits-Clos* in case he was there.

"*Mais non*, Excellency," was the response at the door, the Baron is most often at Bonrepos now. If the survey for the canal is finished, I am certain you will find him there."

When he reached Bonrepos, he found the renovation complete and the Riquets in residence. He was shown into Riquet's cabinet where he found the Baron studying sketches of the artworks planned for the interior of the manor.

"Excellent news of the survey results," beamed Bourlemont as they met. "There can be no doubt that your plan will go forward now."

"It would seem so, Monseigneur," replied Riquet. "Is it only to share the joy of this news in person that you have honored me with this visit? Now that this herculean restoration is nearly completed, I am better able to receive you in a manner befitting your station," he added with a broad smile.

"No, actually, I am come to invite you to Paris to meet with Minister Colbert. Now that the King's technicians have verified the scientific data supporting your proposal, I believe it would be wise to explain your plan in more detail to the Minister."

"Excellent!" agreed Riquet heartily. "I actually have several proposed routes, one of which I find clearly superior, yet I believe it would be prudent to provide the Minister, and thus the Sun King, with options. The plan that I prefer is the one supported by Commissioner Boutheroüe. It is the route we have just surveyed. It carries the feeder *rigole* past the *seuil de Graissens* to the *seuil de Naurouze*. This will mean that the canal will not directly serve Revel or Castres, but there will be fewer locks and it will better serve the capital and, in fact, all of Languedoc."

The Archbishop showed no reaction to the suggestion that Revel and Castres might be abandoned.

"As anxious as I am to hear the details," said the Archbishop, "we must be off with haste to Paris. The King is hosting a preview of his renovation at Versailles, and I want to arrive in time for you to meet with the Finance Minister before the festivities begin."

With that, Riquet tasked Gerome with assembling minimal adequate luggage for the trip and spoke briefly with Catherine, then the three set out for Paris and the Louvre. The Sun King was born at the Chateau Saint Germain, and that was his primary residence during the years of struggle with the canal and with the renovation and expansion of his father's hunting lodge at Versailles. But the King's court had, for a time, been relocated from Saint-Germain to the Louvre, and that was where Bourlemont and Riquet planned to meet with Colbert.

It was not to be. Colbert was very busy trying to keep the King's treasury solvent. Fraud, embezzlement, wars and, not least of all, the renovation of Versailles had severely drained the treasury and Colbert was struggling to restore it. This gala was not helping.

Bourlemont and Riquet, indeed, arrived at the Louvre in time to meet with the great man before the days of celebration at Versailles, but he had no time for them. Riquet, who had not been invited to the gala, was obliged to wait patiently in Paris until the celebration concluded.

Happily, his new son-in-law, Jacques de Lombrail, Lord of Rochemontès, had been made Treasurer General of France, and he and Marie had settled in Paris. Marie welcomed the serendipitous visit from the father she loved so dearly, and the days passed quickly.

While Riquet bided, Bourlemont celebrated with the King's court at Versailles. He managed to secure a commitment from Colbert to meet with him and Riquet thereafter. When that time came, the meetings went on for days. Riquet presented his three alternatives along with cost estimates and estimated time to complete the project. Colbert, like Boutheroüe and Riquet, was drawn to the route from Toulouse to Naurouze, thence to the Mediterranean. He spent much of his precious time going over the details of Riquet's proposals, clearly invested in the ultimate value of the project despite the staggering cost during a time of severe strain on the treasury.

"I believe the *Chevalier* should inspect the various possible routes for the canal and the planned route of the mountain *rigole* and of that of the plain," he said at last. "His concurrence would mean much to our King."

"I stand ready to guide him at his convenience," agreed Riquet. "I shall await him in Toulouse, if that is your pleasure."

"I shall so advise the *Chevalier*," agreed Colbert.

Eight

The Dam.

Riquet returned to Toulouse with Bourlemont and awaited Clerville at *Rue des Puits-Clos*. When the *Chevalier* arrived, the two, accompanied by Gerome, set out for Naurouze thence across the plain to Revel and the Sor, thence into the *Montagne Noire* to the Alzau. Clerville was only interested in the route from Toulouse to Naurouze, not deeming the others to be worth consideration. He judged one route to be disproportionately beneficial to Castres and the other to favor Bonrepos too heavily for comfort. Like Boutheroüe, he favored the route that best served the capital.

"It seems you may have found the solution to commerce between the two seas that eluded even the great Leonardo," allowed Clerville at last.

"I do believe I have," replied Riquet. "Your affirmation is most encouraging. All France respects your knowledge of engineering. I anticipate great benefit from your counsel."

"I'm not sure 'all France' agrees with you," Clerville demurred, "but I do enjoy the confidence of the Sun King and his Council.

As they examined the various streams and catchment points, Riquet posed the question of the relative benefits of higher versus lower catchment points.

"We plan to build reservoirs at the catchment points on the mountain," opened Riquet. "I was hoping for your advice regarding optimal placement of the catchments and reservoirs. Our *géologue* has confirmed suitable bedrock for the dam sites, but we are uncertain whether it might be better to relocate them lower on the mountain to lessen the gradient of the *rigole*. Larger dams would be required, but more storage would result."

"I see," replied Clerville. He had little to say beyond that as they retraced the route of the *rigole* back from the Alzau. Clerville had no argument regarding the suitability of the catchment sites or the viability of the dam sites and offered no opinion regarding possible relocation. Then, as they were nearly back to Revel, Clerville reined in his horse in the valley of the Laudot River, just south of Revel near a small tenant farm known as "Saint-Ferréol." He had paused here briefly on the way to the Alzau but had not declared his purpose as he studied the verdant river valley. Now he shared his thoughts.

"I would propose one large dam rather than many small ones," he announced. "If we were to dam this valley, we could capture more reserve than all of your *Montagne Noire* dams combined, yet still provide storage well above the elevation of the *seuil de Graissens*. If we collect the waters here, excess from one stream would compensate for reduced flow in another. Our resources would be stronger combined. Also, the construction logistics would be simpler here in the valley than high in the *Montagne Noire.* The place is barely inhabited, and I believe you will find sound footing for such a dam at the base of that stone outcropping."

"An ambitious notion," observed Riquet.

"This whole project is an ambitious undertaking, *monsieur*; were you not aware? Great minds envision great works. I had been led to believe that yours was such a mind. *N'est ce pas?*"

"I believe I can rightfully claim the mind of a visionary, *sieur*," Riquet replied in indignation, "and primary responsibility for the King's interest in this enterprise. My father, Guillaume, was wont to say that one has two choices in life. One can look upon the ills of the world and despair, or one can envision the world as it might be and strive. In this enterprise, I have chosen to strive against great odds and the opposition of small minds."

This brought a subtle smile from Clerville and there was a faint hint of admiration in that smile.

The dams of the various streams of the *Montagne Noire* would be mundane engineering projects. The dam Clerville envisioned would be the most massive ever built. It seemed to Riquet that such a proposal would only compound the perception that this whole endeavor was unrealistic. Not comfortable with such a grandiose plan, Riquet's concerns were eased some by the fact that the plan was not his, but Clerville's, and if Colbert (or Louis) balked, he had a more modest proposal to bring forth.

"If you can convince the King, *sieur*, and if you will show me the way, I shall adopt your plan gladly," he concluded.

"The Sun King is a great King," replied the *Chevalier*. "He will see the wisdom of this plan and not shy from the challenge it presents."

They waited in the valley while Gerome rode to Revel to fetch one of the Commission's *géologues*. After thorough inspection of the valley floor at the base of the stone outcropping Clerville had indicated, the *géologue* confirmed that the bedrock was shallow there and composed of high-quality stone, running uninterrupted across the floor of the valley for one half mile. It would offer a solid footing for the dam.

After spending the night in Revel, they returned to Toulouse whence Clerville left for Paris to report his findings to Colbert and the King.

* * *

Riquet now briefly turned his attention to the career of his first-born, Jean Mathias. Matty had just turned twenty-six and had an established law practice in Toulouse. Riquet had seen to his sons' educations by providing tutors for them at an early age. His vision for Matty had been a legal career, for Pierre-Pol, the military. While Matty received instruction in the former, his brother trained in the martial arts and studied military strategy.

Now, to advance Matty's career Riquet bought him a seat in the Parliament of Toulouse, realizing that the Parliament would be instrumental in the approval process for the construction of his canal project. This intrusion into the world of the nobility of the sword stirred resentment among many in Parliament, but it secured for Matty a place in the society of Toulouse and for his father a friendly voice in Parliament.

Nine

The Route from Naurouze.

The next order of business was to stake the centerline of the canal from the Stones of Naurouze to the Mediterranean. Clerville's plan was to connect the canal to the Aude River near Trèbes, just east of Carcassonne. From there, the Aude would provide passage to the Robine Canal which passed through Narbonne to the Mediterranean.

To Hector, this plan suffered the obvious flaw of incorporating a live river channel into the canal, but he planned to make that argument to the full commission rather than debate the issue with Clerville, a native of Narbonne.

Even Clerville was opposed to using the live channel of the Fresquel. He agreed that it was too small and subject to unacceptable fluctuations to be of practical use. He supported Hector's plan to shadow the Fresquel to the point just before Trèbes where the canal would join the Aude. Next, therefore, the route to Trèbes needed definition.

Hector reconstituted his survey crew and he, Riquet and François struck out for Naurouze to continue the route survey to the Aude. Riquet had ordered a new supply of oak posts which were on hand when the party was ready to proceed. There was no fanfare this time as they set out from Bonrepos, just weary anticipation of the hard days that lay ahead. Hector Boutheroüe was included in the goodbye hugs between all members of the Riquet clan, having come to be fully regarded as family.

At Naurouze François' monument references proved invaluable. To establish a starting alignment for proceeding they needed to recover two posts they had previously set. Having been set flush with the surface for their protection, none were visible without discovery. One was simply covered by windblown leaves and was easily uncovered using François' reference measurements from blazes in two nearby trees. One reference measurement only gave them an arc along which to search, but the second gave them an intersection of two arcs to pinpoint the location. The second post was buried under the trunk of a tree that had fallen in one of the storms that had ravaged Languedoc that summer. The axemen were needed to expose it. Fortunately, the fallen tree was not one of those they had chosen as references.

They proceeded southeasterly from Naurouze, toward Castelnaudary, holding to the south of the Fresquel and above the floodplain. As they approached Castelnaudary, Boutheroüe reviewed his notes of their progress from Naurouze.

"We have dropped sixty-five *pieds* in only one hundred thirty *arpents* to Castelnaudary," he said. "I fear we shall need eight locks between here and the summit, but I believe we can cluster at least half in the first thirty *arpents*. Clustering in staircase locks minimizes the traffic impedance, almost as if it were only one chamber."

"Still he insists on *more* locks rather than *deeper!*" thought Riquet. But he chose not to rekindle that bootless argument with Boutheroüe. He had discussed the issue privately with both Clerville and Andréossy and knew that, in the end, they would side with him.

In the morning they continued eastward passing Castelnaudary a half-mile to the north, about halfway between the town and the Fresquel. From there, the land fell quickly, dropping thirty-five feet in less than a thousand.

"This stretch is going to require an extraordinary staircase," mused Boutheroüe.

"Will it still seem almost as one?" asked Riquet somewhat facetiously.

"It will require a great volume of water," replied Boutheroüe, ignoring the gibe. "I'm not sure the pound behind it will be adequate."

Two days later they made Villepinte and quartered for the night in real beds. At supper, Riquet revisited the staircase supply problem.

"The current route brings the canal close to Castelnaudary, but not through it," he said. "What if we were to construct a large harbor at Castelnaudary, as a reservoir for your 'extraordinary' staircase, and reroute the canal to better serve the city as well as our staircase?"

"A sound engineering plan as well as commercial," agreed Boutheroüe. "But both Colbert and Clerville seek to avoid cities as detrimental to their military transport goals."

One of the key values of the canal to the King, Colbert and Clerville was as a secure passage for the Royal Navy from the Mediterranean to the Atlantic. They sought a means to move warships between the two seas quickly and without exposure to foreign navies. Riquet was more interested in commerce.

"It is at least worth considering," Riquet insisted. "We might even ask the city to help with the costs."

"Indeed."

Costs were of great concern to Riquet. This was bound to be a costly enterprise, and any economy he could devise would augur in favor of the Sun King's ultimate authorization to proceed. Also, he had initiated some preliminary conversations with Colbert regarding the possibility that Riquet would help fund the project in return for which the King would establish the canal right-of-way as a fief under Riquet's Barony to be held by his family in perpetuity. Riquet foresaw the potential for rich returns on his investment, but he could also see that even a small share of the costs of construction would be a daunting expense for one man no matter how wealthy. For his part, Colbert saw the advantage to bestowing a private entrepreneur with a vested interest in maintaining the canal going forward. He viewed Riquet's proposal as analogous to Hector's relationship to the Canal Briare which had served France well for generations.

In the morning they faced a summer storm so cruel that they agreed to shelter in the village until it passed. Villepinte lay to the north of the Fresquel river and their intended canal alignment lay to the south. Seeking respite in the village, they had forded the river, leaving the wagons on the survey line under guard. With the advent of the storm, re-crossing the swollen river seemed a risk not worth taking.

Waiting for the waters to subside, Riquet passed the time writing letters, both business and personal. He wrote Colbert of their progress, omitting any mention of his plans for harbors at Naurouze and Castelnaudary, intending to wait for some future moment when he felt the time was right to advance the somewhat tangential projects. Before he presented a formal proposal for either port, he wanted to give himself time to prepare persuasive arguments for incorporating those cities into the route of the Sun King's military canal. He correctly saw Colbert as being very conservative and knew he would need strong arguments for these proposals.

The storm lasted several days and eventually Riquet and Boutheroüe found themselves playing *piquet*, a card game in which scores were tracked by small oak pegs in an oak board drilled with two parallel rows of one hundred holes each in a loop pattern. Each player had two wooden pegs. One pair was natural oak in color; the other was stained dark to differentiate between players. In posting a score, a player would move his back peg ahead of his front peg leaving open holes equal to his score minus one between the pegs. A key element of *piquet* was auditing the pegging of your opponent to verify that scores were posted correctly. It was not uncommon for players to "haul wood"; that is, to peg a point extra. If discovered, they could feign innocence, having accidentally over-pegged. Under-pegging was rare. Riquet never "hauled wood." He was a meticulous accountant in *piquet* as in business and scrupulously honest.

Card games can be very revealing of character, and Boutheroüe came to realize what a truly ethical man Riquet was, overcoming his prejudice toward tax farmers. Having initially assumed the *fermier* to be greedy as were so many farmers of the *gabelle*, he now realized that his initial judgement might have been undeserved. Minister Colbert, who harbored the same prejudices, would not learn better until it was too late.

In time, the weather cleared, and they were able to safely re-cross the Fresquel and continue the survey toward Trèbes.

They followed the valley of the Fresquel River southeasterly, holding to the south and above the floodplain until August found them just north of Carcassonne. They decided to seek real food and real beds inside the city walls. The guards were especially heartened by this plan as it meant relief from the sentry duty they were obliged to stand while the party camped.

As usual, word of their arrival spread quickly and as Riquet, Boutheroüe and Andréossy were finishing supper at their *auberge* a delegation from the city *Consuls* arrived at the inn. The spokesman for the delegation had a round rosy face and an equally round belly, both suggesting a fondness for food and wine more than labor. He greeted Riquet as an old friend, somewhat surprisingly, as their only previous contact had been in connection with the *gabelle*. After some brief cordialities he stated his business.

"The *Consuls* would like you to meet with them tomorrow at a time of your choosing," he said.

"To what purpose?" asked Riquet.

"We wish to discuss the route of the Sun King's Royal Canal vis-à-vis Carcassonne," was the reply. "We should like to discuss the possibility of serving our city's trade and transportation needs."

"Possible, but expensive," offered Boutheroüe.

"But you are willing to discuss it?"

"Of course," said Riquet. How would ten tomorrow morning suit your *Consuls?*"

"Ten it is, then," said the spokesman. Then, bidding them all a good night he gathered his entourage and left as quickly as he had arrived.

When they were gone, Hector expressed his reservations.

"As we discussed regarding Castelnaudary, the Sun King's primary goal in building this canal is to be able to pass warships from sea to sea in safety. He is hoping to avoid proximity to cities along the way. You are planning ports in Gardouch, and Castelnaudary. You envision building a new city around the reservoir at Naurouze. Now you are considering re-routing the canal to engage Carcassonne?! The King and Colbert both will assume, perhaps rightly, that you have lost your mind."

"You must attach a price to the revision that will placate Colbert and the King," replied Riquet. "I shall tell you in confidence that in the ages to come, I believe our canal will be used far more for commerce than for military transport. I intend to serve our King with this enterprise, but I shall also endeavor to best serve the people of Languedoc."

"My service is to the Sun King, first and foremost," replied Hector. "I shall calculate a price that is certain to compensate our Sovereign for exposing his canal to the city.

The full body of the *Consuls* was assembled to meet with them the next morning, and it seemed that some had more interest in the discussion than others.

"As I understand the plan," said one, "you will join the canal to the Aude near its confluence with the Fresquel just downstream from here, thence the Aude will be maintained in navigable condition as far as the ancient fork of the Aude which is now the Robine Canal. Then the *Canal Royal* is to pass through Narbonne, by way of the Robine, to the sea."

"That is indeed the plan," agreed Riquet.

"We would like to discuss the possibility of bringing the King's canal closer to our city," said another. Why not join the Aude upstream from Carcassonne, thereby providing our city ready access to the commerce carried by your canal?"

"Because, *sieur*," explained Boutheroüe, "there is a ridge between the valley of the Aude and the valley of the Fresquel that would be a challenging obstacle to that route. At this point in the route it would be regressive to step the canal over the ridge with locks. The only acceptable approach would be to cut through the ridge. That would be quite expensive."

"How expensive?"

"I prepared an estimate last night in anticipation of that question. The additional cost would be approximately one hundred thousand *livres*. With the Sun King's permission, we shall agree to change the route if your city will compensate us in that amount."

Some of the *Consuls* harbored Languedocian reservations about granting the King in Paris military access to the city. The price tag swayed most of the rest and the proposal fell to the majority in opposition. Instead, the route continued to follow the Fresquel to its confluence with the Aude. Goods could be carted between Carcassonne and the canal for transport, and the city's defenses would remain secure.

Bypassing Carcassonne, the survey continued down the Fresquel valley to the Aude. If the live channel of the Aude was to be improved to navigability, this would be the end of the cut canal, and ergo the end of their survey. Confident that the Royal Commission could be convinced of the folly of using existing river channels for transport, Boutheroüe wanted to plan for a parallel canal cut just above the floodplain taking from the river only the water needed for alimentation.

"Our work is not yet completed," he cautioned. "We must continue our survey as far as the Robine. We must insist, to the extent we are able, that the Aude not be incorporated into our canal. The use of live channels is just folly."

"If you cannot convince the Commission of that fact, no one can," agreed Riquet. "We should proceed as you say to establish a route for a parallel channel as far as the Robine. You are willing to use the Robine?"

"It is not a live channel. It is an abandoned fork of the Aude which has since been maintained as a canal by the people of Narbonne and so may serve our needs."

They continued the survey toward the Robine, the final leg that would connect the *Canal Royal* to Narbonne and thence to the sea. To avoid crossing the Aude, they held to the north of the river, crossing the Fresquel just before the confluence of the two rivers.

The next obstacle they faced was the Orbiel River, just before Trèbes. Reluctantly, Boutheroüe was planning to cross both the Fresquel and the Orbiel at grade, using downstream weirs on the rivers to bring the river water level up to match that of the canal. He knew there would be issues when the rivers were in flood, but he saw no alternative.

After crossing the Orbiel, they tarried in Trèbes for a few days while Gerome replenished their post wagon from a mill on the Orbiel. Then, continuing eastward, they held close to the eastern edge of Trèbes and continued along the northern slopes of the valley of the Aude, keeping the course above the Aude's floodplain, to Puichéric and on to the Pechlaurier Rock, a stone palisade abutting the left bank of the Aude where the river passed through a narrow defile.

"These cliffs will be troublesome," observed Boutheroüe. "We shall be cutting the channel from stone, but only after this mountain has been removed. The right bank of the Aude would be no kinder. There is no easy passage through this defile."

Once past the Pechlaurier, Hector noted that their route had fallen one hundred sixty feet in five hundred forty chains from Trèbes to Argens.

"Another twenty locks," moaned Boutheroüe. "and I saw no place to group them more than three in a set. Maybe four at the most."

"As you have said all along, Hector, *mon ami*," Riquet consoled, "'we shall need an adequate number of lock chambers for our descent to the Mediterranean, bothersome as they are.' We cannot change the elevation of Naurouze and therefore must descend six hundred *pieds* to meet the sea. The only way to reduce the number of locks needed, as I have said before, is to make them deeper."

"Which seems irresponsible to me," growled Hector.

They continued through Roubia and Saint-Nazaire to the junction of the Aude with the Robine Canal. This would be the eastern terminus of their survey. Happily, the terrain dropped only slightly from Argens to the Robine, a distance of some two hundred chains. Clerville's plan was to improve the Robine canal to carry the Sun King's canal into Narbonne and follow the Robine thence to the Mediterranean.

Upon reaching the Robine, Boutheroüe felt the need to investigate the viability of the old canal, enlisting the aid of one of the chainmen.

"That brass you carry shows you which way is down, does it not?"

The chainman smiled as he considered the question.

"If you mean my plumb bob, yes, it does that precisely."

"Well, grab some extra line, and let's see if it'll tell us how far down is down."

Puzzled, the chainman did as he was directed and soon found himself on a bridge over the Robine just downstream from its junction with the Aude.

"I want you to dip your brass into the canal just till you feel the bottom but keep the tension in your line."

He did.

"Now let's retrieve it and see how much line is wet."

The canal was only three feet deep.

"As I suspected," said Boutheroüe. "Silted up. This canal will need to be dredged constantly to clear the sand deposited by the Aude."

This gave Hector grave second thoughts about the wisdom of tying their route to the Robine. The people of Narbonne had struggled since Roman days to keep this fork of the Aude navigable, ultimately, in the previous century, transforming it into the Robine Canal.

Hector's reservations were compounded by the knowledge that Narbonne was no longer intended to be the ultimate destination for the canal. The King had proposed a new port as the eastern terminus of the *Canal Royal*. Narbonne would only be a stop along the way. Clerville had been commissioned to build the King a new Mediterranean harbor at Cette, a small fishing village on the *Étang de Thau.*

Cette lay on the narrow outer boundary of the *Étang,* on a narrow band of sand separating the lagoon from the Mediterranean. The village, since renamed Sète, lay nestled at the base of Mont Saint Clair, a mountain of pink marble anchoring the sand spit. Clerville wanted to build the King's port on the lee side of that mountain. Colbert wanted it on the windward side, the seaward side, to provide quick and easy access from the Mediterranean for ships seeking shelter. The issue was argued before the King and Colbert prevailed.

From Narbonne, the canal would run north through the coastal marshes and through the *Étang de Thau* to Sète. Hector had never favored the idea of driving the canal north from Narbonne through the marshy coastal lowlands. The route would be flat, true enough, but the marshlands would contribute their own impediments to progress. Boutheroüe favored a more direct inland route running northeasterly from the east side of the Pechlaurier Rock toward Béziers and then Sète, an option he planned to promote to the Royal Commission. But for now, he chose apparent acquiescence to Clerville's plan. If commissioned, the *Canal Royal* would require excavation of one-hundred-fifty miles of canal from Toulouse to Sète. The excavation would surely begin at the Garonne in Toulouse and there would be ample time to debate the best route from the Pechlaurier Rock to Sète.

These reservations notwithstanding, for the purposes of presentation to the Royal Commission, the centerline survey was complete, and Riquet was elated. In less than six months they had traced a viable route from the Garonne to the Mediterranean and encountered no barriers to the project. There were definite challenges, but no actual barriers. As they made their way back to Bonrepos, Riquet was anxious to prepare his proposal for the Royal Commission. They were scheduled to meet in November, and that would give him the time he needed to craft the findings of their journey into a formal plan for construction of the canal.

He found great comfort in the certainty that five key players: Colbert, Clerville, Boutheroüe, Bourlemont and Andréossy all favored proceeding with the grand enterprise.

Ten

Briare.

With the survey completed, Hector grew anxious about being away from Briare for so long. He was welcomed warmly by the Riquets at Bonrepos but that only made him miss his own family more. He decided to return home and invited Riquet to travel with him to Briare to view the operation of his canal and its locks.

"I need to confirm that there are no major operational problems and it would be an opportunity for you to see how the locks work and how we manage the traffic."

"I would be most pleased, Hector," agreed Riquet, "Let us depart in the morning if the weather holds."

The weather held, and they set out at daybreak: Riquet, Hector, Gerome and André. It was a journey of more than one hundred sixty leagues, so they traveled by coach and brought a dozen armed guards for security.

Seventeenth century France was traversed by an interlaced network of mail routes peppered with post stations where horses were stabled to provide fresh mounts for riders carrying the mail, much like the pony express of the American west. Those horses were available for rent to gentlemen of means. Hector recommended that they follow post routes to ensure the availability of fresh teams along the way.

Their route took them west to Toulouse, where they exchanged Riquet's team for post horses. Gerome promised the stationmaster a generous reward to keep Riquet's team well fed and watered and out of the post rotation.

From Toulouse they proceeded north, along the post route, to Cahors. They approached Cahors from the west, crossing the Lot River on the *Pont Valentré*, an impressive piece of stonework featuring a tall guard tower at each end and a third tower in the center of the span. The guard at the gatehouse recognized Hector and waved them through without hesitation.

They spent the night in Cahors. The inn was a great stone structure with a roof of slate, set behind a stone wall that enclosed a great carriage house, also of stone, where they housed their carriage and boarded the team. There was a large fireplace in the dining room and the innkeeper was not stingy with the wood. The warmth was welcome. The ceiling was low and the huge beams that supported the first floor above were exposed to view, adding to the ambiance of cozy comfort. They enjoyed a fine supper of *confit de canard* but encountered a serious issue with the wine.

"*Aubergiste!*" called Riquet. "I fear you have served us ink in place of wine! It is as black as the devil's heart and tastes as if stirred by his own vile finger!"

"*Mais non, monsieur,*" replied the indignant innkeeper, "that is the color of *Côt Noir.*"

The *Côt Noir* grape would later come to be known as Malbec, which is to this day the signature full-bodied, tannin-rich, black wine of the Lot river valley and Cahors and one of the five grapes of Bordeaux.

"The robust flavor does not please every palate," the innkeeper admitted, "but it was specifically chosen by the Pope in Avignon to be the wine of communion in the days when that city was the seat of the Holy See. Perhaps *monsieur* would prefer a more mundane Bordeaux?"

"Chosen, no doubt to limit consumption," grumbled Riquet. "Yes, if you will, a more 'mundane' Bordeaux would be most appreciated."

After supper and several glasses of wonderfully mundane Bordeaux, as they climbed the stairs to their rooms, Gerome asked Riquet, "I have always wondered, how it is that the "first" floor is always at least one flight up and not the one you enter from the street?"

"I believe," he replied, "it is because "first" refers to the first floor with accommodations. The ground floor has always been assigned to business, storage, or livestock, partly because the residence one floor up is easier to secure."

Early in the morning, they traded their post horses for a fresh team and resumed their journey. They crossed the Dordogne River and continued north to Brive, lodging for the night inside the city wall. The next morning, they continued north to Limoges, crossing the Vienne River on the Pont Saint Martial.

"The river is high," noted Hector with obvious trepidation. "It often floods in concert with the Loire. A bad omen."

"Having come this far," replied Riquet, "we must persevere and hope for the best."

They again lodged inside the city wall. The *auberge* might have been built from the same plan as the one in Cahors. It featured the same stone structure, exposed beams and warm fire. The stew was full-flavored, and the wine was rich and abundant. They enjoyed a peaceful, rejuvenating night's rest.

In the morning, Riquet proposed a brief shopping excursion.

"I want to find an enameled copper piece for Catherine while we are here," said Riquet.

"I know the perfect shop," replied Hector.

With Gerome and André in tow, they strolled through the narrow, cobbled streets of the city to a small shop specializing in the enamelware for which Limoges was famous. The shop was in a stone and beam structure similar to the inn, and there was a small fire burning in the fireplace on the far wall. The use of the space was far different from the inn. The room was filled with shelving and the shelves were filled with the works of artisans, mostly pottery and enameled copperworks. Many of the larger copper pieces were hung on the walls.

"A truly impressive inventory," thought Riquet.

The shopkeeper greeted Hector like an old friend and, learning their purpose, disappeared into a back room, reappearing shortly with a stunningly beautiful serving plate of enameled copper. It bore a profusion of poppies and lavender in colors so vibrant they seemed to be three dimensional – even four, in that Riquet imagined he could smell the lavender. It was a unique artwork and Riquet was duly impressed.

"A piece for the true connoisseur," proclaimed the shopkeeper.

"Beautiful, indeed," agreed Riquet, "but at what price?"

"For a friend of *Monsieur* Boutheroüe," plied the shopkeeper," a mere pittance: eight *livres*, ten."

"And if I were not accompanied by the illustrious *Monsieur* Boutheroüe, could I have it for five?" asked Riquet with a laugh.

"If you had not arrived with 'the illustrious *Monsieur* Boutheroüe,'" replied the shopkeeper indignantly, "you would never have seen such an exquisite piece. But if you came seeking a bargain, *monsieur*, please explore the shelves and walls of my humble shop. There are many to be found."

"No, no, no," laughed Riquet, "I shall gladly pay your price. I meant no offense. It truly is an exquisite piece. I thank you, *Monsieur le Marchand* for your special consideration. I am certain that my wife will love it."

From Limoges, they continued north, spending the night in Châteauroux. The next morning, they left the post route and turned to the northeast to Bourges. Bourges lay on the post route from Clermont to Orleans, so they were able to secure a fresh team for the next leg of the journey which would bring them, finally, to Briare. As they approached the city, they passed a queue of a dozen barges moored to posts set along the bank of the Loire. Arriving in Briare, they found the canal traffic stymied by the flood waters.

"You see," said Hector, "we cannot open the flood locks to admit traffic to the canal without admitting the destructive flood waters. As you can see, the Loire is a river of sand. The flood waters would bring enough sand to fill the canal overnight. This would require extended closure to dredge the channel."

"Clearly," replied Riquet, "and this is the sort of interruption we can expect if we use the Fresquel or the Aude for our canal. We must *not*."

They crossed the canal into Briare, noting the totally arrested canal traffic, and found the street along the quay of the Loire inundated. Hector's offices were on higher ground and he was able to satisfy himself that there were no operational issues requiring his attention. Floods were common on the Loire in the fall and winter, and his crew were accustomed to protecting the canal from the high water.

Hector persuaded Riquet to stay awhile hoping for abatement in the flood waters that might permit the canal to reopen. This would provide him with the first-hand observation he had traveled so far to experience.

Within a few days, the Loire shrank enough that the canal could be opened to traffic. Hector invited Riquet to join him for an inspection tour up to the summit to see how the locks worked, how alimentation was provided and how excess waters were expelled. The inspection tour consumed the greater part of the day. When Riquet was satisfied that he had seen what he had come for, they returned to Briare.

Knowing that the Royal Commission was scheduled to meet in November and fearing that deliberations might last through year's end, Hector had decided to remain in Briare to spend some time with his family. Riquet bid Hector farewell the following morning and set out for Toulouse under clear skies.

He endured longer days on the return trip, stopping for the night just once in Limoges more to rest the guard than for himself or Gerome, who enjoyed the relative comfort of the coach.

Upon their return to Toulouse, Gerome retrieved Riquet's team from the post station, rewarding the station master as he had promised.

Meanwhile, Riquet stopped by Bourlemont's residence to report what he had learned on the journey. The Archbishop received him in his cabinet and his valet served them a rich smooth Fronton.

The Monseigneur's desk, like his coach, was a work of art produced by woodworkers who clearly loved their craft and knew their medium. The wood chosen for each piece had clearly been selected for the beauty of the grain pattern which had been enhanced by the finishing process. Riquet guessed that the piece must be older than either of the men seated at it.

After brief cordialities, Riquet came right to the point.

"Hector's experience is truly essential to this enterprise," he told the Archbishop.

"That does not surprise me," replied Bourlemont. "*Monsieur* Colbert is no fool. He chose *Monsieur* Boutheroüe to serve on the Royal Commission for good reason. If the Sun King is to sponsor this bold venture, it is imperative to him, and therefore to Colbert, that it succeed."

"As it is to me," replied Riquet. "It is for me the dream of a lifetime. I have pledged most of my fortune to the King to prove my belief in success."

"If you succeed," assured the Archbishop, "I am certain that you will be richly rewarded for your risk.

"On a lighter note, will you attend Christ's Mass here in Toulouse?" he asked.

"We expect to, Monseigneur. When I leave Your Excellency today, I shall return to Bonrepos. My family is there now, and we shall attend services here again this year at *Cathédrale Saint-Étienne*. But for now, I must ask your leave to return home."

"Go with my blessing, my son, and may God bless you and your family with a joyous Christmas this year and for years to come.

Christmas was joyous, indeed, that year. Prior to attending midnight Mass in Toulouse, the Riquets enjoyed a sumptuous *reveillon de noel* feast at Bonrepos. Their table was spread with poultry, ham, salads, cake, fruit and wine. Catherine had prepared a large *bûche de Noel*, baked, as was the custom, to resemble a yule log. She served it on a stunning enameled copper serving plate from Limoges.

Eleven

Deliberations.

With the commencement of the survey, the Royal Commission had posted notices on church doors and *mairies* in Languedoc inviting competitive proposals for construction of the canal. Three other proposals were submitted, but they lacked the insight of Riquet's plan and were summarily dismissed. Riquet's plan was the only one deemed to bear further investigation and carried endorsement from Commissioners Clerville, Boutheroüe and Andréossy.

The three had met with Riquet earlier in the week to review his final plan prior to presentation to the Royal Commission. Clerville, Boutheroüe and Andréossy had examined the plan meticulously. Without their support, the Commission would never endorse the plan nor would the King. As the three pored over the plan, Riquet realized he was holding his breath.

Clerville produced a map of the canal showing the route through Narbonne, lock locations and sizes, dams and reservoirs for the feeder canal and, to Riquet's astonishment, the ports at both Naurouze and Castelnaudary which he had not included in his final proposal. Riquet could barely control his shock at the sight of this map.

"Is this your work, François?!" he demanded.

"It is," intervened Clerville. "It was produced for the Commission pursuant to his duties as *géomètre*."

"I should have had an opportunity to review it prior to publication! It contains information that I was not yet prepared to share beyond the four of us. Going forward, I may have need of a *géomètre* who is less free with privileged information."

"François is most loyal to you," assured Clerville. "I am certain he would not have included any information he knew to be secret. The worst he can be faulted for is excessive honesty. I am not sure there even *is* such a thing."

"Indeed, I would not," affirmed François. "I certainly meant no offense. I was unaware that any of the plans I have depicted were confidential. My only intent was to help advance this grand enterprise."

"I see you have not yet abandoned your pusillanimous plan for multiple dams," charged Clerville on completion of his scrutiny.

"And yet," added Hector, "the inadequate number and overly optimistic size of the locks you are planning is nothing short of reckless. The lock walls will never bear the burden you plan to trust to them."

"Neither François nor Nicolas shares your concerns," returned Riquet. "We all favor the greater depths to require fewer locks and thereby minimize the delay in traffic flow that each lock represents.

"You have both made your concerns clear," he continued, "on both points. I have given much consideration to both the lock sizes and the reservoirs. Ultimately, if my proposal is sanctioned by the King, I shall be the one responsible for implementing it. I must submit the proposal that I deem most likely to succeed.

"This is that plan," insisted Riquet. "Can you support it?"

"If you three are all agreed that locks that deep are advisable," conceded Hector, "I shall support your plan and hope that I am wrong."

Clerville said nothing.

* * *

On November 7th, 1664, the Royal Commission met in Toulouse to consider the plan prepared and submitted by Riquet.

The King's Royal Commission was comprised of three dozen noblemen, clergymen, city fathers, legislators and King's *intendants*, official representatives of the Sun King. The only members who brought any real technical knowledge were Clerville, Boutheroüe and Andréossy. Also in attendance was the entrepreneur, Pierre-Paul Riquet. The meeting was led by the *Chevalier* de Clerville, but Minister Colbert, a member of the Royal Council, was recognized by all present as the senior representative of the King. They met in the main hall of the *mairie* of Toulouse where Andréossy's map of the proposed route had been displayed on an easel for all to examine.

"Gentlemen," began Clerville, calling the assembly to order, "you have all had an opportunity to read *Monsieur* Riquet's proposal and to examine the proposed route of the *Canal Royal*. Are there any questions?"

In response to the ensuing clamor, he turned to the Sergeant of the Guard who pounded the butt of his pole axe on the floor until order was restored.

"All those who have questions will please rise. I shall hear your concerns one by one if you remain in order."

Half the assembly took to their feet.

"*Monsieur* Nivelle," called Clerville.

Nivelle, a member of the Parliament of Toulouse, addressed the assembly.

"I am concerned about the use of the city moat for this canal. Will there not be flooding in times of storm? Will our city wall not be endangered?"

"The canal will be designed," replied Clerville, "to divert excess flows into natural channels for the protection of the canal itself. There will be no threat to your moat nor to your wall."

Unappeased, Nivelle continued.

"This is nothing but a flight of fancy," he charged, "and one of enormous expense!" Pointing accusingly at Riquet, his voice rose even louder. "This man knows nothing! Nothing of water, nothing of canals, nor does he know anything of locks! He will never see this work come to fruition!" This last was more prophetic than he could know.

"This notion should be abandoned entirely!" yelled *Monsieur* Pouget. "You confiscate prime farmlands to satisfy this *fermier's* futile dreams of glory! Stay with the sale of salt, *Monsieur* Riquet. That is something you know how to do."

"That is the question," replied Clerville calmly but firmly, "that our King has entrusted to this body. It is not yours to decide, *Monsieur* Pouget, but a decision to be reached by consensus. His Majesty hopes that this bold undertaking will prove to be a boon to the people of Languedoc and, indeed, all Occitania. The Sun King is a man of vision as is the Baron Riquet. Are you not?"

Unwilling to openly question the King's judgement or to face down the *Chevalier* who was known for his skill with a sword as well as with battlements, Pouget returned sullenly to his seat.

"This is no flight of fancy, gentlemen," continued Clerville. "It is a well-conceived plan for communication of the two seas. This entrepreneur has found the means to accomplish this connection where many great minds before him failed. And who here dares say that the *Chevalier de Clerville* knows naught of what he speaks?"

His challenge being met with silence, he continued. "That said, as a soldier I do have concerns about using a moat for any other purpose than defense."

Using his poniard as a pointer, he indicated an alternate route on the map that would pass to the east of the moat and connect to the Garonne north of the city.

"I would propose to reroute the canal so that we do not come within four *arpents* of your moat and join the Garonne at the Sept-Deniers meadow half a league downstream from *le Bazacle*. What say you all to that?"

Le Bazacle was an ancient ford of the Garonne. Not really a bridge, not really a dam, more of a weir crossable by carts, but not by boats. It marked the upper limit of navigability for the Garonne. The Sept-Deniers meadow, so named because the church had leased the pasture from the city since the middle ages for the annual price of seven *deniers*, lay just one mile downstream from the ford. There was a general murmur of agreement, a vote was called for, and the amendment was approved. The canal would give the city wall a wide berth.

One of the *Consuls* of Castres who owned a mill on the Sor River was next to speak.

"Is it certain that the *Montagne Noire* will provide enough supply for your canal without depleting the Sor?"

"*Au contraire*," replied Clerville, "this plan will help maintain a constant flow in the Sor."

"And how does your *fermier* plan to lift these waters to the stones of Naurouze," demanded one member of *Les États du Languedoc*. "Will machines be required? Who will maintain them?"

"Monsieur Riquet's proposal is quite clear on that point," assured Clerville. "The collected waters will reach Naurouze by natural flow alone."

One of the Consuls of Carcassonne who owned a woad farm that lay in the path of the proposed route was next.

"If this work proceeds," he asked, "how much of my land will be taken and how will I be compensated for the loss?"

"The channel of the canal will require sixty pieds," said Clerville, "but the taking must be twice that width to allow for tow paths, berms, tree plantings and lockkeeper's buildings.

"We plan to mark the boundaries of the taking once this body has recommended whether and how to proceed.

"As to the amount of compensation, I must refer you to the Finance Minister."

"The King has authorized me," offered Colbert, "to assure you that you will be compensated fairly for the taking. Before an exact amount can be determined, the taking must be appraised for each holding that will cede land to the right of way. The appraisal will commence once the boundaries are marked. The Sun King would have none of his subjects harmed by this enterprise."

These responses seemed to address the concerns of many. The number of the assembly standing diminished quickly.

The Baron of Castres took the floor next.

"This plan calls for digging new channels parallel to rivers that would seem themselves to be adaptable for navigation. Is this expense truly necessary?"

Riquet himself fielded this one.

"This decision was born of the apposite experience of Commissioner Boutheroüe with the Canal de Briare. The use of live streams will soon cost more in maintenance and interruption of commerce than would be spent on these parallel channels."

Boutheroüe nodded agreement.

"The Fresquel is *peu de chose*," continued Riquet, "and not worth the effort to establish and maintain navigability.

"The Aude is inconstant, full of stones and badly set," he said, "and of a sort that one could not render navigable except for small flat bottom boats, so that we are all agreed that it would be better to dig a new canal along its shores, at enough distance and elevation to not fear floods from the river."

"The Robine is three *pieds* deep," offered Boutheroüe. "The Aude constantly carries sediment into it. If adopted as our route to the Mediterranean, it will need significant initial dredging and constant effort and expense to maintain navigability."

"It should be noted," he added, "that between Narbonne and Cette the coast is pocked with salt marshes that will impede excavation of the channel and confound construction of the towpath. These are lands such as we took great pains to avoid in the valley of the River L'Hers."

"These marshes harbor the miasma that brings the fourth fever," added Riquet. "Our workforce will be decimated by the *malattia de mal aria* which I myself contracted there and which still lays me low from time to time."

"We would fare better turning north after the Pechlaurier Rock," offered Hector, "to take a more direct route through Béziers to Cette."

At this point the entire assembly had returned to their seats but the room still held a low murmur of one-on-one conversation.

"I propose," declared Clerville, "that this full assembly inspect the proposed route within the context of the questions raised here today. When we reconvene, we shall be better armed to make a decision that will best serve our King and our people."

In the weeks that followed, the commissioners visited the proposed route of the canal and its feeder *rigoles*. They confirmed the detriments presented by the existing channels of the Fresquel and the Aude, and the problems that the coastal marshes would contribute.

Clerville ordered Andréossy's route centerline modified to bypass the moat and meet the Garonne at Sept-Deniers. He ordered the right-of-way boundaries staked based on the new centerline for purposes of the appraisal for the taking.

By the end of the month the Commissioners had concurred with the inadvisability of using the existing channels, and even changed their minds about routing through Narbonne. The consensus was that a more direct route to Sète avoiding the coastal marshes would be best.

Perhaps the only draw offered by Narbonne was its proximity to the mouth of the Aude. If the Aude was deemed unusable, then Narbonne lost its appeal.

In the end, the Commission decided to adopt Riquet's plan for alimentation and adopt his route as far as Saint-Nazaire but thence northeasterly to Béziers and Sète. Construction of the section from Toulouse to Trèbes would be sanctioned provided that Riquet could demonstrate the feasibility of his alimentation plan. Confident of success, Riquet volunteered to construct a trial *rigole*, at his own expense, to prove that the waters of the southern face of the *Montagne Noire* could, indeed, be rerouted to join waters from the Sor and from there, by natural flow alone, provide adequate alimentation for the summit locks on the great divide at the *seuil de Naurouze*. He anticipated that he could complete the trial for about two hundred thousand *livres*, a sum that he could easily afford and a commitment that he expected to be two-edged: he believed it would establish him as the clear choice to build the canal should the King decide to proceed. He expected that the cost of the trial would be the best investment he had ever made.

Even with that generous concession, the Commission wanted to limit their exposure in case some unforeseen obstacle arose. If the trial succeeded, they would recommend that the King authorize construction of the canal, but initially only the section from Toulouse to Trèbes, roughly the west half.

The route from Saint-Nazaire to Béziers was accepted in principle but would not be formally adopted until Riquet could lay out a specific route that could be shown to be buildable. Like the King, they wanted to proceed cautiously.

"Their own engineers have verified the alimentation plan," Riquet objected privately to Hector. "What will it take for them to be convinced?!"

"I think they have made that clear," replied Hector somewhat sympathetically. "When they see abundant water flowing to the *seuil de Naurouze*, they will be convinced. Even if they are not convinced the Sun King and Colbert will be. The feeder *rigole* needs to be built eventually, and you and I know that it will succeed. For now, we must be patient and persevere."

But the canal would be routed to Béziers: Riquet's hometown. He could not believe his good fortune. If only his father were alive to witness it.

In fact, if his father had been alive, he might yet have opposed the project. Many prominent citizens of Languedoc did. Perhaps they resented being required by the King to relinquish lands as right-of-way for the canal, as did many in Toulouse; perhaps they saw it as a boon to trade for cities other than their own, as did many in the abandoned Narbonne. Some just resented Riquet for trying to rise above his station by way of this improbable undertaking which promised to suck millions in taxes from the people of Languedoc. For myriad reasons they formed a tacit conspiracy to undermine him at every turn, hoping to make Colbert and the Sun King regret having placed their trust in this upstart tax farmer. They were sadly successful.

Colbert was a soft target for the campaign to undermine Riquet. Despite the integrity he had demonstrated for decades farming the *gabelle*, the entrepreneur could not escape the stigma of all the thieves Colbert had known to hold that position in the past. Even after Riquet's thirty-five years of scrupulous service to the King, Colbert was inclined to ascribe dishonesty to the *fermier* even though he was guiltless.

Riquet's struggle to build the foremost engineering achievement of the seventeenth century was an engineering challenge, to be sure, but in the end, the political challenges would prove greater.

Book III

Blood and Stone

Twelve

1665

On May 27, 1665, Riquet received authorization from the King's Royal Council to cut the trial *rigole* from the *Montagne Noire* to the Sor River, and from the Sor to Naurouze, as required by the Royal Commission to demonstrate that water would, indeed, follow his proposed route. Noble birth imbued more credibility than did science in the culture of the Sun King, and noble birth was a quality that had not yet been ascribed to Riquet. The King's Councilors, like his Commissioners, wanted to see the water flowing before they would fully accept the science.

An edict was issued ordering cooperation from the owners of the lands the *rigole* would impact, under the threat of "corporal punishment."

Riquet quickly assembled a work force and began construction of the trial *rigole*.

"Form them into brigades," advised Clerville, "with forty men to a brigade or sixty women. Assign a Brigadier to head each. Assemble *ateliers* comprised of five brigades each and led by a *Chef de Atelier*. Any skilled workers (engineers, stone cutters, masons, smiths, carpenters and the like) will be in addition to the base force of forty but subject to the same command and control.

"For every two ateliers, you must assign a *Côntrolle Sédentaire* to audit attendance at the worksites.

"You will eventually employ thousands in this endeavor and this structure will be critical to maintain order and verify payrolls.

"You can pay the brigades of sixty women the same as you pay forty men, their values being equivalent. The skilled workers must be paid according to the rate their skill demands and separate from the base pay of the brigade.

"And young Andréossy would be well chosen to lead them all. He is born of good stock; he is totally loyal to you; and he has shown impressive leadership skills in his work for the Commission.

"All shall be as you say," replied the Baron. "I had not foreseen the value of your military experience, only your engineering expertise. But your advice will greatly simplify management of such a host. I had considered François for second in command but was not certain of the choice until you concurred."

Riquet persuaded Bourlemont to write Sofia Soler's parish priest on his behalf. He was reasonably certain that she was illiterate, so it seemed the best way to reiterate his offer of employment. Also, engaging her priest as an intermediary would lend credence and respectability to him and to his proposal. The Archbishop was happy to accommodate him and wrote asking Sofia's priest to inform her that the project Riquet had previously discussed with her was indeed under way and asking if she and Olivia would consider helping him with it. The missive carried with it an implied endorsement of the entrepreneur's character that could not be overlooked.

* * *

Sofia Soler did not know what to think when Father Vilar asked her to stay after Mass. She assumed one of her neighbors must have complained but could not imagine what that complaint could be. When the priest told her that he had a message for her from Monseigneur Bourlemont, Archbishop of Toulouse, she was dumbfounded.

Enough time had passed since Olivia lost her hand that Sofia had assumed Riquet's need for their services had either been a hollow promise or had simply not materialized and she had dismissed that conversation from her mind. She could not imagine that the Archbishop even knew she existed. That he would have a personal message for her was inconceivable.

"There must be some mistake!" she protested. "I am Sofia Soler (as if the priest had mistaken her for someone else). What would His Excellency have to say to me?"

"The Archbishop seems to think that Baron Riquet has offered you employment. *N'est-ce pas?*"

"*Oui*, but it was years ago. I thought the offer forgotten. It is renewed?"

"It would seem so. The Archbishop deems the work to be valuable to the church and to France and he vouches for the character of the Baron. It seems that you, Sofia, are blessed with an opportunity to represent our little village in an endeavor sanctioned by the Sun King himself. It would be unseemly to decline."

"When I spoke of this with Tomás years ago, he agreed reluctantly, but we have not mentioned it since. I will have to seek his permission anew."

"You can tell him that you have my support if that will help."

"Thank you, Father, I shall try."

"You should take *Le Brise Noire* so that you will always have a way home," insisted Tomás when it was decided that she must go.

Le Brise Noire was the name he had given to the Ariegeois stallion that had found them during the war. He was drawn by a salt lick they had set out for the sheep. When

165

Tomás found him, he was saddled, but the saddle hung alop, the cinch having loosened as he lost weight. His ribs were easily countable. Foraging on land grazed by sheep was not ideal.

Tomás saw that the saddle was stained with dried blood and there was an ugly scabbed-over wound on his withers and another on his left hindquarter. Tomás picked an apple from the tree in the yard and approached the stray slowly. The stallion's appetite overcame his uneasiness and he eagerly devoured the fruit from Tomás' hand.

Although he and Sofia could never afford a horse, Tomás had friends who owned them. He had learned how to judge quality and could see that this was an exceptional animal despite his sad condition. He gently took the rein, led the stallion to the well and drew a bucket of water which the horse nuzzled greedily. He carefully removed the Spanish military saddle and set it aside.

"He is clearly a war refugee," he observed. "A fine animal. I am certain he is Ariegeois. I am also certain that his owner has no further need of him."

As Tomás and Sofia gradually nursed the animal back to health Tomás built a stable in the barn. In time, Tomás began to take him out occasionally to "stretch his legs." As the stallion regained his strength, he also regained his speed, eventually prompting Tomás to dub him *Le Brise Noire.*

Tomás cleaned up the saddle, but the steed wanted no part of it. He had a violent reaction to the very sight of it. Tomás did not mind. Riding bareback gave him a feeling of unity with the horse.

Thus, when word came from the Archbishop that Sofia had been called to help the Baron of Bonrepos in an enterprise sanctioned by God and by the King of France, they agreed that she must go and Tomás insisted that she take the stallion to ensure her safety on the road and her ability to return home whenever she chose.

Sofia bade a tearful goodbye to her daughter, Caterina, reminding her that she would be responsible for their home and Sofia's share of *rigole* maintenance while she was away.

"I'm not sure how long I shall be gone," she cautioned, "but I expect to be home ere summer's end. Mind your father and Olivia as well. Know that, wherever I am, my thoughts are of you and your father and I love you both dearly."

She had not ridden the horse much, but she took to riding naturally and was confident that the animal loved her and would do her bidding. She packed a few personal items and laded them on the stallion. After a few reassuring caresses, she took hold of his mane and vaulted onto his back. He bore her weight with ease and responded to her slightest touch on the reins. A gentle touch of her heels to his ribs and they set out through the foothills of the Pyrénées for Toulouse.

From the great steed's first stride, Sofia rode as if she had been born on horseback. Once they reached the great valley, her horse found his stride and fully emulated the breeze he was named for. The ride to Toulouse was much easier than she had anticipated.

In Toulouse she called on the Archbishop seeking directions to Bonrepos.

"Welcome, my child," greeted the Monseigneur. "Thank you for your prompt response to my appeal. The Baron will be most pleased to see you. His great work has just begun, and he expects your skills to be invaluable to the project."

"Father Vilar was most persuasive, Your Holiness."

Bourlemont smiled. "'Monseigneur' will do, child. Now let's get you pointed in the right direction and not keep the Baron waiting."

She arrived at Bonrepos with the ides of June. Riquet was surprised but pleased to find Sofia in his parlor.

"If your offer of work still holds true and the pay is as you promised, I have decided to give it a try." she said.

"Excellent!" he exclaimed, "I shall put you to work this very day. The Sun King has ordered me to build a *rigole* of extraordinary length and I should very much value your opinion of the route. Is Olivia with you?"

"She could not be persuaded. If you don't mind, though, I am quite drained from the ride, and could use a night's rest."

"*Bien sûr!* You shall be my guest here tonight and tomorrow we shall get you settled in Revel; I have an apartment there you can use. Tomorrow will be soon enough to begin your part in this great play."

The next day, she and Riquet rode to Pont Crouzet on the Sor and began tracing the route of the main feeder *rigole* back toward Naurouze. Riquet was impressed by the magnificent Ariegeois stallion that had brought her from the Pyrénées. It had a coat as black as obsidian and the way it glistened showed that it was well cared for by someone who knew how.

"A fine animal," observed Riquet.

"He is that," she replied. "He came to us haggard and bloodied. Half-starved and half wild. A war refugee by our guess. My husband saw his worth right off, so we nursed him back to health."

"He looks like he can fly."

"My husband calls him L*e Brise Noire.*

"He insisted that I take him so that I would always have a sure way home."

As they rode, a question occurred to Riquet. "Who will maintain the *rigole* that feeds your village while you are here building this one for me?"

"Olivia's daughter and mine have worked with us for the last six years," she replied. "Your man left us short-handed, if you take my meaning, so we added four more hands to our little crew.

"The girls still have much to learn, but Olivia is there to teach them still."

At one point where the route stakes dropped into a valley Sofia asked, "How do you plan to get the water up the far side?"

"We'll build a wooden aqueduct to carry the flow across the valley at this elevation," he replied.

"If the ancients had done such as that, our town would not have water today, the wood having rotted out long ago."

"I see," Riquet sighed. "Stone would be better," he winced, "but much more expensive. This project is painfully costly already."

"I think the ancients would have simply run the *rigole* up the valley and crossed at its head, holding the slope and the flow gentle all the way. The longer route means naught to the water."

"And the extra work would be nothing compared to the price of stone. You are proving your value already!"

Riquet was so impressed by this insight that he was moved to write Colbert to reassure him saying that he had found a way to avoid costly aqueducts, thereby lengthening the route of the *rigole*, but reducing the cost of construction and maintenance. He was expecting to bring the trial *rigole* in on schedule and under budget:

> *I have ridden my work of all blockages*
> *of all aqueducts and tunnels, and I lead it*
> *by the surface of the earth, past*
> *depressions and valleys, and by natural*
> *slopes so that I make the thing easy to*
> *build and easy to maintain; and I relieve*
> *the rigole project of about four hundred*
> *thousand livres of expenditure, which those*
> *structures were predicted to cost.*

Riquet had four hundred forty men and women at work already. He and Sofia found François near Naurouze supervising the construction of the trial *rigole.* Spades were being soiled by the hundreds. Riquet introduced Sofia and explained her recommendation.

"Sofia, it is my pleasure to introduce to you François Andréossy, my second in command. François, this is Sofia Soler, a master, perhaps I should say *mistress*, of *rigoles* from the Pyrénées.

"Sofia has observed that we can avoid aqueducts if we simply follow the contours of the land as we pass from the Sor to Naurouze. What say you to that?"

"Of course!" cried François. "We have *carte blanche* from the King for any lands we deem necessary, so the additional length is not an issue. I should have thought of that!"

"As should I, *mon ami*," replied Riquet. "but this is too great a puzzle to be solved by one mind. It will be the collective achievement of all who have contributed and all who have yet to contribute to it. Do you think you can put Sofia to work?"

"At once! I shall assign an *arpenteur* and a *nivelleur* to her to translate her plan into stakes for the *terrassiers.*"

(The *terrassiers* were the soilers of spades. They did the actual digging of the canal and transported the earth out of the channel.)

Riquet's brow furrowed some.

"Be sure you pick men of good character," cautioned Riquet, "as I already have an investment in Sofia's security that I would not want jeopardized."

François immediately selected an *arpenteur* and a *nivelleur* and four laborers to serve as Sofia's crew. He made it clear that Sofia would be in command, much to the dismay of the men.

"She has special skills," affirmed the Baron, "much as you do *Monsieur le arpenteur,* and can guide you to the most efficient route."

In response to the grumbling he announced, "Any man who cannot abide working for a woman may leave now and will receive half pay for today but will not be hired back."

The grumbling stopped.

Once Sofia and her crew had been dispatched, François explained the plan for construction of the trial feeder *rigole* to the Baron.

"We started at the low end," he explained. "So, when it rains, or if we should strike a shallow water table, the water will not fill our ditch. It can just flow on down to Naurouze where it can join the south fork of the Fresquel."

"An excellent plan," agreed Riquet.

By mid-July Riquet had assembled a workforce over one thousand strong and was making better than expected progress. As she was integrated into the workforce, Sofia was not subject to the pejorative pay structure for women, but, like other skilled workers, she was paid as Riquet had promised.

* * *

As the work progressed, François was impressed with Sofia's leadership skills and decided to put her in charge of the *atelier* building the *rigole de la montagne*. As *Chef de Atelier* she assigned duties and made decisions regarding the route and construction techniques. This caused resentment among many of the men who bridled at taking orders from a woman. There were many women in Riquet's workforce, but the men generally referred to them as "*femelles*," a term correctly applied only to cows, sows and ewes. The term was intended to equate the female laborers to farm animals. It would have been hard enough for many of the men in her *atelier* to adjust to seeing Sofia as an equal. Accepting her supervisory authority was nearly impossible for some.

She was a handsome woman, but by no standard beautiful. She had the solid frame of one who has worked hard all her life, birthed and raised children and seldom rested. Her skin was more like leather than velvet, tanned by sun and wind, and the creases at the corners of her eyes were born more of squinting than of laughter.

"I'd like to give that one a poke to see if she giggles," said Garth to one of his *terrassier* chums as she passed by assessing progress.

"Have a care, *mon ami*," replied his pal, "she's near old enough to be your mother and she's tight with the Baron."

"Hey, now," warned Garth, "you leave my mum alone and I won't talk about yours or the way she makes her livin'."

That ended the discussion, but not the base thoughts Garth harbored of one day showing this bossy *femelle* her proper place.

One afternoon Sofia slipped away to relieve herself in the forest, far enough from the jobsite to avoid observation. As she was rising and adjusting her small clothes, she found herself face-to-face with Garth. His pants were around his ankles and his tunic was raised to reveal an erection of which he was obviously very proud.

"If you're through drainin' it, I can put it to better use," he grinned.

Smiling, she stepped toward him, reached down and gripped his scrotum firmly enough to make him wince. When he tried to free himself, she squeezed harder until he dropped to his knees with a cry of pain. Her hand strength was the result of a lifetime of shearing sheep and milking sheep and goats. She leaned forward and in a low, even voice told him:

"On our farm in the Pyrénées, it falls to me to castrate the rams when the spring brings too many. I used to use a razor, until I found that one quick twist and yank would do the job. Would you like me to show you my technique?"

"No!" he howled. "No! No! No! I am sorry *Madame le Chef!* Let loose and I will never trouble you again!"

"You don't trouble me a bit," she scoffed.

She released him, and as he scurried off to rejoin his fellows, she turned to see a giant of a Moor standing nearby who had apparently been watching the drama unfold. He was one of dozens of Moors in Riquet's workforce, a stonemason who was undoubtedly the tallest.

"Mon dieu!" she thought. "This one must be seven *pieds* tall. This giant will be more of a challenge to subdue."

"*Bonjour, Madame*," he opened in a voice so resonant that she felt it more than she heard it. "I am called Majiq. *Monsieur Le Baron* asked me to see to your safety. I saw that one follow you into the woods and thought I, too, should follow. I was waiting to see if you needed help. It appears you did not."

Majiq was indeed seven feet tall. His skin was as black as the coat of *Le Brise Noire*. His hair was close cropped in tight curls and his smile and his eyes were big and bright. There were creases at the corners that Sofia guessed were more likely born of laughter than squinting. His roots ran to the Tutsi of Lake *Nyanza*, at the root of Africa's horn, but his grandfather had migrated to the quarries of North Africa where his father learned the skills of a quarryman. At twelve Majiq had been apprenticed to a stone mason and that was the trade he brought to Riquet's grand endeavor.

"No, thank you, Majiq," laughed Sofia, "I've dealt with worse than that one in my time, but thank you."

"Was that true, he boomed in a low voice, "what you said about the rams and all?"

"No," she laughed, "of course not! Why would anyone be so cruel to an innocent animal? I was ready to give it a try on that one, though. With rams, you just tie cord at the top of the sack and they drop off in a few weeks. They never miss 'em."

A low hearty laugh rolled forth from deep in Majiq's chest. "I thought not, but I guessed you might be willing to test the 'technique' on Garth there. Well, now you know that I shall never be far if you need me. Call out and I'll be there."

"*Merci*, Majiq, that is comforting indeed."

As it happened, from that day forward, it seemed to Sofia that there were fewer undercurrents of rebellion in her *atelier* and she even imagined that she was granted a certain degree of respect by the men in her command. The phrase "*Oui, madame le Chef*" took on a new flavor of sincerity.

* * *

The rains impeded progress that summer. As with the roads, rain turned the clay of the *rigole de la plaine* channel to sticky muck. Once hammered into place in the *rigole*, the clay was the ideal soil for a watertight channel, but during construction it was nearly impossible to work when saturated. Riquet's contract called for a ditch only two feet wide, just to prove that water would follow the route as designed, but in the face of the complications presented by the inclement weather, Riquet made another bold decision.

On a routine inspection of the worksite he found François rain-soaked and covered in wet clay.

"It is nearly impossible to work this muck in the rain!" he snarled. "And we lose half of it down stream to Naurouze. Would that we could wait for the rain to cease before pounding the clay in place, but only God knows when that might come to pass."

"It makes no sense," mused Riquet, "to struggle to seat this muck in a two-foot wide channel only to have to dig it out some months from now to expand the size of the channel."

"Indeed," agreed François, "we know the route is viable. This 'trial' is only to comfort the non-believing nobility. Here on the plain we should build it full size. It will save time and money in the end.

"And, if we build it wide enough and deep enough and install a few simple locks, we could use it to transport timbers and stone from the mountain."

"An interesting thought," agreed Riquet. "It has pained me deeply that our new route abandons Revel. What you suggest would facilitate our enterprise, true enough, but it would be a lasting link to the world for Revel. If the Dark Mountain can supply a sufficient quantity of water, we might even link to Castres one day."

Riquet decided to not only build this portion of his trial *rigole* full size so that once the clay was pounded into place it would not need to be disturbed again the following year, but wide enough and deep enough to provide navigation for small barges from Revel to Naurouze. He was, after all, certain of the success of the trial. He ordered it widened to twenty feet and deepened to six. He also decided to build a port at Revel to handle small shipments of stone and timbers from the mountain to the *Bassin de Naurouze*. He would call it Port Louis.

François estimated that about a dozen simple wooden locks would handle the gradient. Not wanting to spend time and money on the locks, which would only be needed for navigation, Riquet simply had log sills set where locks would be built to create small cascades at the drop points. This temporary measure would suffice for proof of the plan.

The *rigole de la montagne*, however, he held to the original two-foot width, seeing no potential there for navigation, and finding that it passed through more stone than clay.

This bold decision to make the trial *rigole* navigable did little to further delay progress, and eventually saved thousands of *livres*. Riquet had rightly reckoned that the additional expense now, which he could easily afford, would pay huge dividends later. His business sense would not allow him to ignore the long-term savings to be derived from investing more now. He realized that his *rigole* canal might even generate income one day.

By October, water flowed in quantities that could leave no doubt that the summit locks could be kept full. Ever the skeptic, Colbert sent two of the Sun King's *intendants* to verify Riquet's claim. When they found Riquet's twenty-foot wide channel in place of the two-foot wide channel they expected, they assumed that they had misunderstood the specifications. Finding a larger *rigole* carrying more water than they had expected, they had no problem confirming the success of the trial to Colbert.

With the trial *rigoles* completed, Riquet offered Sofia a respite.

"You are welcome to winter in Revel if you like," he offered, "but I expect you will want to return home."

"*Oui sieur*, she agreed. "I sorely miss my family."

"Will you promise to return once we are authorized to proceed with the canal?" he asked. "I can make good use of your skills in that endeavor as well. You have proven to be an able *Chef de Atelier*."

"I expect I shall be able to continue. When will that be?"

"Probably not until after the first of next year.

"Majiq plans to winter near Perpignan. If he were to escort you home, it would be a great comfort to me. Also, I could then send word to him when we resume work and he could retrieve you as well."

"I would welcome his company. I encountered no trouble on my journey here, but, as you have said, the roads are not safe."

Majiq rode a beautiful snow-white Arabian mare. The four of them made an image worthy of Henri Matisse as they journeyed to Sofia's village. The snow had not yet come to the low passes, so the ride was not difficult. Sofia introduced Majiq to her family and explained that he would be returning in the spring to escort her back to Toulouse. Like Riquet, Tomás was comforted knowing that she would have an escort for the trip.

Beyond her personal safety, there was the money. As *Chef de Atelier* she earned one hundred *livres* per month. She had the simple tastes of her Pyrénées lifestyle and had saved most of her salary. When she showed it to Tomás his eyes widened even beyond the reaction he had when he heard of the Bishop's summons.

"It is a fortune!" he cried. "Surely this is more than you were promised?"

"Indeed," she smiled proudly. "I have been made a *Chef* over two hundred men and women!

"It is a grand enterprise," she told him. "We shall be building a canal all the way from Toulouse to the sea! It must be seventy or eighty leagues!"

"Mon dieu!" exclaimed her astonished husband. "It will take years to dig a ditch that far! How long will you be gone?!"

"I must abide as long as is required of me, my love," she consoled. "Think of the money. Once I return, you may never need to pick grapes again. The Baron has assured me that I shall be allowed to return home during the harvest season when he expects the workforce to be lost to the vineyards and woad fields."

Thirteen

1666

In February of the following year Riquet met with Colbert to discuss the Commission's findings in detail and to negotiate a plan going forward that would be acceptable to both Riquet and the King. Colbert invited Clerville to join them.

"I fear," began Clerville, "that your canal will not serve to pass the King's galleys from sea to sea. The expense of a canal that size would be too great, and once the galleys arrived in Toulouse, they would find too little water in the Garonne to carry them to Bordeaux except in times of flood. The Garonne is navigable, indeed, but for most of the year only for barges and other flat-bottomed craft, not for great sea-going warships."

To Riquet, this was a death sentence for his canal; his heart sank.

"But as an avenue for commerce," continued the *Chevalier*, "your plan is eminently feasible. The canal would be a great boon to commerce in Languedoc and, in my opinion, benefit all France."

Riquet's spirits rose some. His main goal had always been commerce. The plan to transport the Royal Navy had been the King's and Colbert's. But now the King's own military expert, head of the Royal Commission, was saying "no" to warships and a solid "yes" to commerce. This would be the best of all possible outcomes. He looked to Colbert for a reaction.

"Commerce is reward enough," decided Colbert, "if the plan is workable."

Riquet's heart soared.

"I am convinced that it is," Clerville affirmed.

"Before I can recommend to the King that we move forward with your plan," Colbert cautioned Riquet, "I shall need the *Chevalier* to prepare a detailed cost estimate for the canal from Toulouse to Cette and, if you will, *Monsieur le Chevalier*, a similar estimate that addresses only the feeder *rigoles* and the portion of the canal between Toulouse and Trèbes."

"You will recall," suggested Clerville, "my recommendation for one great dam on the Laudot at Saint-Ferréol instead of the many small ones proposed by the Baron. Would you prefer that I estimate the cost of the one great dam or the many little ones?"

"The small ones seem less risky," ruled Colbert. "Let us not make this great challenge even more challenging."

"I shall do as you have directed," replied Clerville, "but it will take me no small amount of study and perhaps six months to prepare."

"So be it," agreed Colbert.

"For my part," offered Riquet, "I have already invested a small fortune in this trial *rigole*. It has clearly succeeded, and I would like some assurance that the King will entertain my participation as a partner in this grand endeavor."

"Yes," affirmed Colbert, "he and I have discussed that option and I believe the King sees the value of creating a private incentive for ongoing maintenance of the canal similar to *Monsieur* Boutheroüe's interest in the *Canal de Briare.*"

"Also, if I am to take on such great personal financial risk," continued Riquet, "I would ask assurance that the nobility of my Italian ancestors will be rehabilitated as we have discussed and that the canal will form a fief to be held by the Riquet family in perpetuity."

"I shall so recommend," granted Colbert. "I sense that the King leans in favor of your rehabilitation petition.

"So, *Monsieur le Chevalier*," he concluded, "the powder is in the prime hole and the wick is in your hand."

"At your command, *Monsieur* Colbert." Clerville left the room with an air of purpose and Riquet followed with a sense of confidence he had not felt since Hector had first implied his support.

* * *

Riquet was bold but not foolhardy. He had deferred the expense and, perhaps more importantly, the investment of time required to build his Port Louis at Revel and the locks of his *rigole* canal until he was more certain that his grand enterprise would move forward. The meeting with Colbert and Clerville gave him the assurance he needed, so while he waited for Clerville's report, he proceeded to build the port and the locks required for navigation on the expanded *rigole de la plaine*.

By spring, Port Louis and the locks were finished and Riquet organized a celebration of the inaugural navigation from Port Louis to Naurouze. The Archbishop of Toulouse, the bishops of Comminges and Saint-Papoul, as well as the King's *intendant* for Languedoc, Claude de Bazin de Bezons, seated on a boat drawn by horses, drew gaping stares from the locals as they sailed by.

* * *

Le Chevalier Louis Nicolas de Clerville did not have the requested estimates in six months. He needed eight. His detailed estimates predicted costs of 3,677,605 *livres* as far as Trèbes and a total of 4,897,562 *livres* for the entire project. Despite the fact that the consensus on the Royal Commission was to take the route north from Saint-Nazaire toward Béziers, Clerville's estimate still stubbornly indicated Narbonne as the eastern terminus. Also, his estimate included twenty reservoirs as opposed to the fifteen proposed by Riquet, possibly intended to budget for the one great dam he still envisioned on the Laudot at Saint-Ferréol.

Before the Sun King could issue an edict to authorize the first phase of construction, details of finance and ownership had to be hammered out. That process proved far more problematic than the engineering had been. Who will pay? Who will benefit? The King and Colbert were both mindful that it was always easier to extract taxes for war than for public works.

The report of the Royal Commission was announced by the King's Council at Saint Germaine along with the King's plan for financing the project. Not wishing to inhibit open discussion, the King opted out of the meeting. In the King's absence, Colbert chaired the deliberations. The *intendants* of Languedoc, Guienne and Roussillon had been invited to participate along with various other officials of Occitania. Also in attendance were Riquet, Clerville, Boutheroüe and Andréossy.

François had modified his map to show the route as adopted by the Royal Commission bypassing Toulouse at the start and running north via Capestang to Béziers and Sète at the end. The plan still showed the small catchment reservoirs and not Clerville's great dam at Saint-Ferréol. Colbert had François' map mounted on an easel for the Royal Council's inspection as they gathered and, after some informal discussion centered on the map and its contents, he opened the meeting of the Royal Council. He announced the Sun King's intent to proceed with the project and His Majesty's desire that the project should be funded by the *États* that would benefit from the canal, in partnership with the crown and the entrepreneur as well.

"The King has agreed to indemnify all lands taken for the canal," he declared. "Those lands shall become the fief of the entrepreneur the Baron of Bonrepos. That fief shall pass to his heirs in perpetuity.

"The King expects the costs of construction to be borne in equal shares by the Crown, the entrepreneur and the provinces that will benefit from the canal."

The Syndic of Bordeaux bridled.

"Even if Monsieur Riquet manages somehow to successfully complete this ambitious undertaking," he seethed, "the canal will not pass through Guienne. We should not be asked to pay for a project that does not benefit us."

"The canal will benefit Guienne greatly," rejoined Colbert. "The link to the Garonne will allow Bordeaux to barge goods to Marseille, not just Toulouse. That said, His Majesty does not envision any additional assessment against Guienne on account of this great undertaking. He expects that the funds collected in Guienne for the *gabelle* will be adequate for your contribution.

"The King intends that those funds will contribute to the Crown's third of the costs. The Baron Riquet has agreed to bear one third and the *États du Languedoc* will bear one third."

Monsieur de Fleury, the treasurer of the *États du Languedoc*, voiced objection. "*Le Chevalier de* Clerville has estimated the costs for construction to be more than three million *livres* from Toulouse to Trèbes alone," he argued. "That would mean that our treasury would be held to account for over one million *livres* for a project that has little chance of ever coming to fruition!"

"The Sun King is convinced that it will succeed," returned Colbert. "Surely you are not questioning the wisdom of Louis the Great?"

He was, of course, but, of course, he did not dare say so. "Of course not," he replied contritely. "It is only my conservative nature that forces me to anticipate all possible outcomes. Clearly the King's Royal Commission has done a thorough study of the plan, and if His Highness is satisfied, I would not presume to bander judgement with the Sun King."

Only Riquet was fully satisfied with the plan. Clerville still favored one great dam instead of many small ones and Boutheroüe was still concerned that the oversized locks would not survive the hydraulic forces they would encounter in operation. But all were obliged to accept both the engineering specifications and the funding plan as the King's will.

So the Royal Council decided that the King's treasury would pay one third of the costs, the States of Languedoc one third, and Riquet, himself would be responsible for one third. In return for his investment, Riquet would receive the canal as his fief. He and his heirs would have the right to build houses, mills, docks and warehouses in the canal right-of-way and collect taxes and tolls, as well as miscellaneous other rights attendant to governance of the fief such as issuance of hunting and fishing licenses. This fief would be unique in all Europe being one hundred fifty miles long and only one hundred twenty feet wide. Also, Riquet's contract as *Fermier General* of Languedoc would be expanded to include the territories of Roussillon and Cerdagne. This seemed a boon but would prove to be a financial disaster.

Privately, the King had agreed to grant Riquet's petition for letters of rehabilitation of his family's former Italian nobility, restoring to the Baron of Bonrepos, in the eyes of the King, nobility of the sword.

Construction of that portion of the *"Canal Royal des Deux Mers"* which would connect the Garonne at Toulouse to Trèbes, and completion of the feeder *rigoles* for the summit locks comprised the "First Enterprise." The King, through Colbert, was withholding commitment to the "Second Enterprise," finishing the canal from Trèbes to Sète, until the first half was a *fait accompli*, or at least until all doubt as to the viability of the plan was laid to rest.

Once the question of funding was settled, Clerville requested an audience with the King to revisit the issue of storage: whether one large dam would, in the end be safer, cheaper and more effective than many smaller ones. The King granted the audience but wanted Colbert and Riquet involved in the discussion.

"The logistics alone favor Saint-Ferréol, Sire," insisted Clerville. "Stone, timber and even labor can reach a worksite in the Laudot valley much more easily than multiple sites high on the Dark Mountain.

"And when completed, the reservoir I am proposing will hold nearly as much water as the entire canal. There will be no fear of summer shortages."

"If I may, Sire," offered Riquet, "I confess that I have not felt comfort with this plan since first it was conceived but while building the trial *rigole* in the mountain we indeed found the logistics quite difficult, and if Your Highness is undaunted by the challenge of constructing a dam of this size, never before seen, and if the *Chevalier* can provide plans for a structure that will contain such a terrible force of water, and if the cost of construction is not prohibitive, I believe it might indeed be the best option."

"If we were easily 'daunted,'" replied the King, "this entire enterprise would have been stillborn."

The trace of indignation prompted silence from all in the room while the King pondered.

Finally, having reached a clear decision, the King declared, "If you can produce a plan, Nicolas, that will hold within the budget approved by our Council, you shall have your great dam."

Clerville produced a plan and Riquet included the dam in the valley of the Laudot at Saint-Ferréol in his final bid of 3,630,000 *livres* for the First Enterprise.

Riquet's bid, in agreement with the *Chevalier's* estimate, was accepted and on October 7th of 1666 the King signed an edict calling for construction of the First Enterprise and Riquet was authorized to commence his grand adventure.

Unfortunately, Riquet's optimistic specifications for the number and size of the locks had not been corrected and the entrepreneur would later come to deeply regret his hubris in that regard.

Riquet was on hand for the signing of the edict, and the construction of the *Canal Royal des Deux Mers* was underway.

Riquet immediately set about building a workforce of over two thousand men and women, ten *ateliers* in all. Initially, his focus was on completion of the feeder *rigoles*, but by January he had begun work on the Laudot dam at Saint-Ferréol as well. The basin for the reservoir had been excavated, the bedrock that would hold the foundation of the dam exposed and he was ready to commence with raising the great dam.

He wrote to Majiq and summoned him to return Sofia to Revel and when they arrived, he reconstituted her *atelier* and put them to work expanding the *rigole de la montagne*.

Fourteen

1667

In January of 1667 Isaac Roux began work on the outlet culvert Clerville had prescribed for the Laudot dam. The culvert was a three hundred seventy-foot-long masonry structure enclosing the channel of the Laudot. The structure was six feet wide and eight feet high. It followed the course of the Laudot and would allow the river to flow unobstructed until the dam was completed. There was a valve built into the culvert which could be closed to block the river and fill the dam or opened to drain the reservoir for maintenance. As construction proceeded, a second culvert would branch off above the first to allow clear water to be tapped for the canal. A second valve would select either the upper flume for alimentation or the lower flume for maintenance of the dam and the reservoir.

* * *

Riquet was willing to gamble with his own fortune in this grand enterprise but not with his children's futures. The letters he had received from the Sun King rehabilitating his family's Italian nobility imparted to the Riquets a royal claim to nobility of the sword. The mood in Toulouse was already set, however, and the King's endorsement did little to sway attitudes of the old noble families.

He had established Matty in the Parliament of Toulouse, and now sought for him a wife who would strengthen his standing in the society of the capital. He chose Claire de Cambolas, a mature woman from a noble family, and Matty was well pleased with the choice.

On the eve of the launch of the construction of the *Canal Royal des Deux Mers*, Riquet emancipated his eldest son; that is, he gave him legal identity as his own man. This would help protect him from debts incurred by his father on behalf of the King. He also gave him the house on *Rue des Puits-Clos* in Toulouse, reserving only a small apartment in the back for himself and Catherine to use when they needed accommodations in the city.

The next day, Jean-Mathias and Claire were married in the *Cathédrale Saint-Étienne de Toulouse.* The wedding was attended by an elite list of Toulousain dignitaries drawn more by Claire than by Matty.

Later the same year, for the same reasons, he emancipated Pierre-Pol, now a Captain in the elite King's Guard.

In the years to come Pierre-Pol would distinguish himself in the King's Guard and, to further establish his nobility, his father would buy for him the Barony of Saint-Felix and the County of Caraman. The Barony would entitle him to join his brother in the Parliament of Toulouse, that body so important to decisions regarding progress of the canal.

* * *

It was April before Roux's culvert at Saint-Ferréol had progressed to the point that they could start on the foundation for the dam itself. Riquet invited Archbishop Bourlemont to ceremoniously place the first stone and to bless the work. As they awaited the Monseigneur's arrival that morning Isaac explained Clerville's plan.

"This will essentially be an earth dam, but there will be three stone walls to hold it in place. This upstream wall will be our first line of defense. It must be absolutely watertight to prevent the imprisoned water from escaping under the earthworks and undermining the whole structure. To create a positive bond between the wall and the bedrock, we are cutting a channel one *pied* deep in the bedrock to receive the first rank of the stone. As you can see, the first wall of the dam will be nearly fifty *pieds* thick, and when completed it will be sixty *pieds* high where we are standing.

"There will be a ten-degree bend in the middle to follow the course of the bedrock along the valley floor. Each of the three support walls will be constructed as the Romans did: outer shell structures of stonework infilled with a mixture of waste stone and hydraulic concrete. The infill will have to wait for the arrival of your shipment of pozzolana clay from Italy. Do you know yet when we can expect delivery?"

"I have had no word," replied Riquet. "But I am bound for Perpignan, thence Cette. There may be news."

Pozzolana clay was an essential ingredient in hydraulic concrete. Born in the volcanoes of the Apennine Peninsula, it was the crucial ingredient that allowed Roman concrete to set underwater and gave it its exceptional strength.

Clearly impressed with Clerville's plan, Isaac continued, "When completed, this first wall will be a massive rampart against the massive weight of the water it will hold in reserve. The center wall will be higher. Rooted nearly an *arpent* downstream, it too will be let into the bedrock. It will only be 18 *pieds* thick, but it will rise one hundred fifty *pieds* above the bedrock.

"The third wall will support the back of the earthworks. It will be twenty-five *pieds* thick and rise ninety *pieds* from the culvert. It will be rooted in the bedrock one more *arpent* back from the center wall."

"Is the stone you are using taken from the Bassin de Naurouze?" asked Riquet.

"No," Isaac replied somewhat emphatically. "This is granite from the *Montagne Noire*. Harder to work, but..." He paused for thought. "...harder. Stone for *le durée éternelle*. But we may use the Naurouze stone for the third wall. It will bear a lesser load."

"And the material excavated from the *rigole* that you are stockpiling just there, it is for the earthworks between the walls?" Riquet guessed.

"Yes. That and the tailings from our quarry and the earth removed from this basin that will hold the reservoir. The clay has been kept separate for use in sealing the front of the earthwork."

* * *

As the foundation for the dam was being laid, Riquet was in Perpignan, the capital city of Roussillon. Roussillon had been ceded to France just six years earlier at the end of the Franco-Spanish War. Riquet had been given the contract to administer the *gabelle* in Roussillon, ostensibly to supplement funding for construction of the *Canal Royal*. But the new territory had been a drain on his resources rather than a supplement. He was obligated to make periodic payments to the King but was having difficulty collecting from the people of Roussillon. The King's monopoly on salt was even less popular in the newly yoked Roussillon than it was in Languedoc. With salt from Spain available for one tenth the King's price, Hugo

Hérault had had difficulties enforcing the *gabelle*. He had been more strict than compassionate. Heads had rolled – literally. Riquet was meeting with the King's *intendant* for Roussillon, Charles Macqueron, to answer for Hugo's severity. Hugo had, indeed, acted severely, but not without provocation.

* * *

Two leagues west of Prades, deep in the foothills of the Pyrénées, the road passed through a dense pine forest. Hugo and his men had stopped a wagonload of goods bound for Prades from the hills near the Spanish border. They were in the process of searching for contraband salt when Hugo heard a shriek from one of the female passengers and turned in time to see one of his men withdrawing his hand from under her skirts.

It was necessary to search women travelers in regions where smuggling was rampant as they often concealed contraband salt beneath their clothing. Unlike many enforcers of the *gabelle*, Hugo, in keeping with Riquet's guidance, would not abide inappropriate liberties.

"Ease off, Donald," ordered Hugo. "I doubt she has any salt hidden in her cunny. You're authorized to search, not fondle. If I catch you at that again you're done."

As they were checking the last of the bags for salt, they were suddenly attacked by Miquelets.

The Miquelets were guerrilla bands of former militia raised to defend villages from whichever side was currently pillaging them during the Franco-Spanish War. With the war's end, some militiamen returned to their farms; those without farms formed rogue bands who would prey upon travelers, much like the renegade ex-soldiers of Languedoc. Unlike the brigands of Languedoc, they were selective, preying only upon outsiders and never upon their countrymen. As a result, they enjoyed tacit support from the people of the Pyrénées.

The Miquelets tended to view Riquet's *gabelous* as the Sun King's pillagers.

The rebels had emerged from the forest and opened fire without warning, dropping two of Hugo's men and wounding a third. They then rode off at a gallop toward Prades.

"To horse, men!" shouted Hugo. "We'll run them down!"

By the time his men were mounted the rebels were out of sight, but the tracks of their horses were easy to follow until they reached Prades. The streets of Prades were cobbled, and they lost the tracks of the Miquelets once they entered the city. There was no sign of the tracks where the road left the east edge of the city. They checked the town livery stable and found no sign of horses that had been ridden hard recently. They proceeded to the *mairie*, and on the way gathered up two local men of about thirty years of age.

"Hold them here," commanded Hugo. He burst into the Mayor's office.

"Your fucking Miquelets have just murdered two of my men!" charged Hugo. "My men and I will have a mug on you at that bar across the way. If you don't produce the assassins by the time we're finished, one of yours whom we now hold will be finished as well, if you take my meaning."

"They are not *my* Miquelets!" protested the Mayor. "I have no idea who might have done this. It's not reasonable to expect me to solve this crime in the time it takes to down a mug of wine!"

"It's no matter to me if you do or you don't," insisted Hugo. "Two of yours will pay for two of mine. I'm giving you a chance to make it the right two. Next time we're attacked it'll be ten of yours for each of mine."

"Two?" asked the Mayor. "I heard you say 'one' before?"

"After we do the first, we'll have another mug and give you another chance before we do the second."

After the first mug, Hugo stepped into the street leading the town cobbler by his hair. He quickly released his terrified prisoner and with one swift motion separated his sword from its scabbard and the cobbler's head from his shoulders. He struck the blow from the front to avoid interference from the man's thick dark hair. The severed head lifted slightly then fell to the street face-up. The cobbler's eyes blinked three times, then remained open in a fixed gaze toward heaven.

The Mayor was at a loss. Even if he knew where to begin looking, which he did not, he saw no way he could possibly meet Hugo's demand. It might be politically unwise for him to try. To even try might have repercussions for him or even his family. His protests failed to move Hugo.

By noon the heads of two unlucky townsmen lay in the street.

As Hugo and his men departed, he shouted out to no one in particular, "It's your Miquelets have done this! Remember this day if ever you think to attack officers of your King!"

The Mayor appealed to Macqueron and Macqueron appealed to Colbert. Colbert confronted Riquet with the complaint and Riquet responded with a frank assessment of the culture of Roussillon.

"Murders are as common in Roussillon as bread and wine. No human power could prevent this sort of men killing each other, and you may therefore infer that my *gabelous* face the same fate. In this country my agents must always be on guard; they kill just as they are killed; it is the only way they can perform their duties."

Colbert was appalled by Riquet's frank acceptance of the inevitability of the killing and directed him to meet with the *intendant*, Macqueron, and find a way to reduce the bloodshed.

* * *

"Your men are leaving a trail of blood through Roussillon," Macqueron charged.

"Much of it their own," replied Riquet. "They are here on the Sun King's business. When your people attack them, they attack the King! Perhaps a larger force would deter rebellion?" Riquet knew he had little hope of producing a larger force; most able-bodied men at arms had been conscripted for the War of Devolution in the north.

"Perhaps it might," replied the *intendant*, knowing how unlikely it was.

"Perhaps your own men at arms could escort my men and provide some assistance against the Miquelets?"

"Perhaps we simply need to put three or four to the wheel as a lesson to the others," replied Macqueron.

"Perhaps," agreed Riquet, "but to do that we would need to *capture* three or four. They attack my men like lightning bolts, then melt into their villages before the thunder claps. The answer is a larger force, which *you* should provide as *you* seem unable to maintain order. A visible display of your support for the Sun King would not be without value as well."

"Have your man report to me," conceded Macqueron. "I shall assign a score of men at arms to escort him. And I shall issue a proclamation that any attack on agents of the Sun King is an attack on Roussillon.*"

Turning to leave, Riquet paused, then turned back to face the *intendant*.

"Perhaps if I were to meet with representatives of these belligerents," he offered, "some sort of compromise could be reached that would end the bloodshed?"

"It seems worth a try," was the response. "I shall make it known that you are willing to negotiate. And will your words carry the weight of the Sun King?"

"The King wishes an end to the mayhem as much as do I," assured Riquet.

Riquet passed the word to Hugo with regrets for the men he had lost already, and also passed along the suggestion to make an example of three or four of the rebels.

"They are ghosts," replied Hugo. "Either we kill them, or they vanish like fog on a sunny day."

Later that year Riquet engaged in negotiations with leaders of one of the main groups of Miquelets. An agreement was reached granting them partial relief from the *gabelle* and promising the King that his *gabelous* would go unmolested.

Riquet wrote Colbert of his success, reaffirming his belief that one could "with a sheet of parchment and a little wax do as much good as the iron and the fire could do harm."

For a time, Hugo and his men enjoyed a fragile peace.

197

* * *

Returning from Perpignan, Riquet stopped in Sète to check on the pozzolana. On François' recommendation, he had ordered fifty tons of pozzolana clay from Naples, anticipating that he would have extensive need of it over the course of his enterprise. He found that the shipment had arrived and gave the importer instructions for distribution.

"Have ten *muids* carted to Toulouse immediately," he directed, "ten to the site of the Laudot dam at Saint-Ferréol on the Revel plain and hold the balance until I send for it."

* * *

As the dam and the feeder *rigoles* progressed, it took months for the King to acquire the properties subject to taking for the main channel starting at the Sept-Deniers meadow near Toulouse. Clerville had assigned a crew to stake the boundaries of the land to be taken for the canal and the fief that would hold it. Then, in the name of the King, he ordered them appraised. After that process was completed, the lands had to be reappraised immediately to account for improvements. On the first pass, the Sun King's appraisers had assigned the same value to lands bearing orchards or mills as they assigned to bare land. That plan was *ne marche pas* for the owners who resented having to cede their lands to the canal at any price.

The land required for *Le Écluse de l'Embouchure* at the western terminus of the canal, the lock that was the link to the Garonne river, was taken first and construction of that lock began. François supervised construction of a temporary coffer dam to divert the Garonne from the canal excavation. In September, with the coffer dam completed, Riquet's *terrassiers* began excavation of Clerville's revised canal alignment which bypassed the city moat in favor of Sept-Deniers.

On November 19th, 1667, a dedication ceremony was held on the field of Sept-Deniers and in the dry trench of *Le Écluse de l'Embouchure*. Three hundred feet of canal ditch had been dug sixty feet wide and ten feet deep, ramped up to the surface on the east end. This was less than half of the excavation required for the lock but deemed adequate for ceremonial purposes. This would be the amphitheater for the ceremony.

A temporary chapel had been erected in the field and Riquet's entire force of six thousand *terrassiers* and crafts men and women attended. They were assembled by *ateliers* like Roman legions, including the workforce from Saint-Ferréol and the feeder *rigoles*.

All the leaders of the capital city turned out and the contention over the value and viability of the canal was given a day of rest. The city elite formed a procession of coaches from the capitol to the chapel where Monseigneur Bourlemont gave the benediction. The dignitaries then marched solemnly down the ramp and into the ditch for the ceremonial setting of the first two stones.

It was a beautiful, warm, sunny day but came on the heels of six days of rain and the floor of the trench was mud. Planks and canvass had been laid out to protect the fine shoes and hose of the elite and a carpet of red serge had been laid down the center for the clergy and the *Capitouls*.

Riquet rode proudly along the brink inspecting his *ateliers*. Monseigneur Bourlemont blessed the ceremonial first two stones of the lock foundation, then passed one to the President of the Parliament of Toulouse and one to the *Chef de*

Capitouls of the city, who in turn ceremoniously set them in place with mortar served from a silver trowel. Cannon and muskets roared salutes and there were shouts of "*Vive le Roi.*" All was right with Toulouse.

Praise be to God; the coffer dam held, and the Garonne did not intrude on the ceremony.

As construction proceeded, the lock itself proved to be less loyal. Over Boutheroüe's ongoing objections, Riquet had specified a rise for the lock of eighteen feet, meaning that to meet design specifications for the minimum canal depth the lock walls rose twenty-six feet from the foundation. As Hector had predicted, the lock dimensions were too ambitious.

To facilitate construction of the lock walls, scaffolds were erected for the masons. Stones and mortar were lowered to the masons via a system of ropes and pulleys.

As *Le Écluse de l'Embouchure* neared completion, Boutheroüe was on site watching the walls rise, convinced that the lock was too deep, and dreading the collapse he deemed inevitable. Riquet was in Toulouse to provide the archbishop with a progress report on the Saint-Ferréol dam. He decided to stop by to assess progress on the Garonne lock.

He arrived at Hector's side just in time to hear the deafening scream of stone grinding on stone. Then the screams of the men. Both Riquet and Boutheroüe gaped in horror as they saw the walls buckle and collapse. When the walls and scaffolds went, one mason caught hold of a rope and pulled himself to safety. Three others fell into the pit and one of them had his skull crushed by the avalanche of stone. Another, luckier, escaped with only a broken leg. The luckiest was spared serious injury, receiving only minor cuts and bruises.

As the *Chef de Atelier* was seeing to the injured men, concerned by Riquet's pallor, Hector invited him to join him for a mug of wine.

"Your color needs restoring," he said. "You have had a grave shock."

"I'm suspending work," intoned Riquet numbly, "until I understand the reason for this disaster."

When the wine had been served and Riquet's color had returned a bit, Hector employed some wry humor to broach the subject of the collapse.

"Perhaps the first two stones were not set correctly," he offered. His reference to the ceremony of the first stones mixed dark humor with a measure of smug satisfaction which was out of character but perhaps forgivable in consideration of the ongoing struggle he had pressed with Riquet over the issue of the maximum safe lock size.

Riquet smiled grimly. "It appears you were right all along, Hector," he admitted. "My design was optimistic. A man is dead because I did not heed your advice. I am persuaded. This will mean nearly twice the number of locks I planned for, but I am persuaded.

"If we make *Le Écluse de l'Embouchure* a double, do you think it will stand?"

"I do," agreed Hector.

"We shall," agreed Riquet, still a bit dazed.

It took three months to replace the great lock with a two-chamber staircase. When the walls appeared ready, they decided to test them with water from the Garonne. While Riquet watched, they pumped water from the river to fill the second chamber of the double. He did not breathe until he saw, with great relief, that the walls were holding. But when they opened the sluice gate to let the water from the second chamber fill the first, the walls of the second chamber bulged and tipped inward. Draining the first chamber to meet the river level had the same effect on that structure. Removing the water left only the inward pressure from the earth that was being held back by the lock walls, and the walls could not withstand it. Riquet nearly wept.

No lives were lost this time, but the repeated failure was disastrous to his credibility as it was to his budget. This was but the first of many locks he would need to build for this great work, and he began to wonder if his dream was doomed.

Fifteen

1668

Adding to Riquet's dismay, the treasurer of the *États du Languedoc* in Montpellier, *Monsieur* de *Fleury*, seized upon the lock wall failures as a pretext for withholding funds, accusing Riquet of incompetence and failure to meet contract requirements.

Indeed, Riquet's struggles with engineering were compounded by seemingly endless struggles with financing brought on by the intransigence of some of the very people he sought to serve.

He was not receiving income from Roussillon commensurate with the price he was required to pay the King for that contract, the lock failures were running his costs over his budget, and when the *États* withheld his funding his wealth, great though it was, eroded quickly. It was difficult for Riquet to meet his obligations to the crown while also financing construction of the *Canal Royal*. Riquet would eventually be forced to sell several properties in order to meet his obligations.

That spring Riquet received a letter from Colbert demanding that his payments for the *gabelle* be brought current. Riquet's contract as *Fermier General* required him to pay a fixed amount to the treasury regardless of collections. Salt profits from Roussillon had been severely compromised by the ready source of contraband from Spain and Hugo had his hands full trying to enforce the King's monopoly. In addition, *Monsieur* de Fleury continued to withhold funds earmarked for the canal on specious grounds.

Riquet repeatedly requested Colbert's help freeing the funds he was due from the *États*. Colbert, for his part, was still unsure of his *fermier* and reluctant to plead Riquet's case to the King.

Ultimately, he decided that, having chosen this man to advance the King's interest in this grand endeavor, he must support him fully or risk his failure. If Riquet failed, that failure would be shared by Colbert and by Louis the Great. That was unacceptable.

After the festivities at Versailles, the court of the Sun King had resettled at Saint Germain pending completion of the renovation. Colbert found the King in his cabinet poring over the plans for the expansion and renovation of Versailles.

The King's favorite color was evident in his cabinet. The draperies were dyed blue with the woad of Toulouse and blue velvet tapestries hung from the walls. The moldings and cornices were gilded as were the carved contours of his cherrywood desk.

"*Bonjour*, my dear Colbert," moaned the King. "We hope you have not come seeking funds. Four years into this 'renovation' at Versailles we fear it will bankrupt us before we ever again spend a night there."

"Not exactly, *Majesté*, but I must tell you, Sire, Baron Riquet has again requested Your Majesty's help in extracting funds from the Treasurer of Languedoc, which funds he asserts are being speciously denied due to the unfortunate events at *Écluse de l'Embouchure. Monsieur Requête*, if Your Majesty will forgive the pun, does have a point." (Riquet's requests for aid had become so frequent that Colbert, more suspicious than sympathetic, had taken to referring to him as "Pierre-Paul *Requête.'*)

"Our mother and Cardinal Mazarin knew how to deal with ambitious tax farmers," replied the King. "We believe there was a gibbet involved."

"I share your suspicion of tax farmers, Sire, but Archbishop Bourlemont has assured me that *Monsieur* Riquet is above reproach: a meticulous accountant and completely scrupulous. Although I remain wary, I believe his complaint is legitimate."

"Do what you can," the King conceded, "to shake loose the funds *Monsieur 'Requête'* has been promised. But encourage him to manage expenses for this First Enterprise and to not further burden the Royal Treasury. This hunting lodge may bankrupt us yet."

In response to pressure from Colbert, Riquet finally received the first of the eight annual payments he was due from the *États du Languedoc*, for construction costs related to the First Enterprise. The payment of 150,000 *livres* was inadequate, but a start. What he really needed was to fix the cash flow problem that was Roussillon.

* * *

Exasperated and embarrassed by the failure of the downscaled locks at *Le Écluse de l'Embouchure*, Riquet turned to Clerville for advice. Clerville was in Marseille engaged in the construction of Fort Saint James, so that was where Riquet sought his counsel. In his absence, work could proceed on excavation of the channel, but the lock would not be rebuilt until he found a way to preclude another collapse.

Before leaving for Marseille, Riquet tasked François and Isaac with inventing a new lock design that would be less prone to collapse. The groundwater near the Garonne made the first two locks particularly problematic but even the double at Bayard, fifty feet above the riverbed, was unstable. He needed an expedient solution to his ongoing embarrassment at Sept-Deniers, but beyond that, he needed a design that would not fail under normal conditions.

"This *Écluse de l'Embouchure* will be the death of me," he moaned to Clerville. "I'm killing stonemasons and wasting time and money. My reputation is in the mud as well. There must be some way to construct locks that will stand against the pressures of earth and water. Have you any ideas at all?"

"Not every problem can be solved with engineering," warned Clerville. "But I believe this one can. Drive a wall of piles into the floor of the lock chamber at the base of the lock wall. Tight like the fingers of a hand. They will hold the mud while you excavate to bedrock, or at least hardpan. Then fill your excavation with rock and cement to the design elevation for the floor of the lock. This will provide a solid foundation for the walls and for the doors. It would be best to employ pozzolana clay in the concrete, but if you can block the river and the ground water adequately you can succeed without it."

"I shall try as you recommend. I have asked François and Isaac for a better standard design. If you have any inspirations that would improve the design, I would be most pleased to hear them.

"I fear," replied Clerville, "that your issues with lock chambers will not benefit much from my brute force methods, *mon ami*. My *forte* is design and construction of massive defenses. By comparison, your locks are delicate structures."

He grasped the old Baron's shoulders and made direct eye contact.

"Isaac is a wizard with stone," he reassured. "I am confident that he will find a solution."

"If your wall of piles gets me out of Toulouse, I shall be, once again, in your debt, Nicolas."

Returning from Marseille Riquet stopped in Montpellier to petition the King's *intendant*, Claude Bazin de

Bezons for help with the intransigent treasurer of *Les États du Languedoc*.

"How fares your canal, *Monsieur le Entrepreneur?*" asked the *intendant* when they met.

"Grinding along," replied Riquet. "Grinding along. We have encountered and conquered many obstinate obstacles made of stone. We have yet to prevail, however, over the most obstinate of all: your treasurer, *Monsieur de Fleury*. He uses dissemblance and chicanery to deny me the funds I am due. The canal would progress with ease if he would simply release the funding the King has assigned to my works. Have you the power to move him?"

"As you are no doubt aware, I have the power to *re-*move him. But he has many powerful sympathizers who would not look kindly on such an act. Perhaps the King or even *Monsieur* Colbert…?"

"Minister Colbert, who speaks for the King himself, has tried repeatedly with little success.

"I have, at last, through the Minister's efforts, received the first installment for the First Enterprise, which was owed to me two years ago, but I have received nothing since then. I am hard pressed to meet my obligations to the King while retaining enough to pay for materials and labor needed to advance my enterprise. If you cannot move this great troll, I fear that all we have invested in this grand enterprise may come to naught."

"I am sorry to confess that if such should be the result of the treasurer's intransigence many in Montpellier might applaud him."

"That is a sorry confession, indeed. They would see the bulk of their countrymen suffer to serve their petty jealousies."

"Has it not always been so with men of power and privilege?"

"For the most part, that is the truth, but for my part, I believe that the Sun King and his Minister are both striving to improve relations with Languedoc and to improve the lives of her people."

"I am sure they see it that way," replied Bazin. "The prevailing view from Montpellier is, unfortunately, not the same."

"I am only asking for funds I am rightfully due," insisted Riquet. "It is malfeasance of his office for *de Fleury* to deny me my due."

"I shall do my best to persuade him, but I cannot promise results where Colbert was unsuccessful."

Riquet left the *intendant's* office feeling that he'd taken the sharp end of the pike.

* * *

Upon returning to Toulouse, feeling an urgent need to show progress, Riquet ordered the locks rebuilt per Clerville's instructions, using the recently arrived pozzolana clay.

In November of 1668, one year after the initial dedication ceremony, a second ceremony was held. Water from the Garonne was again pumped to fill the second chamber, Bourlemont blessed the work, and Pierre Campmas was on hand to open the sluice and spill the water from the second chamber into the first. The water was cycled through both chambers and the walls held. The successful rebuild was, at last, a belated major victory for the beleaguered entrepreneur.

The War of Devolution had ended, freeing thousands of soldiers to the labor market, and Riquet's workforce had swelled to eight thousand souls. Excavation and construction were proceeding apace.

He had also hired a score of ex-soldiers to reinforce Hugo, but the *gabelle* was still producing more rancor than revenue in parts of Roussillon where the local leaders of the Miquelets had not participated in Riquet's negotiations. The drain on Riquet's finances was devastating and he received little sympathy from Colbert and the King.

* * *

Riquet had sorely needed the victory at *Le Écluse de l'Embouchure*. Finally constructing locks that did not immediately collapse served to incrementally restore his severely damaged credibility.

In June, Clerville had produced a revised cost estimate for the Second Enterprise, which would include continuing the canal from Trèbes to the Mediterranean and construction of a new port at Sète. He also solicited bids for the project.

Riquet was greatly disappointed to learn that the Second Enterprise had been put out to bid. He had assumed that if he succeeded with the First Enterprise that the second would come to him as a matter of course. Apparently, Colbert was still not convinced that he was the man for the job. His failures at *Le Écluse de l'Embouchure* had embarrassed Colbert and the Sun King, himself, as well as Riquet and had served to strengthen the case of his detractors. He wondered if he would ever win back the Minister's trust.

While *Le Écluse de l'Embouchure* was undergoing its final reconstruction, he was preparing a proposal for construction of the Second Enterprise.

First, he needed to confirm the route from Saint-Nazaire north through Capestang to Béziers. He and François rode the route together, departing from the original survey near Saint-Nazaire and heading northerly toward Capestang thence northeasterly to Béziers and, ultimately, Sète.

"It appears to me," observed François, "that we may be able to hold our elevation constant as we traverse this route with one very long pound. Until the Orb valley, of course. At that point we shall face a precipitous drop.

"The Répudre river will not be crossed easily. I'm thinking we might want to cross it with a *pont du canal*. It has been done once before to my knowledge. There is a canal that crosses the river Lambro near Milan on such a bridge. I believe it has served for centuries. Not far beyond the Répudre we must cross the Cesse, which might also require a *pont du canal*.

"We shall also need to find a way past the Ensérune ridge without adding locks."

"I do not doubt that you will find the best path," assured Riquet. "I find the idea of canal bridges intriguing. We must discuss that option more. As long as you are certain that there are no insurmountable obstacles, I can put together a bid that will be close enough to reality."

His proposal was not conceived in total darkness. He knew the elevation drop from Trèbes to sea level. From that he knew how many locks he would need (at fifteen thousand *livres* per lock) and from Trèbes to Saint-Nazaire he knew approximately where they would be built. Also, he could accurately estimate how many leagues of canal would need to be excavated. He based his proposal on that data. He judged that any portion of the route needing to be cut from stone would compensate him with stone for the labor of the cutting.

As he prepared his bid, the magnitude of the transformation that his dream had undergone fully struck him. He had envisioned a short canal with a few locks connecting two very proximate rivers. As it had evolved, this enterprise, connecting Toulouse to Sète, would ultimately entail the excavation of an astounding one-hundred-fifty miles of canal. The realization was daunting, but he would not shy from the challenge.

As daunting as the scale of the excavation might be, its cost was predictable. The biggest unknown was the eventual cost of completion for the destruction-prone jetty for the port of Sète. Colbert's decision to build the new port on the windward side of Mont Saint-Clair introduced the ferocity of the Mediterranean as a huge risk factor.

Sixteen

1669

Fortunately for Riquet, before he had submitted his proposal, Clerville's estimate of 5,832,000 *livres* was published in order to induce bidders. No other bidders came forward. Still unsure of the costs required to build a structurally sound lock and despite the wild card that was the jetty at Sète, Riquet submitted a bid that matched the published estimate, which exceeded the guess he had cobbled together on his own. In January of 1669, his bid was accepted and the contract for the Second Enterprise, completion of the canal from Trèbes to Sète, was his. Now his obligation for one third of the costs had risen to three million *livres*, which represented a significant majority of his wealth. The need to control construction costs and to generate revenue from the Roussillon *gabelle* became even more urgent.

Reluctant to adopt Clerville's piling wall as standard procedure for lock construction, Riquet continued his quest for a new lock design that would not collapse. Meanwhile he focused on clearing and excavating, postponing lock construction until he was convinced that the structural problem was solved. He wanted no more debacles like the Garonne lock. That being said, the first six locks past *Le Écluse de l'Embouchure* were already built or under way. If he suspended work there, in the shadow of the ramparts of Toulouse, people would notice. So, he carried on with those locks and with construction of the port at Saint-Sauveur, hoping for the best.

The specifications for the locks called for them to be walled with alder wood except for the entry lock from the Garonne, which was to be brick. The Garonne locks had already been upgraded to stone rather than the signature red bricks of Toulouse, and to insure against another embarrassing collapse, Riquet ordered all locks to be constructed of stonework.

* * *

In the spring, Colbert sent Clerville to check on Riquet's progress. Upon arrival at Saint-Ferréol, Clerville found Isaac Roux in charge of construction and, on inspection, found that the dam was rising straight and true.

"Where is Campmas?" he asked Roux, curious about the *fontainier's* absence. The two had seemed inseparable since the survey of the routes of the *rigoles*.

"He is up on the Dark Mountain inspecting progress on the enlarging of the *rigole de la montagne*," Roux replied.

"You seem to be making good progress here," said Clerville. It looks as if you will finish on time."

"Barring any unpleasant surprises, it will be so," Roux assured him.

"Pierre had an idea I have incorporated into the design of the dam. I was certain you would approve. We have encased a lead pipe in cement entering the dam two *toises* above the river channel. It passes through the dam and exits downstream near the Laudot. Pierre calculates that the water pressure from the reservoir, when full, will produce a column of water fifty or sixty *pieds* high. It will be a dramatically beautiful display to celebrate this great work."

"Indeed! An excellent idea. *Monsieur* Campmas is truly talented.

"How is the *rigole* progressing?"

"On schedule," said Roux. "The *rigole de la montagne* is troublesome but will be finished on time."

"Troublesome?"

"Yes, in some places the channel must be carved from the stone of the mountain; slow work. In others, the ground is so porous the channel must be sealed with clay or stonework to be watertight."

"And where is the Baron now?"

"I believe he is at Saint-Sauveur inspecting progress on the port.

"Now, if you will excuse me, I must go and inspect the sealing of the upstream fill. As I expect you know, we are encasing it in clay six *pieds* thick with granite facing for protection against wave action."

"Yes, that was my specification. Water will never pass that barrier in a century. *Bonne chance* to you and your men! Fare well!"

When Clerville arrived at Saint-Sauveur the Baron was not there but the port was nearly completed. The excavation had produced dry solid footing for the walls, so Riquet had decided to proceed, cautiously, with construction of the port. Like the first six locks following *Le Écluse de l'Embouchure,* suspension of construction work here, in the shadow of Toulouse, would be noticed.

Clerville reported to Colbert that the work was proceeding according to plan.

* * *

At the time, the Baron was in Béziers. His sister, Madeleine, had written to tell him that her husband was very ill. Paul Mas was more brother than brother-in-law to Riquet and the Baron lost no time reaching his bedside.

"You must not leave me now that my grand enterprise is commenced," he chided. "Your help with the *gabelle* frees me to focus on this great work. You are to be honored at the opening ceremonies.

"I need you; Madeleine needs you."

"If God wills," Paul replied weakly. "It is a thing beyond my power to decide. When God calls, peasant or King, we must go.

"It pleases me to know that I have been of some service to you in this grand adventure for which you will be long remembered with great honor. Thank you, my brother, for coming so far to say goodbye.

"It has been one of the great pleasures of my life to be your friend, yes, and brother. It pains me deeply to leave you and your sister in this untimely way. Give my love to your children, which love is as if they were mine own, and, of course, to Catherine."

With that, Riquet's most trusted friend since his days at school in Béziers, fell into a sleep from which he would not wake.

* * *

As the First Enterprise progressed, the main channel made a significant impact on the lands through which it passed. Leaving Toulouse, the channel was fifty-six feet wide at the surface. The sides sloped inward to a width of thirty-six feet at the bottom. The bottom was six feet below the design water surface. In the beginning it was a garish scar on the French countryside, which further infuriated Riquet's detractors. Riquet envisioned the beautiful blue ribbon that it would be one day, lined with shade trees, winding its way through the beautiful countryside of his beloved Languedoc. But that would take time.

The leading edge of the excavation was ramped to facilitate removal of material which was used to berm the sides of the channel to protect adjacent lands from flooding. The excavated material was loaded into wicker baskets to be born out on the heads of the *terrassiers*. Any excess was sold locally to fill marshlands. Riquet was no engineer, but he was a smart businessman.

A ditch was cut along the outside toe of each berm to direct any excess waters to the nearest natural watercourse. A narrow ledge was cut on each wall of the channel, just below the design water level, where reeds would be planted as protection from the erosive action of the waves generated by canal traffic.

As the ugly scar scrabbled through the landscape within sight of Toulouse, Riquet's masons followed the *terrassiers* struggling to build the locks that would eventually enable navigation from sea to sea. Having found solid footings for the locks at Bayard, the Port at Saint-Sauveur, and the double at Castanet, Riquet decided to authorize construction of the Castanet locks even though they were not subject to Toulousain scrutiny. But as they were finishing the second chamber, three days of heavy rain resulted in the collapse of three of the four lock walls. One of the three caught two men beneath it as it fell. As if ordained by God, Riquet once again arrived at the site just in time to witness the collapse. He was despondent. As he was contemplating how to proceed, one of his stone masons approached him.

"May I have a word, *Monsieur le Baron?*"

"*Bien sûr*," said Riquet. "You're one of the Medailhes brothers, are you not?"

"Oui, *Monsieur le Baron*, I am Michel. My brother, Pierre, is that one, there. They just pulled the stone off him. I think his leg is broke."

He pointed to his brother, nearly a twin, still in the muck of the trench.

"If so, he'll receive full pay while it heals, I promise you."

Despite his feudal authority, Riquet was an innovator in humane working conditions. He pioneered the concept that, under certain conditions, holidays, sickness and the like, one might still receive pay even though not required to work. These policies, combined with the generous pay he offered, earned him a stable workforce, but even more resentment from the other lords of Languedoc who eventually convinced Colbert to bring pressure to bear forcing him to substantially reduce wages. This, of course, made it more difficult for Riquet to maintain the large workforce that Colbert expected.

Sensing that he had not addressed the issue that had prompted the meeting, the Baron asked, "Beyond that, how can I help you?"

"In Fréjus, our hometown, there is a retaining wall was built by the Romans, so they say. It's stood for centuries, *sieur.*"

"Yes, the Romans were superb stone workers," replied Riquet.

"They were indeed, *sieur*, but I'm thinking there might be more to it than that."

"*Oui?*"

"Well, the wall's not straight, *sieur*, she's curved. Like an arch for a bridge, she is, only lying on her side. I'm thinking maybe she bears the weight of the earth the same as the arch bears the weight of the bridge."

Medailhes was tall and muscular from years of hard work. He outweighed Riquet by forty pounds. But at that moment, grasping immediately the import of the man's insight, Riquet dismounted, grabbed him by the shoulders and gave him a French kiss. Not the kind that involves the tongue; the kind where you seem to be having trouble finding the mouth: missing wide left at first, then wide right.

"If this solves our lock wall problem, as I believe it will, you have work here for the duration of this project at double pay, and once the canal is completed I shall find you and your brother work at Bonrepos for as long as you like. I shall have *Monsieur* Andréossy revise our lock design according to your insight, then we shall see!"

Andréossy designed the gateposts on the Castanet locks much thicker than the walls, as all the weight borne by the wall would be transferred via the arches to the gateposts. He also called for a one-piece granite threshold for the lock doors to bear that load. The new design was not just stronger. The parenthetical plan also provided more room at the surface to accommodate traffic. Riquet was well pleased and made the design the standard plan for the rest of his locks.

* * *

Late that fall, with the aid of François Andréossy, Riquet finalized his plans for the new city at the Basin of Naurouze and tasked Matty with their presentation to Colbert at Saint-Germain. He saw the assignment as a means to introduce his son to Colbert and the court of the Sun King.

While in Toulouse, he stopped to see the Archbishop and report on the progress to date. His patron seemed to have aged considerably since his last visit.

"You are well, Excellency?" he asked, trying his best to mask the concern that struck him.

"As well as can be expected at my age," replied the cleric equivocally. "What brings you to Toulouse?"

"In part, I have come to report on the progress of the *Canal Royal*," replied Riquet.

"The locks are nearly finished as far as Castanet, and I believe the River L'Hers can provide adequate alimentation for the canal from Castanet to the Garonne.

"If you think it would not be unwise, once that section is complete, we could try opening the canal for trade to that point."

"Absolutely," agreed Bourlemont. "The sooner we can show some benefit from this bitterly controversial enterprise the better. (pausing) "You are confident there will be no more failures?"

"We should couch it as a test," hedged Riquet. "If the test is successful, we shall simply declare the canal open for trade between Castanet and Toulouse. Or, for that matter, between Castanet and Bordeaux or even Paris."

"Yes," agreed the archbishop with a weak smile, "Let us not forget the benefit of the link to the Garonne that so publicly debased you, my friend."

Riquet spent the night at his apartment at *Rue des Puits-Clos* with Matty, who had postponed his departure until the morning. He was having a glass of port wine with Matty in the den by the fire when a messenger arrived from Bourlemont requesting his immediate attendance. With deep foreboding, he left his port unfinished and accompanied the messenger to the archbishop's residence. He found his friend and mentor bedridden and ghastly pale.

"I fear that I shall not see our great work come to fruition," wheezed the Archbishop.

With a somber genuflection, Riquet knelt by the old cleric's bedside, took hold of his hand and kissed his ring.

"Of course you will," he insisted. "Of all people you must. Without your vision and influence this grand enterprise would still be nothing but an old man's dream."

"I fear that I shall not," whispered Bourlemont. "I know My Father's will. My work for him on this earth is finished but for this:

"You must never lose heart in the face of your attackers. Your cause is just. The Lord will ensure that you complete this work. He will help you to overcome whatever obstacles come your way. My role as your mentor has come to an end, but the *Chevalier* de Clerville is a true friend to you and to the *Canal Royal.* Heed well his advice. Young Andréossy, too, will help you to find your way. You and I shall not speak again on this earth, but I feel blessed to have known you.

"Now I would rest some."

"The blessing has been mine, Monseigneur," replied Riquet, teary eyed. "I shall take my leave for now."

He released the old man's hand and rose to depart.

One indulgence the Archbishop had allowed himself was a fine Murano mirror that hung on the wall of his chamber. Riquet caught sight of his own reflection as he passed out of the room and was stricken by how much his own countenance resembled that of the bedridden cleric.

The next day Riquet received word that his patron had passed. All other concerns were pushed aside by grief. Riquet became suddenly aware of how insignificant his struggles with the canal seemed in contrast to the loss of his brother-in-law and his mentor, both in the same year. As his dream was fast becoming reality, he was painfully aware that it would never have been possible but for His Excellency Charles-François d'Anglure de Bourlemont.

Seventeen

1670

Intending to share with Clerville the solution to the bane of the collapsing locks, Riquet headed for Sète to inform the *Chevalier* of the new design and to check the progress on the jetty for the port. He arrived to find Clerville gone and Ponce Alexis de La Feuille de Merville in charge of the port construction.

La Feuille was an *ingénieur géomètre* and trusted protégé of Colbert. The Minister had recently assigned him to Clerville as second in command regarding oversight of the *Canal Royal*. Riquet found him to be a gentleman of fine manners and courtly grace. He felt that they might have been friends under different circumstances, but he more and more resented Colbert's obvious implications that he needed to be watched. Colbert couldn't trust Riquet simply because he was a tax farmer, and in Colbert's experience, that occupation was equivalent to "thief." The entrepreneur saw de la Feuille as just the latest of the Minister's minions sent to spy on him.

"The Cette quarries are in operation carving out the pink marble of Mont St. Clair," Alexis reported. "And barracks have been constructed for the workers. Clerville has left for Saint-Ferréol for another inspection of progress on the dam."

"I'm sorry I missed him," said Riquet. "I have good news to share. I have a new lock design that I am certain will preclude any future failures."

"That will be good news, indeed!" agreed Alexis. "How has the design changed?"

"One of my masons, Michel Medailhes, proposed curved lock walls. Like the arch of a bridge lain on its side."

"*Bien sûr!* That will prevent collapse and provide more room for navigation as well! A most valuable insight."

"How is the jetty progressing?" asked Riquet.

"I expect to lay one hundred *toises* per year if the sea allows it. The pozzolana you provided will help immensely."

Riquet wrote Colbert to report his improvement of the lock design and La Feuille's promise of six hundred feet of jetty per year at Sète. He also reported his acquisition of pozzolana clay from Italy so that concrete could be made that would harden under water, which would facilitate construction of the jetty.

Colbert was heartened by the news of the stronger lock design but was not impressed by the pozzolana plan. He responded with cautions against shortcuts that might compromise the durability of the jetty, preferring the use of large stonework properly set. Once again, he presumed base motives on the part of the entrepreneur.

Riquet, Andréossy, Clerville, and de la Feuille all viewed the use of hydraulic cement as sound construction practice rather than as a shortcut. Also, they all recognized that Colbert's strength was in finance, not engineering, so they proceeded to use the pozzolana.

* * *

The "test" of the section of the canal between Toulouse and Castanet last fall had not gone well. Issues with the lock doors and valves needed to be resolved before the canal could be opened for trade between those cities. On his way back to Toulouse, Riquet found that the lock doors had been adjusted and the new valves had been installed and filled that section once again. This time everything worked as expected. The improved valve design not only did not leak but could be operated with one hand. With the canal opened to trade from Castanet to the Garonne, the completed portion of the canal would aid transport of materials to expedite completion of the remaining section from Castanet to Naurouze.

When trade commenced between Toulouse and Castanet, Riquet was elated to see his vision coming to life, but it deeply saddened him that Monseigneur Bourlemont was not there to share in it.

* * *

That spring, Hugo once again faced outright rebellion from the Miquelets in Roussillon regions that had not participated in Riquet's Perpignan pact. Rapidly losing all patience, Riquet set out, once again, for Perpignan to meet with the *intendant* Charles Macqueron.

In preparation, he met with Hugo at a bar just inside the city gate.

"Well met, my friend," greeted Riquet. "How have you fared since last we spoke?"

"More of the same and worse," growled Hugo. "This is a war zone. Those motherless curs they call Miquelets have taken a toll on my men. It is only by good fortune that I have escaped assassination. Since Prades, they no longer flee to the nearest town, but instead melt into the countryside. We have tried tracking them, but once they disperse their trail soon disappears. They are aided in every way by the locals.

"As to your *gabelle*, you tasked me to be 'strict but compassionate.' There is no compassion in the King's duty on salt. Many of these people are barely able to feed themselves, and the Sun King's price for salt often tips the scales against them. The salt readily available from Spain at one tenth the price is irresistible to people struggling to survive. I am losing my taste for this work."

"Please stay with me until I can see this canal through to the end," pleaded Riquet, "and I promise you that I shall find other work for you. You have served me well, and I do fear for your safety, but if you leave me now, I am lost."

"I'm not going anywhere," assured Hugo. "I won't let those bastards run me off. But I'll not be showing compassion to any Miquelets who cross my path."

"I shall petition Colbert for troops to defend us in this war zone," promised Riquet.

"Also, I shall be seeing the *intendant* Macqueron while I am here. Do you need more men?"

"Always. The ambushes take a constant toll. We've lost six since you last sent men."

"Meet me here again this afternoon and I may have news."

"Perhaps the King will decide to tax his nobles rather than these ragged peasants. That would be good news." Then as an immediate afterthought, "I meant no offense to yourself, *monsieur le Baron.*"

"The first rule of law, *mon ami*, is that laws favor those who make the laws."

"True enough by my experience. Good luck with *intendant* Macqueron."

Riquet left Hugo at the bar and moved on to the *intendant's* offices. He had sent word of his visit and Macqueron was expecting him.

After brief cordialities, Riquet came right to the point.

"I fear your Miquelets are still not tamed, *monsieur.*"

"I wish I could claim surprise," replied the *intendant.* "They are a loosely connected lot and some of the more influential leaders declined to participate in your negotiations. I am certain they do not feel bound by your pact."

"Can you arrange a meeting with them?"

"They did not come before; they will not come now."

"I am left with no recourse but to petition the King for troops to put them down."

"That may be the only way to protect your people," confessed Macqueron.

"Well, then, failing any help with the rebels, can you at least supply my *gabelous* with additional men at arms to replace those lost to the Miquelets?"

"How many would that be?"

"Six, for now. My Captain and I have not spoken since this morning, so the toll may have risen."

The *intendant* smiled. "Done, then. Let me grant you six before it does."

Riquet left the *intendant's* office feeling typically unsatisfied. At least he had arranged reinforcements for Hugo. He took delivery of the promised reinforcements and returned to the bar to meet Hugo.

He again promised to petition Colbert for troops, wished Hugo Godspeed, and set out for home.

He had been but ten days at Bonrepos when Hugo's men arrived leading his horse bearing Hugo draped across the saddle. The Miquelets had finally slain his Captain.

Hugo's sergeant told the story.

"We were just outside Py in the hills south of Prades," he explained, "when they opened up on us."

"I felt the ball pass through my hair that found my Captain's eye."

"Then I felt my knee explode."

He turned his horse to expose the missing limb. His right leg was a match for Gerome's left but for the missing post.

"We buried four of our brothers in them hills," he continued, "but I thought you might want to honor the Captain special, him having served you so well and all." He lowered his head in solemn respect.

"Indeed," agreed Riquet. "He has no family that I know of. He will be interred with mine at *Cathédrale Saint-Étienne*."

Riquet advised his men that enforcement of the *gabelle* would be limited to Languedoc until the rebels could be subdued. He commissioned a carpenter recommended by Roux to fit a prosthetic to the sergeant's truncated limb. Gerome had encountered issues when his own post was first fitted, so he kept a close watch on the process and steered the carpenter away from the errors he had needed to discover the hard way.

In desperation Riquet wrote to Colbert.

"They have slain my Captain," he insisted, "For me his death is the last straw. I shall send no more men to their deaths until the King takes action."

He then set out with Gerome to escort Hugo's body back to Toulouse and post his petition to Colbert.

* * *

The Minister brought Riquet's plaint to the King immediately.

The Sun King turned, at last, to his Minister of War, the Marquis de Louvois.

"How are we to tolerate these impudent Miquelets?!" he implored Louvois.

"You must not, Sire," insisted the Marquis. "If we let them attack your agents with impunity, it is as if they attack Your Highness with impunity.

"These insults must not go unanswered."

"What do you recommend?" asked the King.

"I should think three or four thousand well-trained, properly equipped French *fusiliers* would put a swift and decisive end to their impudence."

The King sent four thousand. They ravaged the border villages mercilessly intending to provoke open confrontation with the Miquelets. Many homes and mills were burned to the ground as examples and Py was razed completely.

Appalled by the accounts of carnage he was hearing, Riquet decided to see the truth of the matter personally. He and Gerome rode south with a complement of a dozen men-at-arms.

He stopped at the *Cathédrale Saint-Étienne* to retrieve Hugo's sword and secured it to his saddle. He stopped at the salt bank for a *minot* of salt bearing the *fleur de lis*.

They smelled the burned-out village of Py before they reached it. The corpses of the villagers still lay where the King's *fusiliers* had left them. A murder of crows was feasting on the remains. Riquet felt suddenly ill but would not be deterred. He enlisted one of the guards to hoist the *minot*, a little over one hundred pounds of salt, onto his shoulder and instructed him to "Salt the ashes of this French Sodom."

There was a large scorched tree in the center of the town square. Driven by anger and guilt stemming from the loss of his Captain, Riquet drew Hugo's sword from its scabbard and plunged it with all the strength he could muster into the root of the tree, into the heart of this vile village.

When the guardsman had emptied the salt bag, he instructed him to climb onto the guard of Hugo's sword and drive it as far into the root as he was able so that it would not be easily removed.

Then he tied the empty salt sack to the hilt and mounted up to return to Bonrepos feeling more empty than satisfied by his vengeance. Riquet had never before seen the ravages of war first-hand. Even when he had provided munitions to the army during the Franco-Spanish war he had done so from a distance. This overdose of reality had deeply sickened him.

"I had hoped," he confided to Gerome, "that my legacy would be written more in stone than in blood."

When, later, the King's men met the insurgents in open battle and were savagely victorious, the victory felt hollow to

Riquet. But, with the exception of a few minor incidents this, finally, put an end to the bloodletting in Roussillon.

* * *

Clerville had been commissioned by the King to govern Oléron, an island off the Atlantic coast near Rochefort. Traveling to Sète from Oléron, the *Chevalier* decided to stop by Bonrepos for a brief visit. He was hoping to find Riquet at home. They had become good friends and Clerville was concerned for the old Baron's health. He found Catherine maintaining the books.

"I hope our King enjoys the gift we are giving him," said Catherine, wearily looking up from the ledgers, "and that his *Canal Royal* will be finished before my husband is."

"You know, I assume," said Clerville, "of the problems with the *gabelle* in Roussillon?"

"Yes," she replied. "What little income we garner is stolen by the Miquelets, but still we must pay our due to the King."

"Have you received word of the King's reprisals?" he asked.

"No, I have not."

"They have been severe and decisive. The plague of the Miquelets may finally be at an end.

"As to the *États du Languedoc* withholding funds, I want you to know that I have written to Minister Colbert on your husband's behalf with the hope that he will bring pressure to bear on the accursed state treasurer to release the funds that are due you."

"People believe," she continued hotly, "that Pierre has taken up this challenge in the hope that it will make him rich. He was *already* rich. This project, in fact, seems to be bankrupting us."

Violently sanding the ledger and slamming it shut, she rose, legs akimbo, and clenched her right fist in Clerville's general direction.

"My husband's desire," she seethed, "– his *idée fixe* – is to create a safe passage for travel and for shipment of goods between the two seas. To that end the inheritance of our children has been impounded to replace the funds so wrongfully escrowed by the treasurer of Languedoc. And my daughters' dowries as well. This canal is everything to Pierre."

To his dismay, Clerville saw tears welling in her eyes.

"Don't ever believe that," assured Clerville firmly. "He is obsessed with this work, that's true. As you know, it has occupied his thoughts since he was a boy. But *you* are everything to him; his *family* is everything to him."

Contrary to Clerville's intention, this brought a flood of tears, but she quickly recovered. He offered his kerchief, which she gratefully accepted, and as she dried her eyes, she sank back into her chair.

"Thank you for that, Nicolas," she managed, "perhaps I suffer the doubts shared by all wives of ambitious men."

Clerville felt that a subject change would be helpful.

"Has he told you of the new lock design?"

"Yes, I have seen the plans. No locks built with the parenthetical shape have needed reconstruction yet. I understand that his inspiration was rooted in our Roman legacy. Have you endorsed the change?"

"*Absolument*! There should be no more collapses. The new configuration is stronger, more stable and provides more room for traffic at the surface than the original straight wall design."

"That will be of immense relief to his mind and to these books. The rebuilds were costly in terms of time, money, and stress. They have been toxic to his credibility as well."

"Well," said Clerville, "there are substantial challenges still to be met, but it is good to have that one behind us."

"Can you stay for supper, Nicolas? Cate and Anne are here, of course, and I am certain they would enjoy seeing you. I know Pierre would wish it."

"You are most kind. I would enjoy that immensely. It would be some compensation for having missed the Baron."

* * *

The First Enterprise was well underway and the contract for the Second Enterprise was recorded. Now François needed to define the route north to Béziers.

In Toulouse, he reassembled the survey party and set out for Saint-Nazaire to begin staking the new route. Using his notes from the survey through Saint-Nazaire to the Robine canal, he recovered monuments on that line just west of Saint-Nazaire to use as beginning points for the survey north. Again, his party included a *géologue* to record soil types along the route.

From the old line they gradually diverged from the course of the Aude and proceeded northerly toward Argeliers and thence easterly toward Capestang, Béziers and ultimately Sète. By following the contours and, assuming that the Répudre and the Cesse would be bridged, they were able to hold the route level through Argeliers and Capestang. As they continued east of Capestang they encountered the rocky Ensérune ridge and turned somewhat southerly, skirting the ridge, to hold their elevation. As they proceeded, the ridge rose to their left and setting posts was difficult due to the shallow bedrock.

"Let's just run levels for a while," suggested François. "Let's see where this ridge is sending us."

Leaving the wagons under guard, they rode east along the toe of the ridge.

The *géologue* brought a long iron rod and frequently tested the soil depth. It soon became apparent that, due to the shallow bedrock, skirting the ridge might be harder than cutting through it. They decided to climb to the crest to see how wide the ridge was.

"No more than three *arpents* at this point," observed François. "But let's continue up the ridge to confirm that it widens to the west. Cutting a channel through that bedrock below will be no day at the Tuileries, and the sooner we cut through and leave this stony ridge behind, the better off we'll be, I'll warrant."

And so, they climbed the ridge. The grade was steep for their mounts, so they rode slowly and with care. At the crest, they encountered the moss-covered stone remnants of an ancient fortified city.

"A city of the ancients," observed François. "These must have been the people who drained the swamp at *Montady*."

"Where?" asked the *géologue*.

"Come with me," said François, "I think I can show you where."

He led him to a point on the north side of the ridge where they could look out over the verdant valley to the north. There was a great round field of wheat, more than a mile wide, cut into many thin wedges like slices of a great pie.

"That is – or was – the *Étang de Montady*," explained François. "It was a perched water table, a stagnant pond shrouded in miasma until the ancients drained it. Those radial lines you see are drain channels leading to the central well. The well drains through a tunnel into that valley we traversed as we sought a route to bypass this ridge."

"The drain tunnel passes under this stony ridge?" asked the *géologue*.

"Oui."

"Where is the outlet? Can you show me?"

"I believe I saw it as we passed," said François. "It's late. Let's plan on making camp near there for the night."

They rode back down to rejoin their party and backtracked toward the point where François remembered seeing the outlet.

He had no trouble finding it and directed the party to make camp nearby. As they made camp, the *géologue* was rummaging in his saddlebag. He eventually produced a candle. After supper, as it grew dark, he lit the candle in the fire and started for the mouth of the drain tunnel.

"Don't you want to wait for morning?" asked François.

"It won't be much lighter inside the tunnel in the morning and if there are bats, I'd prefer to make my inspection while they're out," replied the *géologue*.

François decided to join him in exploration. The drain was large enough for them to stand erect, but they ducked instinctively despite the adequate headroom. They had not gone far when the *géologue* passed the candle to François. Taking a small pick from his belt he chipped a sample from the wall of the tunnel.

"Sandstone," he said. "If this is typical of the stone forming this ridge, cutting through the ridge should be easy.

"Do you smell that?"

"I do. What is it?"

"Bat shit."

They quickly returned to camp and sat by the fire sharing a bottle of wine. The moon was new, there was essentially no ambient light, and their little fire did not diminish the spectacular display that was *le Voie Lactée*. The humbling view of that broad white band across the night sky induced pensiveness.

"Cutting a tunnel to drain the lake that way would seem challenging," mused the *géologue*. How would they have done it, exactly?"

"They could have constructed a wooden tube," suggested François, "roomy enough for well diggers. They would have sunk it in the center of the pond, bailed it dry, dug into the bedrock, then tunneled to daylight.

"On the other hand," he mused, "I would never be comfortable digging that well, much less the tunnel, knowing all that water was perched above me looking for a way into my shaft. I would start the tunnel from this end.

"First, I would sink a steel shaft, perhaps with an auger bit, into the center of the lake some depth into the bedrock. A good bit could be persuaded through the sandstone. Then I would make horizontal and vertical measurements to some point in this valley that would be suitable for the outlet. I would then tunnel from that point toward my auger bit, planning to reach it at the desired depth. Once my tunnel reached the sunken end of the shaft I would return to the lake and mark the auger's location with straddle points, then withdraw the auger. Then I would either wait for the lake to drain through the bore hole, or enlarge the drain at once, depending on how slowly it drained and how long I was willing to wait.

"The challenge would be boring through the bedrock."

"The stone is quite soft," offered the *géologue*. "It might be done. In fact, for our purposes a tunnel through the ridge might be best. We shall be higher than the drain when we reach this point and our tunnel could pass right over the ancient drain.

"The most challenging aspect will be preventing the ridge from collapsing onto the heads of those cutting the tunnel."

In the morning they projected the route across the ridge where it appeared to be narrowest, taking the route northeasterly toward Béziers and planning to cut through the ridge one way or another. Anticipating the possibility of a tunnel, François had elevation benchmarks set on each side of the ridge. Except for the ridge and the river crossings, the route remained level so that no locks would be required until they came to the Orb valley, where it dropped down more than sixty feet to the Orb River and Béziers.

"The descent to the Orb is going to require an extraordinary staircase," observed François. Probably eight chambers."

From the Orb, less than forty feet above sea level, the canal would pass easterly to cross the Hérault river north of Agde and on to the *Étang de Thau*. The route would then continue north through the lagoon to Sète.

Carrying the survey across the Hérault, François employed some geometry in the Euclidean sense of the word. A post was set on the survey line west of the Hérault. He sent two laborers across the Agde bridge to set a post on line across the river. A temporary marker was set on the west bank two chains upstream from the survey line and the angle between the three points was recorded. François then moved to the temporary marker and measured the angle from that vertex to the posts straddling the river. From those two angles and the distance measured along the west bank, he was able to calculate the distance across the river without direct measurement. Now the rest of the party could also cross comfortably by way of the Agde bridge.

Once past the Hérault, there were no more significant obstacles until they reached the *Étang de Thau*. This, then, was the effective terminus of their survey.

With the survey completed, Andréossy prepared a map of the route for presentation to the Royal Commission along with the *géologue's* report. François also prepared a separate report for Riquet's eyes only in which he confirmed the major challenges he foresaw in constructing the direct route through Béziers: shallow bedrock, crossing the Répudre and the Cesse, the Ensérune ridge, and the eight-chamber staircase required for the descent to the Orb. He reiterated his conviction that the Répudre and Cesse should be crossed via *ponts du canal* and included the observation of the *géologue* that the Ensérune ridge might best be passed through a tunnel. He also warned that crossing the Hérault without obstructing the existing river traffic to and from Agde would be problematic and that no solution to that dilemma had yet occurred to him.

Eighteen

1671

The following January a fierce storm found Riquet again in Sète with la Feuille. The winds and the waves built for hours until Alexis suggested that they retreat to Clerville's quarters: a solid stone structure on the windward shoulder of Mont Saint Clair. Clerville was absent, attending to the governance of Oléron.

The stable, too, was stone so they secured their mounts inside and then took shelter in the house. As the wind screamed around them in their retreat, a two hundred-year-old cypress came crashing down at their door. The heavy slate tiles that comprised the roof of their shelter took up a deafening racket as the wind played them like a huge xylophone. Fearing that the roof would collapse on them, they thought it prudent to seek refuge in the wine cellar. The *Chevalier's* caretaker gratefully accepted Gerome's invitation to join them.

The cellar was cool and a bit damp but in the context of the raging storm it felt cozy to the four refugees. To make the best of the situation they decided to raid the *Chevalier's* wine stores.

"I am sure he would offer it if he were here," reasoned Riquet.

"*Ça marche*," agreed de la Feuille. "I shall accept your judgement on that point."

The caretaker sat in silent acquiescence. He had learned years ago not to interfere in the affairs of those who were above his station.

Four bottles later the four of them finally slept, as the wind still howled overhead. The storm raged all the next day. They found a wheel of hard cheese and broke their fast, washing it down with more wine. Riquet talked of progress on the canal and the feeder *rigoles*, the proven success of his new lock design and the plantings he planned for the shores of the canal.

"We shall plant a buffer of reeds along each side of the channel to protect against the erosive effects of canal traffic. We shall plant shade trees every three *toises* along the shore. Their roots will help secure the banks and their shade will reduce evaporation of the precious canal waters as well as enhancing the comfort of travelers. We shall plant ash, elms, oaks and, where they will thrive, lime trees."

Alexis had little to contribute to the conversation. His thoughts were consumed with worry about the fate of his unfinished jetty and the ships that had sought shelter from the storm behind it.

The wind howled. They looked for another bottle.

"This one from Portugal looks interesting, said Alexis. "I wonder if it's any good?"

"In a storm," replied Riquet, any Port will do."

The next morning, they awoke to clear skies. Clerville's quarters were intact, if not his wine stores. The jetty had not fared as well. It had been halfway to completion when they took shelter but the outer half of that had been wiped clear by the storm.

Dejected, and more than a little hung over, the three men rode down to the work camp to find half of the workmen's quarters destroyed, thirty souls dead and another fifty injured. There were trees lying like jackstraws. Some of them had crushed wagons when they fell. Some had killed horses; most of the surviving stock had run off. They found some of the missing mounts on the lee side of the mountain but were told that many had swum across the lagoon for the mainland so great was their panic.

"We should have stayed to help here," said Riquet, "not cowered in our shelter."

"Could we stop the wind?" asked Alexis. "Could we protect anyone from falling trees? If we had not taken shelter, *we* might have been killed; then who would provide reconstruction?"

"On this point," said Riquet, clearly unconvinced, "*I* shall take *your* word."

The disaster was compounded by the fact that it would undoubtedly convince the Finance Minister that the use of hydraulic concrete had compromised the strength of the jetty as he had predicted. In reality, the Roman cement had strengthened the structure and many ships were spared that would not have survived the storm without the shelter of the new harbor.

This storm would not be the last to challenge Colbert's decision to build the Sun King's port on the windward side of Mont Saint-Clair. The Mediterranean had an avaricious appetite.

* * *

Returning from Sète, Riquet stopped at Castelnaudary to discuss his plan for a port. He had persuaded Colbert that the large basin would be necessary for the proper functioning of the quad that followed. Having abandoned the idea of using the canal for military transport, Colbert had capitulated.

The Mayor of Castelnaudary had keen interest, contingent upon the cost, and Riquet had an itemized accounting for him totaling thirty thousand *livres.*

"I shall submit your proposal to my *Consuls* with my endorsement," promised the Mayor, "then we shall see."

"Your decision will find me at Bonrepos," agreed Riquet.

Continuing toward Toulouse, he found half of the remaining locks leading to the summit well underway following the new parenthetic design. He smiled as he thought how he had struggled and how simple, how *obvious* the solution was. But then wasn't that the way of much invention: obvious once demonstrated?

He saw that the crew working on the lock at Gardouch was battling ground water. There was no solid footing for the walls, and they were employing the pozzolana clay he had sent from Sète to enable the concrete foundation to harden in the watery pit.

"This would not be possible without the pozzolana," exclaimed the *Chef.* "Even with the new design, we would not be able to build locks in this mire without the Roman concrete for a base."

As he continued his inspection of the works, he found Sofia between Vieillevigne and Montesquieu directing the construction of a large settling pond, an intake and a spillway. The feeder *rigole* system was nearly finished and the remaining work would no longer benefit from her expertise. François had assigned her *atelier* to a stream crossing here. There was a single lock under construction, and just up-channel from the lock her stonemasons were building an inlet for alimentation from the stream. Once sediment settled out in the pond, clear water would enter the canal over the upstream wall. There would be an *épanchoir*, a spillway, in the opposite wall of the canal to allow any excess waters from the stream to pass over the canal wall and return to the streambed. At the base of the structure they built a culvert that could be opened or closed depending on whether alimentation was needed for the canal, essentially a smaller version of the one that passed under the great dam of the Laudot at Saint-Ferréol.

"Excellent work," said Riquet. "Is this your design?"

"Oui, *sieur*," she replied, "This was the way the ancients collected clear water in the Pyrénées."

"Once again you prove your worth," he said. "Are your men behaving?" he asked in a voice loud enough for anyone nearby to hear.

"Oui, *Monsieur* le Baron. Majiq is a strong deterrent to bad behavior."

"I trust that you or he will report any form of disrespect forthwith. I assure you it will be dealt with swiftly and harshly." Again, he spoke at a volume that made his words as much for bystanders as for Sofia.

Smiling and tipping his hat, he bid her farewell as he rode on, then suddenly wheeled his horse around and returned to address an afterthought.

"You and Majiq will be leaving me again when the harvest comes?"

"Oui," she replied. "He misses his family as I miss mine. We lose most of our *terrassiers* to the harvest anyway."

"But you will both return in the autumn?" he entreated.

"*Bien sûr, Monsieur le Baron.* You can expect us October first.

It was May before the Castelnaudary city fathers came to agreement and notified Riquet of their intent to pay for the new port. Riquet was proud of his solution to the supply problem for the four-chamber staircase to the east, which would incidentally be a great boon to the city of Castelnaudary. Like his father, he favored solving problems to the mutual benefit of all parties.

Nineteen

1672

Work continued smoothly until finally, early in 1672, the canal was complete from Toulouse to the Naurouze summit, and the waters diverted from the *Montagne Noire*, somewhat augmented by waters from the Sor, flowed in strength from the mountain and through Riquet's *rigole*-canal from Port Louis at Revel to the *Bassin de Naurouze*. Once the gates at the summit were opened, it took six days to fill the canal from Naurouze to Toulouse, connecting Revel to the Garonne, the Atlantic, and the world beyond. Unfortunately, issues with the lock gates again postponed opening the canal to trade for nearly a year.

"Can no part of this labor ever come without woe?" moaned Riquet to François.

"Children are seldom born without pain," consoled his friend. "Resolving the issues with the gates will give us the time we need to finish the dam. I shall feel more comfortable opening the canal to trade with that great reservoir behind the summit locks."

* * *

That August the strain of his life's work again caught up to Riquet. He returned to Bonrepos from an inspection of the dam and would have fallen from his mount if Gerome had not been there to catch him. Matty was home for a brief visit at the time and he helped Gerome steady the sixty-three-year-old Baron on his way to bed. It was another bout with malaria, and it hit him hard. He did not experience his usual quick rebound.

In his weakened condition it laid him flat. Matty feared they might lose him.

It was mid-November before he had recovered enough to consider traveling the canal route to inspect progress, but Matty convinced his father to let him go in his stead. Matty was familiar with all aspects of the enterprises. It had been Matty who had presented Colbert with his father's plans for the great city at Naurouze. The city was never built, but the Finance Minister was well impressed by this intelligent, articulate young man. The Minister's confidence in Riquet's eldest would one day be crucial to fulfillment of Riquet's dream.

At his father's request, Matty now wrote Colbert advising him of his father's grave illness and current stage of recovery.

* * *

The letter struck Colbert to the core. It drove home the vulnerability of the aged salt farmer, for whom the Minister felt great fondness – even admiration – despite the difficulties that plagued their relationship. He expressed his concern in a letter to Riquet:

> *...I have been greatly relieved by the letters*
> *which I have just received from your son...*
> *Although this news has given me much joy, I*
> *shall hope to receive from your hand*
> *assurances of your good health. Think only of*
> *restoring it and be convinced of my*
> *friendship and the desire that I have to*
> *provide you and your family with benefits*

*proportionate to the greatness of your
enterprise.*

The realization struck him hard that this man was the
engine, if not the engineer, driving progress on the great
enterprise, and Colbert knew that well. He suddenly realized
the catastrophic impediment to completion of this work that
the salt farmer's death would present. He assured the Baron
that, in the event of his death, the completion of his great
enterprise would be entrusted to his eldest son.

He responded to Matty separately:

*I have received the letter you wrote me on
the 23rd of this month, by which you advised
me of your father's illness. I was pleased to
learn that he is out of extreme danger, and
that his health is improving every day. Please,
on my behalf, encourage him to give no
thought to the works of the canal until he is
fully recovered.*

*As to you, please visit all the works of the
canal of communication of the seas and work
incessantly to increase the number of the
workmen, which I learn not to be as it should
be. There is nothing of greater consequence
than to advance these works with diligence,
especially repair of the locks, in order to
return at the earliest, convenient and easy
navigation from Toulouse to the Stones of
Naurouze.*

*It is equally necessary that you increase
the number of workers for the excavation of*

*the part of the canal in Lower Languedoc, that
is from Béziers to Cette, because I do not see
that these works are being moved forward
with the force and vigor that your father had
promised. You must also endeavor to make
sure that the two hundred toises of the second
pier of the port at Cette are completed by the
end of this month, as well, your father having
committed to it.*

While Riquet continued to convalesce, Matty diligently monitored progress on the lock doors and on the Saint-Ferréol Dam. When the dam was finished, he authorized Roux to close the valve in the Laudot culvert and fill the *Bassin de Saint-Ferréol*. Once the locks were ready for service, he ordered the canal filled once again from Naurouze to Toulouse.

He assigned a second *atelier* to the excavation in progress between Béziers and the *Étang de Thau*. He also travelled to Sète as directed and found La Feuille doing all that could be done to meet Colbert's schedule in view of the challenges that the Mediterranean continued to throw at him.

Twenty

1673

It was January of 1673 before Riquet felt fully recovered and trade finally commenced between Naurouze and Toulouse.

When that day finally came, at *Le Écluse de l'Embouchure* in Toulouse Cardinal Piero de Bonzi was dressed for ceremony complete with pallium, crozier and mitre as he boarded the first of several boats bound for Naurouze. This was the inaugural cruise opening trade between Toulouse and Naurouze, and between Naurouze and Revel via the enhanced *rigole*. The Toulousain doubters, at last, were silenced. For the Cardinal, it was a round trip of pomp and ceremony. The other boats in the convoy brought goods and passengers destined for Revel or Castres, which they planned to exchange for goods and passengers destined for… anywhere. For Revel, the new canal was a portal to the world.

Riquet and Catherine viewed the ceremony from the shore.

"It is fitting for Piero to bless this occasion," he confided to his wife. "He has been very supportive. But it still pains me deeply that Monseigneur Bourlemont is not here to enjoy the fruits of his vision.

"And Pouget! That bull's pizzle has no place in this ceremony. Had he prevailed there would be no canal."

"God did not will him to win," observed Catherine. "He favored you, *mon cher*. Your dream is fast becoming reality. It will be an incomparable legacy for our children and for theirs."

"I can only hope," countered Riquet, "That it will become reality before it becomes legacy.

"I am quite weary, *mon amour*. Let us return to Bonrepos lest it become legacy today."

* * *

As the canal scoured its way toward Trèbes, François was struggling with the triple staircase coming down from the Naurouze summit on the Mediterranean side. The hydraulics of staircase locks were trickier than single locks. When descending traffic required the first chamber to be drained to fill the second, any variance in volume would either overfill or underfill the second chamber when the water level between the two was equalized. Unless corrected, this would leave the boats or barges either aground or lifted precariously close to the top of the lock doors. Excesses could be spilled out of the second chamber but there was no way to compensate for deficiencies. Having a third or fourth chamber in the staircase just compounded the problem.

He had already completed a single and a double to bring the descent to this point and tested them with water from the summit pound. The two chambers of the double had not been identical but had been close enough to serve. François had checked and rechecked his volume computations for the triple but, as usual, there was enough variance between design and as-built dimensions that by the third chamber they had run short of water. If chamber number two was drawn down enough to equalize with chamber number three, the depth of the second chamber fell below four feet which did not meet the design minimum.

Once chamber one was enlarged, they ran the test again and this time chamber two filled just over a foot above design level, not enough to cause concern. Then when chamber two was equalized with chamber three the resulting levels met the design minimum depth for the canal.

With the triple lock solved, he had only singles before the quad beyond Castelnaudary. On an inspection tour ordered by Colbert, Matty found him testing the last of those.

"And how is your father's health?" asked François.

"He is considerably improved and expects to be reviewing progress in a week or so. Still, I plan to take a more active role in this enterprise and relieve his burden to the extent that I can.

"This stretch is progressing well," he observed.

"Yes," François agreed. "This is the last lock before the great basin at Castelnaudary. It seems to be working correctly."

François and Matty rode together to Castelnaudary where the excavation of Riquet's port was well underway. It was an impressive hole: nine hundred feet wide at the widest point, twelve hundred feet long, and already nine feet deep. There was good stone being quarried from the excavation, and much would be needed for the casements, so the plan was to quarry down at least another three feet if the stone held out. This would be a truly impressive port when completed, with ample supply for the quad staircase that followed and plenty of moorage for ships in transit. Trèbes would be the halfway point in the canal and the Castelnaudary port would have the potential to be a major commercial hub halfway between Toulouse and Trèbes. The stone being pulled from the chasm was an unanticipated benefit from Riquet's ingenious solution to the quad staircase supply problem.

East of the basin the route dropped thirty-four feet in the first eight hundred. This would be the quadruple lock fed by the grand basin of Castelnaudary. François was dreading it.

Based on his experience so far, he had little hope of sizing the chambers perfectly on the first try and he dreaded the inevitable reworking. The *terrassiers* were aided by stone workers cutting the four steps into the channel in preparation for the lock construction. It appeared that much of the stonework would be seated on bedrock, which was good, but unforgiving if revisions were needed.

Once he hammered out the quadruple, the next would be only a double, but the one after that was going to be another triple.

"These staircases are nightmares," he confided to Matty. "Balancing the volumes never seems to translate correctly from theory to stone. I suspect that the curved walls are not aiding the accuracy of my calculations, but I don't see where I'm going astray."

"Won't the descent into the Orb valley require even more chambers?" Matty asked.

"Indeed. No less than eight. A nightmare of nightmares. I should have heeded my father's advice and studied law instead of science."

This brought a hearty laugh from Matty. "The law, too, holds its own nightmares," he said. "You are always trying to persuade someone to do something they are not inclined to do. People can be more stubborn than stone."

François decided to initially line all four chambers of the quad with wood for the process of testing and balancing volumes. That way, if adjustments were needed the volumes could be tweaked without having to tear out and replace stonework. The lock door frames and sills were fashioned from stone as they would not need modification in the balancing process. This worked so well that he resolved to follow the same plan on the coming triple.

* * *

Later that spring Riquet was in Toulouse to draft formal papers to ensure that, upon his death, Pierre-Pol's inheritance would be secure. At the same time, he assigned half of the fief of the canal to Matty. He also negotiated the marriage of his daughter, Cate, to the Marquis Jean de la Valette, the King's *intendant* and governor of Toulouse.

That summer the Riquet family celebrated Cate's marriage to the Marquis in grand style. The Mass was celebrated by none other than Cardinal Piero de Bonzi of Toulouse who had blessed the opening of the canal from Toulouse to Naurouze. The Mass was held in the *Cathédrale Saint-Étienne* in Toulouse and the reception at Bonrepos.

Fresh flowers filled the chateau and garlands draped the perimeter walls of the estate. Riquet was dressed in his finest. There were twenty tables laid with roast pig, duck, lamb and conies, baked casseroles of carrots, corn and beans laced with rich cheeses. There was a barrel of vintage Carignan Jean-Henri and Collette Duvall had put aside for the occasion.

A string ensemble played for those who enjoyed the minuet, the official dance of the Sun King's court. Anyone who showed the slightest interest was pressed into a guided tour of the model *rigole* by their gracious host. Even Hector Boutheroüe and his wife came from Briare to join in the celebration. For a day, the years of struggle fell away from the proud father and he was filled with joy for his beautiful daughter and her new husband.

* * *

As construction approached Carcassonne, Riquet had postponed excavation of the last five miles. He had been approached by three consuls who still hoped to convince their colleagues that it would be worth the cost to bring the canal into the Aude valley upstream from their city. They had asked for time to press their case. But as the allotted time for completion of the First Enterprise dwindled, Colbert sent Clerville to find an explanation for the delay.

"What in Christ's name are you waiting for?!" demanded Clerville.

"There are still Carcassonne consuls who favor the route through the city," replied Riquet. "Now that the King no longer plans to use the canal for naval transport, I am hoping these few far-sighted men will be able to build a majority."

"You have lost your way, *mon ami*," said the *Chevalier* in a somewhat softened tone. "This canal might never have *been* but for your passion and conviction and sacrifice. I know that better than most. But it is not *your* canal. It is the *Canal Royal*. The Sun King and Colbert have shown great patience with the many delays you have suffered. They have given you a two-year extension for completion of the First Enterprise. They, too, are at risk here and need to show results for the tax revenues they have so painfully extracted from the people of Languedoc.

"Now you've got the Finance Minister's wig all knotted up for no good reason!

"You have your ports at Saint-Sauveur and Gardouch," he continued. "You have persuaded Colbert to incorporate the *Grand Bassin* at Castelnaudary. Accept that Carcassonne's ship has weighed anchor without them. Follow the planned route to the confluence of the Fresquel and the Aude. Show

Colbert some results now and it may serve you well in the future."

Riquet was quick to recognize the folly that had seduced him.

"Of course, you are right, Nicolas, I have always viewed Colbert's timeline as subject to the vagaries of real construction issues that are unavoidable. But this delay to accommodate Carcassonne is avoidable and will end today. I shall do as you so wisely recommend. The canal will bypass Carcassonne."

In the years to come, the *Consuls* of Carcassonne would come to bitterly regret their myopia. Only when the city eventually grew to the north would the *Canal Royal* become an integral part of the thriving urban center of commerce that was Carcassonne.

* * *

It was November when Riquet was struck by the news that his sister, Madeleine, had passed just four years after Paul. She and Paul had been more than aunt and uncle to Riquet's children. Having none themselves, they essentially adopted Riquet's as their own. He felt the loss deeply and it reopened the grief of losing his best friend. He resolved to find a way to commemorate Paul for his help in enabling the success of the grand enterprise.

Then Riquet's malaria hit him hard again as it seemed to do whenever he was low. It wracked him for weeks before he felt strong enough to stroll the grounds of his estate once again. He never tired of revisiting the model *rigole* crafted by Isaac Roux, Pierre Campmas and François Andréossy. It conjured memories of debates with Pierre regarding connecting the

Fresquel to the Laudot, a plan he now found amusingly naïve. He recalled long nights by the fire with Isaac planning the renovation of his manor at Bonrepos. He relived his elation at the Archbishop's reaction to their demonstration of this miniature canal.

He wondered at the great good fortune that had come his way – punctuated by tragedy but ultimately enviable. His wife was a brilliant angel who had born him eight children, three taken from him too soon but five now thriving successfully. He had managed to endow them all with the nobility of his Italian ancestors. He struggled under the financial burden of this great endeavor, but it would be his legacy. It would provide his family with security for generations to come.

As the old Baron reached the fountain at the head of his kitchen garden, he drifted back into the moment and his weariness returned. Catherine had come to check on him and she took his arm. Together they strolled into the manor and she escorted him back to bed.

* * *

Once Riquet had recovered enough to ride, he wanted to inspect progress on his life's work. He and Gerome set out for Saint-Ferréol. He was pleased to see the dam completed, full and providing alimentation for the canal between Naurouze and Toulouse. He smiled when he saw the constant flow of traffic being carried on his *rigole* canal to and from Revel. As they continued, he found that all of the locks between the summit and Castelnaudary were finished. The great basin for the port was nearly finished.

The completed quad descending from the great basin was a welcome sight and he found the double completed as well. The Medailhes brothers had the triple well underway and the various singles between there and Carcassonne had been relegated to whichever *atelier* was available as their turn came.

He found François at the Fresquel crossing. The weir in the Fresquel was in place, constructed just high enough to raise the water level in the river to equal that of the canal for the at-grade crossing. Now the stonemasons were building a bridge for the tow path on top of the weir. When completed, the tow path bridge would feature a total of eighteen arches which would allow the river to pass over the weir and yet under the bridge. The tow path ran alongside the full length of the canal to accommodate the horses or mules or, sometimes, men that would pull the barges along. When the canal crossed a river, so must the tow path.

"Where is Isaac? asked Riquet.

"Just ahead at the Orbiel crossing," replied François. "Have you seen his dam?"

"*His* dam?"

"He has built it from the bedrock up. I gave him a brief explanation of the plan and he executed it."

Riquet nodded his head and smiled. "He is a master of stone. I never doubted his success even in so great a challenge. And my son?"

"He is somewhere up ahead engaged in the inspection that you appear to be duplicating. I think he was hoping that you might rest more."

"I'll rest when the two seas are finally joined."

"As I suspected," said François with a wry smile. "Are you hungry?"

François produced a baguette, some cheese and a bottle of wine from his saddlebag and chased a large bullfrog off a moss-covered log in a green glade near the river. Riquet invited Gerome to sit with them beside the Fresquel as they ate, drank, and discussed the way ahead.

"The *Chevalier* is insistent that the canal should join the Aude at Pechlaurier Rock. He deems it to be the best route past the defile," opened François.

"Has he forgotten Hector's admonitions about using live channels?"

"So it would seem."

"And what does *Monsieur* Boutheroüe say?"

"Hector's focus has returned to the *Canal de Briare*, now that the future of this one is secure."

"Is it? I wonder."

"Clerville likely hopes that pulling the canal into the Aude will draw it inexorably toward Narbonne," speculated François.

"Then we must resist that notion. Drawing near to Narbonne will draw us nearer to those coastal marshes. We must not allow the *Chevalier's* affinity for his hometown to draw us that way."

"The only alternative to the live channel of the Aude is cutting the channel through the Pechlaurier Rock. It would be slow and difficult," replied François.

"Minister Colbert has promised me all the gunpowder I need at his price. That should subdue the Pechlaurier Rock."

François refilled their mugs. "Once past the Pechlaurier, we need to cross the Répudre and the Cesse. After that here should be no major challenges until the Ensérune ridge," he continued. "As you know, the route lies on bedrock traversing that ridge, and the best way past the ridge is through it. My *géologue* believes that the soft stone indicates that a tunnel would be possible, although an open cut might be an option."

"We have miners from the *Montagne Noire* in our workforce," agreed Riquet. "They should have no trouble piercing the ridge."

"The ancients, the Visigoths I believe, cut a much longer tunnel to drain *L'étang de Montady*," agreed François.

"Once through the ridge, the next challenge will be the descent into the valley of the Orb," he went on. "The drop into that valley will require a staircase of eight chambers. We can barely balance four. I think I may need to find other work before that day."

Riquet smiled. "I sincerely hope you jest, François. You know I would be lost without you."

"I spoke only partly in jest," replied his lieutenant. "Triples and quadruples are frustrating enough. I have no taste for an eight-chamber staircase carved from solid rock. There will be ample work to engage me elsewhere. I implore you to find another victim for the task. Of course, you would not want to inflict that burden onto Isaac, either."

"I would prefer to have you in charge of it, but if you are unwilling, I shall find someone else. Perhaps the Medailhes brothers. They are magicians with stone."

A brief lull in the conversation produced a cogent question from Gerome.

"Where is the *Chevalier* now?" he asked.

"In Cette, I suppose," replied Riquet without much interest.

"I think not," countered François. "I believe he is in Bordeaux dealing with a problem-plagued renovation of a chateau there."

Suddenly the Baron's brow un-furrowed. His face almost brightened.

"Then I propose that we cut through the Pechlaurier immediately, thereby rendering the issue of the Aude moot. I shall continue directly to Cette where the King has stores of gunpowder I can acquire and bring some to you at the Rock as soon as I am able."

Gerome said nothing.

"The *Chevalier* will not be pleased," cautioned François.

"He will realize the wisdom of eschewing the live channel," returned Riquet with confidence. "If it is a *fait accompli* when he first sees it, how can he argue?"

With the wine gone and the discussion at an end, the three mounted up and continued to the Orbiel where Riquet explained the plan to Isaac, asking him to monitor progress at the Fresquel crossing as well as the Orbiel.

Riquet had a workforce of nearly ten thousand men and women, and there were *ateliers* at work all along the route from Castelnaudary to Pechlaurier. As they traveled, they selected one that was comprised of more miners and stonecutters than most and reassigned them to the Rock. Upon arrival, François put them to work clearing and, to the extent possible, excavating the canal route while Riquet continued on to Sète for the powder.

Arriving in Sète, he found Alexis de La Feuille still struggling with the second pier. Even with the pozzolana, building a wall that would withstand winter storms on the Mediterranean coast was no easy task. But La Feuille was making progress.

Alexis was aware that Colbert had authorized Riquet's use of the powder. He released a wagonload without showing any curiosity regarding where Riquet planned to use it, and Riquet headed back to Pechlaurier. Then, tiring from his travels, he turned toward home, stopping only to have a word with Isaac and pass along François' praise for his work on the dam.

The tow path over the Fresquel was finished, so he and Gerome chose that route for their crossing. It was not quite like sailing on the canal, but it was close. It was a manifestation of the realization of his dream.

Riquet had acquired homes along the route that had the misfortune to fall in the right-of-way for the canal. Their previous owners had been well compensated for the taking, but their homes had become part of the fief of the canal. He often stayed in one or another while on his inspection tours. One such was in Villesèquelande and that was where they spent the night.

While Gerome built a fire, he sat and sipped brandy, too exhausted to even fill his pipe. By the time the fire was fully ablaze, he was asleep.

Twenty-one

1674

Feeling that his project was in good hands, Riquet took some time to rest and recuperate at Bonrepos. After several weeks, Louis Nicolas de Clerville was announced, and Riquet received him in his parlor. After brief, polite inquiries about each other's health and about Riquet's family, Clerville launched his attack.

"I see that while I was busy on another battlefront you have preempted the best route for our canal," he charged.

"I was sorry you were not available to discuss the options, my friend, but felt certain that you would have come to see the wisdom of avoiding the use of a live river channel, once you were reminded of the reasons for *Monsieur* Boutheroüe's vehement urgings against such a course – which were reaffirmed by the Royal Commission."

"It would have been little more than a grade crossing," argued Nicolas.

"Perhaps, but an unnecessary grade crossing. Did you hope it might draw us toward Narbonne?"

"I am at peace with the King's decision. I simply believe the Aude would have been the best avenue through the cut.

"Your route will take you toward the Ensérune ridge. Have you found a way around it?"

"My *géologue* is recommending a tunnel."

"A *canal* tunnel? Folly! Truly *un mal pas!*"

"I guess we shall see. I respect your advice, my friend, but I fear it is tainted by your fondness for Narbonne. Your hometown need not be orphaned by my route. The Robine could be extended to connect to the *Canal Royal*."

Dismissing the obvious pander, Clerville continued his inquest.

"And if your tunnel succeeds, and you reach the valley of the Orb, how do you propose to descend to *your* hometown?"

This forced a sardonic smile from Riquet. "Our plan calls for a staircase of eight chambers."

"*Eight* chambers?! You can barely even balance four! Whom have you persuaded to build this fiasco for you? What desperate engineer has agreed to risk his reputation on such an unlikely challenge? Surely not François?"

"None, as yet, admitted Riquet. "I may need to put it to bid."

"Are you planning another grandiose port for Béziers?"

"No. We shall simply cross the Orb at grade as we pass. The channel is finished from there to the *Étang de Thau*, but for crossing the Hérault. And, of course, once we enter the *Étang de Thau*, we simply pass through the lagoon to Cette."

Finally, the *Chevalier* mellowed his tone somewhat.

"Well, I can see you have thought this through and are not to be deterred from your chosen route. Although your chosen path seems to me to be doomed, I wish you success; so much depends upon it. As always, *mon ami*, if I can be of help, you have only to ask." He rose to withdraw.

Riquet gave a wry smile. "You could build the staircase to the Orb. François has demurred already."

The *Chevalier* laughed heartily. "Anything but that, my friend. You ask too much!"

Riquet escorted him to the door offering his regrets.

"I am sorry we could not agree," said Riquet as Clerville climbed aboard his carriage. "May our next meeting be less contentious."

"And may your conviction serve you well and be not your undoing," replied Clerville as his coach pulled away.

* * *

Matty and Claire lived in Paris now. Colbert had appointed Matty to a judicial position, *Maître des Requêtes.* He was both well-known and well liked at the court of the Sun King. Concerned for the health of the senior Riquet, Colbert was relying on Matty as a potential backup for his dynamic father. He had authorized Matty's absence from his judicial post for as much time as he needed for inspections of the canal works. He hoped to preserve the Baron's health to the extent possible.

In the autumn of 1674, Matty again embarked on an inspection tour of the various works in progress. He found the locks completed from Naurouze to Castelnaudary and the port finished. He authorized the lockkeepers to fill the canal and the grand basin.

Between Castelnaudary and Trèbes, he found the double and triple following the quad were completed and most of the singles. Many of the lockkeeper's houses were either built or under construction as well. The First Enterprise was nearly finished and the Second was underway.

He found François advancing the Second Enterprise as he ground down the Pechlaurier, while the excavation of the long pound was well underway. The long pound was so named because, as François had guessed, with aqueducts at the Répudre and the Cesse and the tunnel through the Ensérune ridge, the canal would run more than thirty miles without a lock. As with the feeder *rigoles*, this would again be a stretch where Sofia's experience would shine, as they cut a course along the natural contours.

The channel between Béziers and the *Étang de Thau* was ready for service save for the Hérault crossing and work was proceeding on the port at Sète as it had been represented to Colbert by La Feuille.

Twenty-two

1675

As his grand enterprise advanced, Riquet more and more felt the need to be closer to the seat of power in Toulouse. In 1675 he bought the estate of Frescaty just outside the ramparts near the *Cathédrale Saint-Étienne* which lay just inside the east gate. Ironically, it was not far from the first post François had set at the beginning of the preliminary route survey. Although Bonrepos was still his sanctuary, he and Catherine and Anne now spent most of their days at Frescaty. Riquet felt better placed to manage his project and inspect progress from this base near the western terminus of the *Canal Royal*.

When Colbert heard of the acquisition, he was livid.

"His pleas for funding are incessant," he fumed, privately to his wife, "yet he has coin enough to buy Baronies and Counties for his sons and an estate wherever it pleases him! I must plead, threaten, and cajole to extract his payments for the *gabelle*, but he manages lavish weddings for his daughters!

"I must ponder whether his detractors may have judged him rightly and he is a charlatan feigning service to the King only to enrich himself. Which is to say '*un fermier de gabelle!*'"

In fact, Riquet weighed each expense very carefully as to cost and benefit. His initial commitment to the grand enterprise was less than two million livres – a price he could easily afford and an investment he deemed secure. But as construction expenses mounted well beyond his (and Clerville's) estimates and the Roussillon *gabelle* continued to drain off resources, it became even more urgent to receive timely payments from the *États*.

* * *

With completion of the First Enterprise, Riquet's entire workforce had been brought to bear on the Second Enterprise, and the work was advancing apace. The triple between Marseillette and Puichéric had been finished, but there were issues with the chamber volumes that the Medailhes brothers were working to resolve. There were still two doubles between there and Puichéric. The lock at Puichéric was a double as well. After that there were yet two more doubles between there and the Pechlaurier Rock which was, itself, followed by a double.

Gradually, the channel had emerged from the Pechlaurier palisades above the Aude. François had stockpiled the stones suitable for masonry separately from the rubble that could be used for filling voids in Romanesque construction of the style used on the Saint-Ferréol dam.

The single at Argens had been finished months ago, so once all the doubles were working the canal would be finished to the beginning of the long pound.

He found François working on the double that preceded the Pechlaurier.

"Have you decided how to cross the Répudre and the Cesse?" François asked. "Will we use aqueducts?"

"I think we must," replied the Baron. "Can you build them for me?"

These would be the only aqueducts on Riquet's canal and only the second and third *canal* aqueducts ever built anywhere. Several would be added in later years, long after Riquet's death, but initially there would be only two. François was convinced that the gorge of the Répudre was too deep and its waters too wild for a grade crossing. Also, the gap was narrow enough that bridging it was feasible. But the aqueduct would be a challenge both in design and in construction. The weight of the canal would be far greater than that borne by any highway bridge, and the structure must be watertight. The Cesse crossing was not so formidable, but a grade crossing would require a weir of unusual height to match the canal water level at that point.

"I think we should seek the *Chevalier*'s advice in designing the aqueducts," said François. "I know we have not earned his love by shunning the Aude and Narbonne, but I believe he will still want us to succeed."

"When last we spoke, replied Riquet, "he did offer me any assistance he could give save building the staircase to the Orb valley. I expect he will help.

"You yourself do not feel up to the task?"

François shook his head resolutely.

"It must be a massive structure to carry the weight of the water, more akin to a battlement than a bridge. A structural failure under load would be disastrous both politically and personally. I shall gladly defer to the *Chevalier*'s experience and wisdom."

"I guess I should seek him out in Cette," mused Riquet.

"He might yet be found in Narbonne," countered François. "He stopped by here late last month and mentioned he had business to attend to there."

"I shall try there first," agreed Riquet.

With the obstacle of the Pechlaurier Rock removed, he and Gerome could pass on horseback, thereby reaching the bridge at Argens to cross the Aude toward Narbonne.

Riquet did indeed find Clerville in Narbonne and relayed François' request for aid in designing the aqueducts.

"Gladly," agreed Clerville. "I have given considerable thought to the challenges you face, and I agree that an aqueduct is the best crossing for the Répudre. I have some definite ideas about how it should be built. You may be pleased to hear that it will employ your pozzolana extensively, both for its hydraulic qualities and for its strength.

"The Cesse is another matter. I recommend a grade crossing for that stream which will allow you to collect the alimentation you will need for the long pound. The Medailhes brothers will have no trouble with that structure.

"But yes, I shall prepare plans for the Répudre aqueduct. Will you wait for them or shall I send them to you?"

"Neither. This will be a major piece of construction, second only to your great dam at Saint-Ferréol. I intend to put it out to bid. If you would be so kind as to have the plans posted here and in Lézignan and Saint-Nazaire along with a request for bids to be submitted to me at Frescaty, that would be ideal."

"I shall do as you request, *mon ami*. There is another thorny problem lying between Béziers and Cette which may have escaped your notice."

"The Hérault?"

"*Oui.*"

"It has not escaped my notice. It occupies my thoughts relentlessly. The canal was to have been completed between Béziers and Cette last year, and we were unable to accomplish that goal due to the quandary of crossing the river without obstructing existing river traffic. Before now we have not needed to accommodate river traffic at crossings, but the Hérault carries constant traffic. I confess that I see no acceptable solution. The weir for the grade crossing must bar traffic on the river to enable the passage of the canal, just as *Le Bazacle* in Toulouse bars the Garonne. The people of Agde will be in open rebellion."

The *Chevalier* smiled. "I have an idea that you may want to consider."

"Absolutely! Please tell me."

"I believe the solution lies in providing passage for river traffic *around* the weir. If we can construct a lock that would allow river traffic bound for Agde to enter a lock at the canal level and be lowered to the level of the Hérault as it is *downstream* from the weir, that traffic could proceed unobstructed to Agde."

"There is a lock already planned near the crossing," agreed the Baron, "but instead of the normal inlet and outlet elevations we would need to provide a third, lower elevation. How? And how do you make the turn toward Agde in the confines of a lock?"

"That is the thorn that pricked me the longest," agreed Clerville. "The answer is embarrassingly simple. Expand the confines of the lock to accommodate the pivot. Construct a *round* lock with the usual inlet and outlet gates for the canal, but a third gate in the wall on the Agde side and a chamber deep enough to lower traffic to the level of the Hérault below the weir. The circular shape would have the same structural benefit as your parentheses, only more so, and support the deeper chamber."

"*Mon dieu, Monsieur de* Clerville! I told you when we first met that you would be an invaluable asset to this project, and you have proven it again. Have you plans and specifications?"

"Not yet, *mon ami*. I wanted to hear your thoughts first."

"My only thought is that you have solved the last remaining puzzle in this seemingly endless chain of dilemmas! Could you perhaps prepare specifications for a bid request to be posted along with those for the Répudre aqueduct? I think it, too, will be worthy of competitive bidding."

"Consider it done."

Feeling his age again, Riquet returned to Frescaty for rest. Within two months he received bids from a partnership comprised of two stonemasons from Narbonne: André Boyer and Immanuel d'Estan. The bids were accompanied by a letter of recommendation from Clerville. They had worked for Clerville previously and he had been satisfied with the quality of their work. He deemed them capable of building the Répudre aqueduct and the round lock at Agde in conformance with his specifications. Colbert had assigned Matty another inspection tour, and he was at Frescaty when the bids arrived, so Riquet sought his legal review.

"These men are endorsed by Clerville," he noted. "If you find all in order, I would ask that you carry these plans to François along with the bids. He can execute contracts, supervise their construction and ensure that the bid specifications are met.

"I am weary beyond words and require rest if I am to see this endeavor through."

Finding all in order, Matty took the bids and began his inspection tour expecting to find François along the way. He found Isaac working on the double at Puichéric. As it happened, Michel Medailhes, inventor of the oval lock design, was working those locks as well, and needed no supervision from Isaac Roux. The latter had been ruminating about a project option that might make better use of his time when, as if in answer to his very thoughts, the Baron's son arrived.

"Ride with me," said Matty. "You are clearly redundant here and I can use you downstream. I carry plans for the *pont du canal* at the Répudre for François and will need you to finish whatever project currently engages him."

"A welcome change," agreed Isaac. "I am as teats on a boar where the Medailhes are working."

He mounted up and joined Matty in his quest.

They found François had finished the double lock prelude to the Pechlaurier and was working on the double at the east end of the palisades. When Matty showed him the bids and Clerville's letter, he was obviously impressed.

"These look like excellent plans, said François. "The *Chevalier* was true to his word."

"It gladdens me to hear that you think so," said Matty. "The Baron would like you to go to Narbonne and engage Boyer and d'Estan to build the aqueduct and the Agde round lock. You will find a store of pozzolana clay at Cette if your own supply is exhausted. Isaac can finish here."

"Pozzolana." mused François. "Of course. I expected we would be using it. This aqueduct looks like a structure worthy of the Romans. It should endure for centuries."

Twenty-three

1676

Boyer and d'Estan brought their own workforce: laborers as well as artisans. They assembled two crews and while Boyer began work on the round lock at Agde, d'Estan tackled the aqueduct at the Répudre. The contracts provided that Riquet would supply all needed materials.

To cross the gorge, d'Estan first set a wall of pilings in the Répudre to isolate the right bank of the stream, similar to the technique used in the final successful construction of the Garonne locks. Next, he had the right bank excavated to the bedrock. He then built a pier using the classic Roman wall design: a shell of stone masonry to be filled with rubble, sand and lime. Instead, however, Clerville's plan called for the fill to be mixed with pozzolana concrete. He repeated the process for the left bank and waited two weeks for the piers to cure before spanning them with a thirty-foot arch built on a temporary wooden scaffold between the two piers. For the actual bed of the canal, he put down a layer of stone followed by a layer of pozzolana cement and, finally, another layer of stone. The masonry walls of the canal channel were thicker than would have been needed for a highway bridge. The extra strength was needed not only to contain the weight of the water but also as defense against the rage of the Répudre in flood.

* * *

While his partner was meeting the challenge of the Répudre, André Boyer was building the round lock per the *Chevalier*'s plans. François kept a close eye on both projects. During an early visit to the worksite of the round lock Boyer suggested a modification to Clerville's plan.

"The extraordinary depth of this lock can be avoided, and I believe it should be. There is room for a single between the round lock and the junction of our connecting link with the Hérault downstream from the weir. Opting to build a single in that connecting link would reduce the depth of the round lock to only sixteen *pieds*."

Intrigued, François considered Boyer's proposal, weighing the benefit of the reduced depth in the round lock against the detriment of an additional lock to be passed by traffic headed for Agde. Each lock was, after all, an impediment to traffic flow.

"Your idea has merit," he agreed. "How will it affect the cost?"

"The quantity of stone used for the single would be similar to that required to deepen the round lock," Boyer mused aloud. "And the difficulty of constructing the round lock would be reduced. Two additional sets of lock doors will be required but we can provide those within our budget.

"I can build them both," he concluded, "for the price agreed for the round lock alone."

"Do it," decided François. "The Baron and I tend to think alike. If I can't convince him of the merits of your plan, it will be my burden. If the *Chevalier* objects, that too will be a cross for me to bear."

* * *

The Répudre aqueduct was completed in September of 1676. In December the first fierce storm of the winter hit, bringing torrents of rain to the hills and valleys feeding the Répudre. The resulting floodwaters carried timbers that battered d'Estan's structure with no mercy. When the waters abated, the left wall of the canal was found to be nearly demolished and cracks had opened in the left side of the bed that would clearly not hold water. Before repairs could be executed another storm ravaged the structure, leaving only the massive piers standing. It had been hard to adequately plan for the power of the Répudre when in full flood. Any weir that might have been built for a grade crossing would have undoubtedly been totally removed by those storms.

As soon as the weather and his health allowed, Riquet rode out to join François on an inspection tour. Arriving at the Répudre, they could not believe how completely the massive aqueduct had been eradicated.

François, in particular, was stunned to see the extent of the damage.

"It appears that I was mistaken regarding the *le durée éternelle* of the *Chevalier's* design. Or perhaps we all simply failed to foresee the force of the Répudre in flood.

"I shall pay for the reconstruction," Riquet assured d'Estan. "The failure is no fault of yours. But double the strength of the left wall."

When the entire superstructure was replaced in the spring, the reconstruction would feature a reinforced wall on the left bank of the canal that exceeded even Clerville's herculean specifications.

* * *

The jetties at Sète were struck by those same storms. Again, La Feuille was obliged to seek shelter in Clerville's keep. The caretaker welcomed La Feuille as he would a member of the family. When the storm passed and he emerged, he once again found much of his work undone.

"It seems there is no end to the voracious appetite of this accursed sea," he growled to his *Chef de Atelier*. "Clerville was right. We should have built the harbor on the lee side of Mont Saint Clair. There is naught to be done but replace what has been devoured with larger stone and more Roman concrete. I refuse to be defeated by *l'eau*."

Twenty-four

1677

In the summer of 1677, with the reconstruction of the aqueduct nearing completion, and having successfully dodged the nightmare of the octad staircase, François shifted his focus to the at-grade crossing of the Orb. The Orb was in its summer ebb and the time was right. The plan was to build a double weir system that would first focus the river channel onto its right bank to receive the canal, then divert the flow to the left bank of the Orb for the canal's exit. The tow path would follow the right bank of the river down to the downstream weir where it would cross to the other side.

Alexis de La Feuille had designed a reusable coffer dam to be placed upstream to divert the river during construction of the upstream weir. It could then be disassembled and reused for the construction of the downstream weir. The coffer dam combined with the reduced flow in the river and the hydraulic concrete enabled construction of the masonry weirs in the live riverbed.

Once past the Orb, the only real challenge remaining was crossing the Hérault. That challenge was nearly met. The round lock had to be built before the weir to avoid interruption of navigation on the Hérault. Upon completion of the at-grade canal crossing, river traffic would need to divert to the canal, and then pass through the round lock which, combined with Boyer's single, would drop Agde-bound traffic to the level of the Hérault below the weir. Canal traffic not bound for Sète or Béziers would exit to the south toward Agde. Eastbound canal traffic continuing upstream on the Hérault could simply choose that route during the crossing, where the canal used the river channel for two thousand feet before exiting, through a floodgate to the east toward Sète.

Once the round lock and Boyer's single in the downstream link were finished, the weir could be built for the Hérault crossing. At that point the canal would be complete between Béziers and Sète. The connection from Béziers to the *Étang de Thau* was finally coming to completion.

* * *

In September, word reached Riquet of the death of *Le Chevalier* Louis Nicolas de Clerville, a man Riquet had come to value as a close friend. His death was sudden and without warning. Riquet was deeply shaken by the news.

Matty was staying at *Rue des Puits-Clos* for a few days while attending to business with the Parliament. His father had invited him to supper at Bonrepos, partly to break the bad news.

"How is Claire?" his father asked at supper that evening. "Has her condition improved?"

"No. In fact it has worsened some, it seems. I'm beginning to think physicians are frauds."

"Clearly, his father agreed, "they do not know as much about these maladies as they claim. Often, it seems, they do more harm than good with their incense and leeches.

"Have you heard that we have lost the *Chevalier?*"

"Yes, it is said that the King was deeply saddened by his death and regretted having distanced him of late."

"It grieves me deeply," he confided to Matty, "to know that he will never see the culmination this glorious work of which he has been so vital a part. First Bourlemont, then your

277

uncle Paul and aunt Madeleine, now Nicolas. It fair breaks my heart."

Matty joined him as he went outside and took a melancholy stroll beside the model *rigole* that he never tired of revisiting. It now seemed like a lifetime since it was conceived. Returning from his stroll he retired without his customary pipe and brandy.

In the way life has of piling on, it was only a few weeks later that his daughter-in-law Claire, ill since April, died, leaving Matty inconsolable. Claire had been to Matty the soulmate that his father had found in Matty's mother. Claire had not been able to conceive, leaving Matty alone and childless. He would remarry years later and eventually he would have heirs, but his father would not know them.

Twenty-five

1678

As the Second Enterprise made its way up the long pound, costs continued to rise and wringing payment from *Les États* continued to be a challenge. Riquet's detractors continued their campaign of calumniation in Colbert's ear. The Baron's investment in his grand endeavor was nearing twice what he had bargained for and he was rapidly descending into debt.

He had come too far to abandon his dream. He could only continue to strive toward success, hoping it would come before his finances totally collapsed.

Unfortunately, Captain Pierre-Pol Riquet brought more grief to his beleaguered father. He had often demonstrated courage under fire, as when he fought at d'Artagnan's side when the legendary musketeer fell at Maastricht during the war of the Netherlands. His skill in the martial arts had brought him to the attention of the Sun King who had appointed him to the Royal Guard. This kept him relatively safe in Paris, but his prestigious position did not provide the bursts of adrenalin that came with warfare. He found life in Paris exquisitely boring. To compensate, he turned to the gaming tables for surrogate excitement and became a compulsive gambler. Like all compulsive gamblers, he was a compulsive loser. He amassed debts well beyond his ability to pay, and for relief he turned to his father for the substantial sum of four thousand five hundred *livres*.

The senior Riquet was far too conservative to countenance this squander of wealth and at first refused to pay.

"Let him rot in jail," he grumbled to Catherine. "He promised the last time that this would never happen again. Let him rot. This squander will not help me plead my case for the financial relief that I so sorely need from the King and Colbert."

"He is our son," countered Catherine.

"He is an unnecessary drain on our finances!" countered the Baron. "We have sold properties in Revel that provided us good income that we might pay for the digging of this great ditch! Must we sell more to finance his card games?!"

"He is our *son*," she repeated quietly, knowing that her husband would find the right course.

In the end, his innate compassion, augmented by Catherine's urging, prevailed. With bitter disappointment, Riquet cleared his son's debt.

Added to these pains, his daughter Cate had produced no grandchildren for her father, a matter of great concern to him. Much of his motivation for the all-consuming endeavor he pursued was his desire to provide security for his children and for generations of Riquets still unborn. None of his children had yet provided him heirs.

In fact, Cate's marriage to the Marquis de la Valette had still not been consummated and she had petitioned the Church for annulment.

To further complicate matters, Jacques de Barthelemy de Gramont, the Baron de Lanta had begun courting Cate even before the Church had rendered its decision. This, of course spawned judgmental comments from the army of detractors who watched Riquet's every move. When the annulment finally came, Cate and Jacques were married, and this union proved to be of the sort Riquet had hoped for all along. It eventually produced a grandson and two granddaughters, although, again, Riquet would not live to see them.

Twenty-six

1679

When the time came to cut the tunnel through the Ensérune ridge, Riquet engaged Pascal de Nissan, a local engineer he knew to have experience in the mines of the *Montagne Noire*. François had set line points and elevation benchmarks on both sides of the ridge as a part of the survey of the inland route to Sète. Once Riquet had definitely decided to cut the tunnel, François had prepared a plan and profile for the miners. Nissan assembled two brigades, each consisting of ten miners, ten carpenters and forty laborers. He gathered the miners and explained the plan.

"Since the tunnel will be level, it's a two-dimensional problem," he told them. "All you need do is cut a shaft on the centerline established by these line points from the route survey. Twelve *pieds* to the left and twelve *pieds* to the right six *pieds* deep from that elevation benchmark and twenty-five *pieds* from floor to ceiling. To provide for the towpath, you will widen the shaft six *pieds* to the right, beginning one *pied* above the benchmark. That shelf will provide the towpath."

He started the second brigade on the far side using the corresponding monuments that would guide the second to rendezvous with the first. As the miners cut through the soft stone, the laborers would carry off the rubble and aid the carpenters in shoring up the friable stone through which the excavation passed.

As Nissan was beginning the tunnel, Riquet's detractors were in Paris lobbying Colbert. Three noblemen of Narbonne had learned of Riquet's intent to tunnel through the Ensérune ridge and the three all agreed that the idea was preposterous. They were beseeching Colbert to prevent it.

"This folly is the most blatant waste of the King's coin yet, in an enterprise that was doomed to fail from the start," declared one.

"This entrepreneur has clearly lost his mind," confirmed another.

"I fear you may be right," worried Colbert.

"This *mal pas* will bring only embarrassment to the you and the Sun King," vouched the third.

Riquet's detractors again found a receptive ear. Colbert's underlying trepidation ensuing from entrusting a major engineering project to a salt farmer, in fact a salt farmer he did not fully trust, constantly troubled his subconscious and, in the face of these alarums, boiled into his conscious mind.

In appeasement and as a precaution, Colbert agreed to send the Sun King's *intendant* for Languedoc, Henri d'Aguesseau, with a team of inspectors to examine the site. They would be empowered to stop work if they found the proposal to be a bad move, *un mal pas*. Colbert wrote to Riquet informing him of d'Aguesseau's mission and ordered him to stop work on the tunnel pending the evaluation of his inspectors.

Fortunately, Matty, too, was in Paris attending to his duties as *Maître des Requêtes*. He was a well-respected and influential gentleman at court and had many friends. One of them related the conversation he had heard between Colbert and the three noblemen of Narbonne.

Knowing it would take some time for Colbert to organize the inspection, Matty lost no time riding home to Frescaty to warn his father of the conspiracy.

He took the post routes from Paris and rode day and night, arriving in Toulouse in the evening of the next day, well ahead of Colbert's letter.

Concerned by his son's abrupt arrival, Riquet asked, "What is it that has drawn you away from Paris this evening?"

"I am here to warn you of nefarious plots against you. I was informed of a meeting between your detractors and the Finance Minister. Colbert has been persuaded to send d'Aguesseau to inspect the site of your tunnel to determine whether you should be allowed to proceed. They are saying that attempting this tunnel is a *faux pas*; indeed, I am told that they used the phrase '*mal pas*'! Colbert has empowered d'Aguesseau to suspend work if he agrees."

"I don't know how to respond," said Riquet, obviously despondent. "I have done my best to serve the Sun King and his Minister well. My principal goal has never been to enrich myself, but only to do well, and to succeed in an endeavor which passed for impossible in the minds of all the world. Colbert's doubts have proven baseless at every turn, yet he accepts as valid the criticism of these high-born princes all the same. If these conspirators persuade him to force abandonment of my tunnel, it will be a disaster. An open cut would waste time and money, both resources I sorely lack, and there is no feasible alternate route."

Pensively, Matty asked, "The work has already begun, *n'est ce pas?*"

"*Oui.*"

"It will take time for Colbert to reach his inspectors. He will surely send them letters which can be weeks in transit. If the tunnel is done when they arrive, how can they deem it ill-conceived?"

Riquet brightened, a sly smile forming in his dark countenance.

"As always, *mon fils*, your advice is wise beyond your years. I don't know if it can be done, but we shall try."

"Now I am spent," confessed Matty. "I must return to Paris in the morning. I have a very important case to hear just three days hence, but I think it best to stay the night. I need the rest badly."

"Of course, but for myself, I must depart at once to act on your advice."

Riquet had Gerome prepare four horses for immediate departure.

"The bay and the roan for me, and two of your choice for you. Choose them for endurance, for we must ride more than fifty leagues tonight."

He knew they would not have post routes to follow and would need their own fresh mounts.

He spoke with Catherine regarding his intentions.

"I have urgent word for Pascal de Nissan that I must get to him as quickly as I can. This will be a long ride for an old man, probably two score leagues at least. Nissan is at Montady and it is there that I must go. Please send Henri after me with the coach. He needn't hurry, I expect to be there for a week or so, but I expect I shall not be up to returning on horseback. Just bid him await me at the house in Capestang. I should be there in a week or two."

As an afterthought, just prior to departure, he stepped into his cabinet and retrieved a tubular leather document case of the sort commonly used only for papers of particular importance and stowed it in a saddlebag.

He took a skin of wine, mounted the bay, and gripped the roan's lead tightly. He chose not to tie it off in case one or the other should stumble. He kicked the bay in the ribs, Gerome followed suit and they were off for Castelnaudary.

This was a trip that Matty might have made in a few hours. At seventy, it would take Riquet longer.

Two hours later, they stopped long enough to change horses In Castelnaudary, Riquet mounted the roan, and they pressed on to Trèbes. Arriving at one in the morning they were able, with some difficulty, to raise an innkeeper who recognized Riquet and was willing, for a price, to provide food and wine for them and water for their horses. They were barely halfway to their destination and the old Baron was already exhausted. After a light meal of bread and cheese and a mug of wine, they retrieved their horses and rode on, Riquet astride the bay once more.

They followed the road, which was much more direct than the canal route, and as the road passed through the Pechlaurier two and a half miles north of the Aude, they changed horses again and pressed on toward Capestang.

Two hours out of Trèbes, the road brought them through a narrow pass. The forest closed in on both sides forming a tunnel of foliage and blocking any light from the moon. They were forced to rein in when their way was blocked by two armed men who obviously meant them ill.

"Where are two such wealthy gentlemen bound in such a hurry on this fine dark night?" asked the first. "And with horses to spare."

"Perhaps you could make better time if we were to lighten your load some," sneered the second.

Gerome acted instinctively. He charged forward while rearing his horse onto its hind legs, thereby shielding both himself and the Baron. It was a technique that had served him well in great battles. As his horse rose up, he saw the pan-flash from the pistols of both assailants, heard the reports, and felt one ball cut his good leg. The other buried itself in his steed's breast. As his horse fell, he slid off its haunches and landed erect despite his compromised legs. He had drawn both pistols mid-descent and now expertly placed one ball in the chest of each brigand.

"I felt expedience was in order," he explained apologetically as they fell.

"It was, indeed," smiled Riquet.

The ball that cut his good leg had spared the bone, so Gerome cut a bandage from the torn pantleg and wrapped his wound. His mount was not yet dead and obviously in pain, so he solemnly drew his poniard and tenderly comforted the beast as he deftly cut both the carotid and the jugular, quickly ending his steed's misery.

They collected the horses that Gerome had so efficiently unburdened, he reloaded his pistols and they continued apace.

They left the "spare" mounts at the Capestang house and continued east, along the north side of the Ensérune ridge, headed for Montady, hoping to find Nissan working with that brigade. Arriving at dawn, they found Nissan and his crew already hard at work. Riquet told Pascal of the devilry afoot and of the defense he had in mind. He had considered various options as he rode and had settled on the one he deemed most likely to succeed.

"I think we should redirect our focus," said Riquet. "we should focus on cutting a pilot shaft no more than five *pieds* wide and eight *pieds* high down our centerline, hoping to finish it before Colbert's inspectors arrive. This should remove all doubt that the tunnel is feasible."

"It is an option I had considered even before this," agreed Nissan. "It will provide verification that our opposing shafts are on track and afford adjustment in the alignment if they are not.

"We could gather two more identical brigades," he added, "so that work can continue night and day."

"Resting each other," agreed Riquet, "as did our horses on the journey here. Speaking of rest, is there a place for me to lay my head?"

Nissan showed him to his tent and the old man collapsed into deep sleep knowing that his engineer would put their plan into action. Gerome took up his station outside the tent. Riquet scarcely moved all the next day.

* * *

"Are you well, master?" asked Gerome in the evening of the next day. "There is hot food if you are hungry and, of course, wine if you thirst."

"Thank you, Gerome, I should eat. I am well rested. In fact, I think we shall go for a ride on the morrow in search of the Medailhes brothers. There is another project that I wish to discuss with them. Is your leg up to it?"

"My leg is fine," replied his valet. "I've had worse wounds by accident."

After another good night's sleep Riquet awoke refreshed and ready to ride again.

They found the Medailhes brothers at the Cesse crossing, which was nearly finished. It was built like Sofia's stream crossing, only more massive. There was a large settling pond upstream, an intake in the upstream wall of the canal, and the downstream wall featured an *épanchoir* to allow excess water to escape back to the bed of the Cesse.

"All is well?" he asked Michel Medailhes.

"*Oui, Monsieur le Baron*," was the reply.

"Well done. When you are finished here, meet me at Montady on the far side of the Ensérune. I have a proposal for you."

"The eight stairs, *Monsieur?*"

Riquet smiled. "You have guessed correctly, Michel."

"We would be honored to build them for you, *monsieur.*"

"Done!

"Instead of meeting at Montady, take your *atelier* directly to the crest of the Orb valley and proceed with construction. You have shown a great talent for building chambers of equal volume, but I fear this will be the ultimate test of those skills.

"If you should need more pozzolana, there should be a store of it in Cette. *Monsieur* La Feuille recently received a new shipment to assist him in his struggles against the avarice of the Mediterranean."

* * *

All worksites were still under the protection of men-at-arms, although there had been no incidents to warrant their presence since construction began. As Riquet and Gerome retraced their path from the Cesse toward Montady, they collected a force of four for a special mission Riquet had in mind.

Sofia more and more felt a strong domestic draw calling her home to her family. She had repeatedly questioned the baron regarding the continued relevance of her special skillset. She had earned enough to ensure her family's comfort for years to come without Tomás needing to take part in the grape harvest. The last bit of contour cutting prior to Capestang was nearly finished under her direction and it was there that Riquet's troop found her. Riquet informed her that he was relieving her of her command and sending her home.

"*Merci, monsieur le* Baron," she grinned. "As I am certain you must know, I am desperately missing my family."

"Majiq is now a *brigadier?*" he asked.

"*Oui,*" she affirmed. "He is most effective and has earned great respect."

"Do you deem him capable of managing the *atelier?*"

"*Oui, certainement,* he is descended from kings."

"You should be the one to tell him that he has been chosen as your replacement. Then, if you will accompany us to Capestang, we can conclude our business."

"What conclusion do you require beyond my return to home?"

"That will be made known to you in due time."

Having installed Majiq as the new *Chef,* she thanked him for watching over her all these years.

"You know where I live," she said. "Once your work here is finished, you and your family must visit us when you can. I have come to greatly value our friendship and Tomás feels that he owes you a great debt as well."

"Perhaps in the summertime?" asked Majiq with a broad smile.

"The hills are most beautiful in the summertime," she agreed. "We will look for you then."

The party proceeded to Capestang and Riquet deposited Sofia and his men-at arms at his Capestang house. His coachman Henri was still there patiently awaiting his pleasure. He continued with Gerome into the village and his salt bank. He expected there would be ample funds on hand for his needs. He procured a purse of two thousand *livres* which pleased the local *fermier* in that it relieved him of responsibility for security for that substantial sum.

Returning to the Capestang house, Riquet spoke privately with Sofia.

"Your special skills have benefitted me well beyond the salary you have received," he began. "I have brought you a supplement that I hope will help you to understand my gratitude."

Retrieving the purse from his saddle bag, he continued.

"This purse contains two thousand *livres*."

Sofia gasped audibly.

"Hush, now," cautioned Riquet in a whisper. "Only you and I know of this, and I recommend that you keep it so. It is a sum that would tempt robbery or even murder. I am sending four men-at-arms to escort you home, men I trust, but even they need not know of it."

"You astound me, *sieur*," she replied in whispered tones. "This is a fortune that you bestow. I should have no trouble buying all the salt I need at the King's price from this day on."

"As to that," he continued while drawing the leather document case from his saddlebag. "if you are asked about the purpose of this conversation, show these. One is an exact copy of the other."

He unrolled two parchments exposing the unmistakable seal and signature of the Sun King.

Sofia's eyes widened in awe. In response to her expression of puzzlement, remembering that she was illiterate, Riquet came to her rescue.

"Yes," he consoled, "I, too, find legal language to be nearly opaque. What they both say is, in essence, that you and yours are exempted by royal decree from payment of the *gabelle* for all time. Neither your home nor your person shall be subject to search and your salt need not bear the *fleur de lis* of the Sun King."

Seeing the tears welling in her eyes he feared she had misunderstood.

"This is a good thing," he reassured, "and should not be cause for tears."

"The tears you see are tears of joy," she assured him. "I do not have words to describe your kindness, only tears."

"There are two copies of the King's order," he continued with some discomfort. "I recommend that you keep one and record the other with your parish priest. I shall not always be master of the *gabelle* in Roussillon, and it would be good for you to have the church know the truth of your exemption."

"If these gifts seem extraordinary, know that they are mere tokens of the deep gratitude that I feel for your unique contribution to the realization of my dream."

He then tasked his men-at-arms with her safe delivery home and said goodbye with this parting request: "Please ask father Vilar to contact Cardinal Bonzi in Toulouse to advise him of your safe return. I would like church records to show that the late Monseigneur Bourlemont's character reference was not misplaced."

This last, he realized, would put the men-at-arms on notice that Riquet would be informed whether Sofia arrived safely home.

* * *

As expected, Colbert's tunnel inspection team was led by Henri d'Aguesseau. When they arrived at Montady, Riquet led them on a torchlit tour through the pilot tunnel. Who could deny the feasibility of digging a tunnel they had just walked through?

"So, this is the *mal pas* we were warned of," observed d'Aguesseau. "It does not seem like such a bad move to me. When do you expect to finish?"

Smiling, Riquet turned to Pascal.

"Six weeks," replied Nissan. "Eight at the most."

The next day Riquet returned to the house in Capestang and, exhausted from his ordeal, boarded his coach with Gerome. With the five surviving horses tied off behind they headed at last for Frescaty. His age was becoming more of a burden with each passing week, and upon reaching Toulouse he retired for a much-needed rest. Matty's time was still divided between his post in Paris and oversight of the works of the great enterprise. François continued the hands-on management of the canal projects still underway and Catherine had all estate business well in hand. Riquet needed do nothing but recuperate.

Twenty-seven

1680

But Riquet's recuperation was slow in coming. At seventy-one, his bouts of fever became more frequent and he was ever slower to recover. Despite the steady decline of his health, he decided to travel to Sète to inspect progress on the port. He and Gerome boarded a barge in Toulouse, taking their mounts on board as well. The perennial breeze refreshed Riquet as did the realization that he was traveling upon the manifestation of his life-long dream. They sailed on his canal as far as Trèbes, then rode along the dry channel (noting the lockkeepers houses nearly ready for occupancy), thence through the Pechlaurier Rock and up the long pound.

They crossed the Répudre on the dry bed of the aqueduct. The repairs to the aqueduct had weathered the winter storms and the channel appeared to be watertight.

The Medailhes brothers had provided a valve in the culvert for the Cesse which was open pending flooding of the canal for navigation. This allowed them to use it as a bridge. Riquet was again impressed with the skill of his star stonemasons.

They passed through the tunnel of "folly" and as they crested above the Orb valley, they found all eight chambers of the staircase nearly completed. At the Orb, they once again boarded a barge to ride to the *Étang de Thau.*

Passing through the round lock just before the Hérault, Riquet was struck once again by the simple genius of Clerville's design. Crossing the Hérault, the tow path was finally broken. Barges crossing the Hérault were pulled along a cable stretched across the river, either taking their tow animals on board with them or walking them over the nearby Agde bridge to pick up the tow path on the other side of the river. The cable also served to deter traffic cascading over the weir just a short way downstream. The sea air was pungent this close to the Mediterranean and seemed to have healing powers.

Arriving at Sète, they found La Feuille still struggling with the breakwater.

"Minister Colbert is not happy," he said.

"Minister Colbert," replied Riquet, "is the one who insisted on the windward side of the mountain rather than the lee. He does not understand that the sea is a hungry body that does not need food to feed itself and that is satisfied only with stones, without being transmuted into bread. In order to satisfy its hunger, gold must be transmuted into stone."

Exhausted, Riquet rested for a week in Clerville's vacant quarters. Clerville's caretaker had been retained by the estate and he welcomed the Baron warmly, knowing how close he and the *Chevalier* had been. While visiting the strong stone structure he remembered with a wry smile his refuge from the storm with Alexis, and with some reverence, the *Chevalier's* contribution to this grand endeavor.

On the return trip he paused in the dry bed of the canal at the entrance to the Paul Mas tunnel, which Riquet had named for his lifelong friend and brother in-law, truly his *beau-frère*. The tunnel was, to Riquet, a microcosm of the canal itself, accomplished despite the impressive array of forces aligned against him. He had chosen this work, the gateway to Béziers, as his memorial to his best friend. He had directed an inscribed stone to be placed above the entrance from the Béziers side bearing his brother-in-law's name and the date the tunnel was completed. He sat for a long while motionless on his horse, admiring the dedication stone and revisiting that summer in Sorèze when he and his sister had gone swimming with Paul in that pond of Riquet's creation.

Finally, Gerome felt compelled to ask, "Are you well, Master?"

"Quite so, at the moment," was the wistful reply. "Quite so."

Returning through Trèbes and Castelnaudary to Toulouse, they found trade flourishing, and canal traffic heavy. Most of the lockkeepers' houses had been finished and stood ready for occupancy. Only one lockkeeper would be required per staircase regardless of the number of chambers.

Reeds had been planted just below water level to mitigate wave action against the sides of the channel. In addition, shade trees had been planted along both sides of the channel. Some of the right of way that buffered the canal was under cultivation by local farmers under tenant farming agreements with Riquet. The canal was steadily becoming a beautiful blue ribbon rather than the ugly scar of its early days.

He decided to rest awhile at Frescaty before returning to Bonrepos. Catherine and Anne were there awaiting his return. While he was there, the fever took him again and he was again bedridden. Catherine was gravely concerned and summoned their physician. She also sent for the rest of their children fearing this might be their last chance to see their father alive. Cate and Marie came immediately, but the boys chose to remain in Paris, thinking this was just one more bout with the fever that had plagued their father since his days in the salt pans of Narbonne.

When the "physician" arrived with his leeches Catherine was appalled.

"Have you none of the Jesuit's Powder?" she pleaded. "In the past it has been most helpful with these fevers."

"With due respect," came the indignant reply, "I believe that *I* know what is best for the Baron. My leeches will drain the vile humors quickly."

"With due respect," she rejoined, "if that is all you have to offer, you may leave at once."

Catherine, certain that this episode was different, summoned a canon of the Saint-Etienne Cathedral who brough the febrifugal powder she requested, but administered the last sacraments as well.

The girls sat at their father's left hand. Anne began to weep silently.

"Where are the boys?" the old Baron asked.

"Serving their King, each in his own way," Catherine replied.

She took his right hand in hers and reminisced.

"Do you remember playing *jeu de cache-cache* in Béziers?"

The Baron brightened some, the beginnings of a weak smile forming.

"And my broken heart each time you left for Sorèze?

"And our joy finding each other in Mirepoix?"

The smile strengthened some.

"And my brother's ultimate inability to resist your charm?

"God willed us to be together. Nothing could have kept us apart. All of our triumphs and our tragedies were destined to be shared by we two."

Riquet's smile brightened a bit more but transformed to wistful as he saw in his mind's eye the people of Languedoc traveling safely from sea to sea. He drifted off to sleep, his great adventure at an end.

Afterword

True to his word, Jean-Baptiste Colbert commissioned Jean-Mathias Riquet, heir to the fief of the *Canal Royal des Deux Mers*, to complete his father's work. Ironically, the abundance of other pressing matters of state prevented Colbert from ever visiting in person the canal that was one of the great banes of his life but possibly his greatest achievement.

In death, Riquet became a "visionary," where in life he was "delusional;" in death a scrupulous salt farmer, where in life he was ever suspected of embezzlement; and in death an unparalleled entrepreneur, where in life he was seen by so many as an impractical dreamer.

On the fifteenth of May 1681, eighteen years after the first spade was soiled and just eight months after the passing of Pierre-Paul Riquet, *Baron de Bonrepos*, a grand procession of dignitaries left Toulouse onboard a regatta bound for Sète. The Sun King's Languedoc *intendant,* d'Aguesseau, perhaps the only participant in the ceremony who had believed in Riquet, took soundings every six hundred feet to verify that the canal met design specifications. On the nineteenth day of that month, a ceremony was held in Castelnaudary to bless the waters of the canal and to officially open it to trade (even though trade had been flourishing between Toulouse and Revel for nearly a decade). The grand opening procession included none of the giants who had made the "impossible" happen. Not even François Andréossy, who was still living, was invited. He lacked the noble status to be recognized for his substantial contribution. Instead the procession was filled, but for d'Aguesseau, with doubters, detractors and tepid supporters who were happy to climb on board the proven grand achievement.

Today, the Ensérune tunnel does not commemorate Paul Mas, Riquet's brother-in-law, as the Baron intended. Less than ten years after completion, the Béziers entrance to the tunnel collapsed into the canal, taking the "Paul Mas" dedication stone with it. The debris was removed, and the entrance was shored up with stone but Riquet's dedication stone was lost forever. Whether through misunderstanding or willful perversion the tunnel is today known as the Malpas Tunnel, even though clearly not a *mal pas*. It was the first tunnel ever to carry a navigable canal.

Southern France is known colloquially as "Le Midi," so the canal is known today as "*Le Canal du Midi*," references to royalty having become singularly unpopular after the Revolution. This exceptional human endeavor is now, rightfully, a UNESCO World Heritage site. Today *Le Canal du Midi* is linked by *Le Canal Lateral* to Bordeaux, the Garonne having been bypassed as predicted by *Monsieur* Boutheroüe.

Today the canal is used more for recreation than for commerce, but it remains arguably the greatest engineering achievement of the seventeenth century; definitely the greatest to have been accomplished by a salt farmer.

Epilog

One hot day in June of 1683 Jean-Henri Duvall boarded a mail boat in Toulouse bound for Bessan. He was accompanied by his wife Collette, his son Jean-Luc and his daughter Evelyne. Their eldest son, Henri, had written Collette to tell her that her mother was very ill and that the doctor advised that the family should lose no time making the journey to her bedside if they hoped to say goodbye. Henri had been helping Matthieu with the vineyard and winery since her father Gaspard had passed five years earlier.

As they sat on deck soothed by the cool canal breeze, they were approached by a middle-aged man with a leathery, weather-beaten countenance that featured creases at the eye-corners that Collette guessed were born of laughter more likely than squinting.

"*Excusez moi, Madame*, he said. "Collette, *n'est-ce pas?*"

"*Oui, Monsieur.* Do I know you?"

"*Oui, Madame*, regrettably so. I am Claude Durant. It was my painful duty to bring you the news of your brother's murder by the Barbary pirates."

"I remember. You have changed some. Allow me to introduce my husband, Jean-Henri Duvall."

"*Bonjour, monsieur*, he replied with a warm smile. You have changed as well, *Madame*, but in your case for the better. You are even more beautiful."

"What brings you to Toulouse, *Monsieur?*"

"Fish. I live in Cette now and have three fishing boats. It has been a good year, and by the *Canal Royal* I am able to sell them, salted, in Toulouse.

"If we had had the canal when I was a boy, your brother might be with us yet."

"He will always be with me in my heart. I should introduce my son, his namesake. And also my daughter, Evelyne."

"Ah, named for your mother. How fare your parents – and your uncle?"

"My uncle is well. My father passed five years ago, and my mother is very ill. It is her ill health that summons us to Bessan.

"By all accounts, travel on the Baron's canal is far safer than by road – and faster as well. But for the late Baron Riquet, my life would have been forfeit to those roads years ago – not long after you and I met."

"*Oui, Madame*, far safer, and, yes faster. I would not think of selling my fish in Toulouse if not for the *Canal Royal*.

"Well, I'll not prevail upon your courtesy any longer. I only wanted to confirm that it was you and not my eyes playing tricks on me and learn what I could of your family who were all so kind to me under the worst of circumstances.

"And you, young man," smiling at Jean-Luc, "it is a noble name you bear which obliges you to be strong, true, and kind as you become a man.

"*Bon voyage* to you all!" he closed as he left them.

"And to you *Monsieur*, farewell!"

Their journey was safe, indeed, and far more comfortable than coach or horseback. Over their one-hundred-thirty-five-mile journey to the round lock at Agde, they were comforted by the cool breeze fostered by the watercourse and the verdant vistas that bordered the beautiful blue ribbon of Pierre-Paul Riquet's dream.

ACKNOWLEDGEMENTS

I am grateful to the French archives for preserving for more than three centuries the many documents that tell this story and to the authors who translated many of them to English. Among the latter are L.T.C. Rolt, *From Sea to Sea*, and Chandra Mukerji, *Impossible Engineering*. Also, I want to thank Monique Dollin du Fresnel, *Pierre-Paul Riquet (1609-1680)*, for compiling an exhaustive biography of the central character. I struggled to conform my story to the historical record and to the extent that I have succeeded, she is responsible.

I also benefitted from the vivid portrait of mid-seventeenth century French culture painted by Alexandre Dumas in his sequel *Twenty Years After*.

I also must thank my editor/publisher Deb Smith for her counsel, without which I would not have dared to publish.

And I would never have found the hubris to begin this project but for Mr. Edwards of Lake Washington High School, who thought maybe I could.

Printed in Great Britain
by Amazon